WOLF

A JESSICA JAMES MYSTERY

KELLY OLIVER

Formatting performed by Damonza.com

Print ISBN number 978-0-692-68535-8
Ebook ISBN number 978-0-692-68536-5

For Rosario, in memory
(September 29, 1938 – February 18, 2016)

PART ONE

CHAPTER ONE

LYING ATOP THE lone desk in an otherwise empty attic, Jessica James chewed at a jagged corner of her fingernail, staring up at the antique cobwebs on the dusty light fixture and wondering how her first year in graduate school had become such a tinderbox. When she ran out of fingernail, she chewed on the skin underneath until she tasted blood, then sucked on her ironclad humiliation. Inspired by the painful pressure of the hard desk against her boney hip, Jessica closed her eyes and imagined a fitting demise for the thesis advisor whose Birkenstocks had stomped on her dream of getting an advanced degree: a quick defenestration, a slow acting poison, or a hard bludgeon to his fat ugly head with the blunt side of an axe. Professor Baldrick Wolfgang Schmutzig, "Preeminent Philosopher" (and World-Class Dickhead) had insulted her for the last time.

Tap. Something hit the attic window. Jessica sat at attention, straining to listen in the darkness. Tap. Tap. She slipped off the desk then tiptoed over to the window and tried to peer out, but all she saw was her round freckled face, messy blonde hair, and startled blue eyes reflected in the thick antique windows. Even during the day, those cataracts of milky glass tainted the outside world with green light, as if everything were tinged with rot. She yanked at the casement, but sealed shut from a century's worth of impenetrable paint, the frame wouldn't budge.

Twenty years ago, Northwestern University had acquired the Victorian mansion and its posh city block. Once inhabited by Chicago's smartest and most fashionable set, now it housed a well-educated group of misfits and oddballs. She hated to think what kind of spirits might haunt this place: anxious graduate students overdosed on No-Doze, suicidal professors denied tenure, shamed secretaries asphyxiated by acetone, clumsy co-eds tripping down the stairs on killer spiked heels. For the past two nights, Brentano Hall's creaky noises, cold drafts, and musty odors had been giving her the creeps, but she dreaded trudging home to Alpine Vista trailer park and its familiar inhabitants, moose-eating rednecks, tree-hugging hippies, and neo-Nazi skinheads. Twelve more sleepless nights before she could slog back to Montana--high, wide and boring.

Tap. Tap. Tap. As pebbles continued showering the window, Jessica jammed her bare feet into her Ropers, threw her fringe jacket over the dirty t-shirt and faded jeans she'd been sleeping in, then crept out of the abandoned office and headed for the narrow staircase. All she needed to top off this week from hell was the campus police busting her for living in the Philosophy Department attic. Galloping down the stairs into god-knows-what in the middle of the night, she thought of her mom's parting words almost a year ago, "Be good." Then holding Jessica at arm's length for inspection, she'd added with a wink, "And if you can't be good, be careful."

Holding onto the banister, Jessica hesitated at the second floor landing, then ducked into the bathroom, scooted across the tiny room to the window, and peered out. Nothing but a sliver of yellow moon against a starless sky. She craned her neck to look down at the side lawn. Nobody. Ping. Ping. Whoever was pelting poor old Brentano Hall was going to blow her cover. So far only the secretary and the janitor knew she was living in the attic, and the janitor had just left a few minutes ago at ten when his shift ended. When the tapping became banging, Jessica dashed back to the staircase and quickened her pace, trying not to slip down the remaining stairs. If she didn't stop the ruckus soon, the campus police would. Bang. Bang. Bang. The projectiles were picking up pace.

Growing up in a scrappy trailer park, Jessica had learned to keep a safe distance from flying objects, especially whizzing vodka-tonics and airborne ashtrays, the fallout from her mother's drunken mood swings. Muscles taut, ready to dodge whatever was thrown her way, her childhood reflexes had outstripped her coordination, and she'd found herself jolting and jerking into adulthood, her pensive watchfulness mistaken for keen intelligence. Along the way, she'd learned, if she kept her mouth shut, eyes open, and ducked, she could slip under the radar, especially when she tucked her long blonde hair up into a cowboy hat and wore her jeans one size too big. Better to stand back and watch, assess the situation and stay out of the crossfire.

Jessica stopped in front of the door to the departmental library, took a deep breath, turned the doorknob, and then inched along the library wall, staying away from the window, still trying to see whoever was out there without being spotted.

"Hang back, follow the leader, and enjoy the ride," her mom always said. Of course, she was giving a poker lesson, but it seemed a pretty good life lesson too. Jessica had tried to heed that lesson for most of her twenty-one years, but eventually her curiosity would get the best of her. Then she couldn't resist poking at a leaky gas-cap, throwing a can of Coke into the campfire, turning her cousin's Ping-Pong balls into gun cotton, or checking to see if horse manure was really flammable. As hard as she tried to be good, Jessica James was constitutionally incapable of being careful, and maybe that's why she was at this very minute running headlong into unknown flying objects being hurled at Brentano Hall.

By the time she'd reached the bottom of the staircase, the tapping and banging had stopped, and now she could hear shouting coming from outside. "Jesse, are you up there? Let us in," a familiar voice yelled.

When she opened the heavy wooden front door and stepped out onto the sagging wraparound porch, she spotted her stoner buddy Jack on the lawn fondling his girlfriend-of-the-month, Amber Bush, a buxom hippy with coils of red hair snaking off her head in all directions, paisley nightgown hanging down to the top of her beat-up Uggs, as if she'd run out of the house in the middle of the night to escape a fire. Amber's mouth opened to say something but soundlessly froze into a perfect O. Jessica had known her long enough not to ask about the sticky brown stuff on her forehead.

"Are you trying to get me busted? Or did you wake me up in the middle of the night so I could watch you make-out?" Jessica shook her head, narrowed her eyes, and pierced her lips. "You guys might as well saddle up and git. I'm going back inside."

"Whoa there. Not so fast, cowgirl. We just scored some killer weed." Jack was hopping from foot to foot. "Wanna smoke it with us?"

"Where'd you get it?"

"At a RatDog concert in Milwaukee." Jack ambled up onto the porch, leading Amber by the hand.

"You went to Milwaukee?" Jessica asked. "Who's RatDog?" She buttoned her fringe jacket and hugged herself to block the brisk June breeze.

"What's left of The Grateful Dead, greatest band of all time,"

Jack said as he grabbed the front door handle and yanked the door open. "They did a mind-blowing 'Scarlet Begonias'."

"It was really cool," Amber whispered, tilting her head to one side, twisting one of her hair-snakes around her finger, and flicking the end of it into her mouth.

"Sorry I asked," Jessica said, rolling her eyes.

"Get inside before the cops see you." She pushed her friends inside the building and closed the door behind them. Before Jack could start another dissertation on washed-up psychedelic rock bands, she headed back upstairs.

Sleep deprived, climbing the uneven stairs was making her woozy, so she gripped the banister tighter. She hadn't slept in two nights and was hoping the dope would knock her out. When she reached the first landing, she took note of the tired hardwood floors, gouged from heavy desks dragged from room to room, and the beautiful carved banister, blackened from hundreds of years of steadying palms. Lingering just beneath the smell of moldy file folders was the faint scent of pipe tobacco from the old days when professors used to smoke in their offices. Now, the few remaining smokers huddled outside under the front awning puffing on Carlton Lights.

With each step of her boots, the ancient staircase creaked and groaned, a familiar lament from the neglected old house. In response, she lightened her step and continued on tiptoe. In spite of its nine-foot ceilings, the mahogany wainscoting and warped floorboards made the antiquated house feel claustrophobic, a sailing ship lost at sea, forever rolling this way and that.

Upon reaching the second floor landing, a wave of nausea hit as she found herself staring at a gold engraved nameplate: Professor Baldrick Wolfgang Schmutzig. She blew at her bangs, clenched her fists, and closed her eyes tight as she marched past the office, but she didn't open them soon enough to avoid tripping on the first stair up to the attic.

"Hey, let's smoke it in Wolf's office!" Jack said. Professor B. W. Schmutzig had given Jack his only B in college.

"Is breaking and entering part of your medical school homework, Jackass?" Jessica picked herself up and continued up the stairs. "Is that why you're studying criminal psychiatry?"

"Watch this." Jack whipped out a credit card and slid it between the doorframe and the lock, popping the office door open.

"Holy Shit! I thought you were joking." Jessica stumbled back down the stairs and grabbed at Jack's shirt, but he'd already slipped through the door and Amber had slid in after him. Jessica had no choice but to follow and shut the door behind her.

"If campus security finds us and I get kicked out of grad school, I'm gonna strangle you blue." Jackass was always pulling crazy stunts like this, and against her better judgment, she always tagged along.

"That which does not kill me, makes me stronger." Jack strolled across the office and shoved some papers off the desk onto the floor, then sat on top of the desk, skinny legs dangling over the side, kicking his desert shoes back and forth against the radiator.

"I love that song." Amber dropped her mammoth purse in a corner on top of a pile of books and sat next to him petting his long wavy hair and cooing into his ear.

"Apricot, it's Nietzsche, *Twilight of the Idols*." Jack pulled a baggie out of his jean-jacket pocket, scrounged around in the fast food wrappers piled on the desk and found a wad of foil. He deftly fashioned a makeshift pipe, filled it, lit it, took a long drag, and then passed it to Jessica. She took the funky pipe and inhaled, holding the smoke in hard.

"Should be, what doesn't kill you sends you to therapy for life," she said, still sucking in air, trying not to exhale. When she finally had to exhale, all the tension of the last week evaporated along with the cloud of sweet smoke.

"You're doing pretty good for a fucked-up cowgirl from Montana. Fresh off the farm, as pert as a morning buttercup and as smooth as a cow's udder, that's how I'll always remember you."

"It's a ranch, not a farm, dumbass." Jessica surveyed Wolf Schmutzig's pigsty of an office and leaned her hip against the edge of the desk.

"Ranch? Farm? What's the difference? You can take the girl out of the country, as they say." Jack's laugh had a smooth smoky quality, and his charismatic smile made him popular with women, at least the ones who liked sexy nerds. Jessica had a penchant for sexy nerds, but so far she'd managed to deflect Jack's charms. More like bronco riding than flirting, they took turns tossing each other to the ground. Besides, until last week, she'd had a boyfriend. After Michael cheated on her, she'd sworn off romance... at least until the end of the summer.

Her ex-boyfriend's infidelity hadn't been the first time she'd had to learn the hard way that every man's admirable qualities (kindness, charm, intelligence, cute butt--you name it) had an evil twin waiting in the shadows to bite her in the ass when she'd least expected it. It hadn't taken a Ph.D. in philosophy to teach Jessica James that virtue was just the flip side of vice. A quick study, she'd already learned that from her limited experience with men.

Jack hopped off the desk and started to unzip his fly. "Speaking of farm animals, how about I take a piss in this barnyard Bald-Dick calls home?"

"Don't be an idiot. No wonder you're studying criminal psychopaths. It takes one to know one." Scooting a stack of papers to one side, Jessica sat on the edge of the desk and turned around to face him.

"Yeah, the world is full of psychopaths, Cowgirl. And

philosophers are some of the best examples. Take world famous Professor Bald-Dick Schmutzig here. He lives in this revolting office," Jack said in a throaty voice, trying to choke back smoke. "Typical philosopher, arrogant asshole living in a fantasy world revolving entirely around his own supposed genius. Bald-Dick is a classic paranoid narcissist, delusions of grandeur and all." Thankfully, Jack had zipped up his fly and taken a seat on the window ledge behind the desk. The pipe had gone out, so he lit it again and passed it to Amber.

"Maybe that's why Wolf told me 'it takes more than intelligence to get a Ph.D., Miss James'. You need to become an arrogant arse-hole like me," she said, imitating Schmutzig's annoying nasally voice and then started giggling. The pot must be working. It dulled the blade of her advisor's razor sharp insult.

"You're too nice to be a philosopher, and much too attractive." Jack's mischievous brown eyes danced as he waved his hand in front of the stack of pizza boxes next to the desk. "But you *are* a slob, so at least you've got that going for you. You'll never be an arrogant asshole… too young, too innocent, mind as pure as the driven snow of a pristine Montana winter."

"More like yellow snow." Jessica stepped over a pile of books and papers and stared down at the jumble of greasy pizza boxes, cheesy hamburger wrappers, and half-full plastic Pepsi bottles. She picked a coffee cup up off a stack of books piled next to the desk and examined the crusty black scum inside, probably nuclear bomb resistant mold.

"Dirty office, dirty mind." She put the cup back on top of a faded journal, then plucked a pencil from a penholder on the desk and used it to poke at a piece of pizza crust, scooting it off the desk onto the floor. Professor Wolf Schmutzig's office was an academic version of those hoarder shows on television, and it reeked like a dead animal in spite of the clouds of spicy pot smoke.

"I think it's admirable the professor lives here," Amber said. "Maybe he's saving money to send to orphans in Tibet, or feed the poor in Africa, or support a family of refugees... or even put his kids through college. Does he have kids?" She was gnawing on some chocolate she'd found amidst the rubble on the desk.

"No, Wolf doesn't have any kids." Jessica took another hit and started to giggle.

"What's so funny?" Amber asked, her mouth covered in melted chocolate.

Jessica couldn't stop laughing. "I'm imagining a baby Wolf with little lamb-chop sideburns, two baby Brillo pads stuck to either side of its tiny face, teeny bulging eyes, petite bulbous nose, diminutive bubble ears, all those miniature balloons bobbing off its baby Einstein head!" As smoke filled her sinuses, a wasabi buzz scalded her scalp and she jerked her hand to the top of her head, pressing down hard to stop the tingling, but then she started laughing even harder.

"Don't forget the mini wool socks and tiny Birkenstocks," Amber added, giggling.

"I have to take a leak," Jack said heading for Schmutzig's bathroom.

"No, you don't." Jessica intercepted him and seized the doorknob so he couldn't get in. When he started tickling her under her arms, she pushed him away, but then Amber joined in, and now both of them were pawing at her. "Stop it!" she cried, tears in her eyes from laughing so hard. "You're going to make me pee my pants!"

Bang. A loud noise startled her. She lurched forward and the top of her head collided with Jack's skull. Recoiling, he yelled, "Fuck that hurt! I think you gave me a concussion. The brain is a soft organ..."

"Shut up, Jack." She glared at him. "Or, I'll aim for another soft organ."

The noise from downstairs was getting louder.

"But concussions can be fatal. I could…"

"SHUT UP, JACKASS!" He stopped mid-sentence, pouted, and rubbed the back of his head. She heard footsteps getting closer. Someone was coming up the stairs. Amber's face stiffened into a hippie Medusa, mouth frozen into that uncanny O, snaky hair slithering to escape her head.

"Quick, turn off the lights." Jessica glanced around the office. "Amber strip! Give me your nightgown."

"Whaa?" Amber's oval mouth didn't move.

"Just do it. Hand it over." Jessica thrust her hand out and waited for Amber to take off her nightgown. Now wearing only her Uggs, Amber was crouching in the corner, hugging her knees to her bare boobs. On hands and knees, Jessica crawled over and stuffed the nightgown under the door to keep the smoke from escaping. She froze when she detected a rattling coming from the office doorknob. *Shit, she'd get a prison sentence instead of a doctoral degree.*

The sound of keys jangling in the lock sent her skidding across the floor towards the bathroom. When Jack yanked open the bathroom door, Jessica's nostrils were assaulted by an acrid odor, the smell of rotting vomit. Rising to her knees, she covered her mouth and nose with both hands. Jack darted inside, pulling Amber in after him. Jessica's ear perked up when she heard the clicking of the lock turning in the office doorknob. She plunged into the dark bathroom, and Jack pulled the door shut behind her. Windowless, the small chamber was completely dark. Back on her hands and knees, Jessica was inching towards where the bathtub should be, when the toe of her boot rammed into something on the floor. The bathroom was probably as messy as the rest of the office. She stood up, breathlessly listening in the darkness, walled in by the stench of death.

The hinges on the office door squeaked and a deep voice asked, "Anybody here?" As light from the hallway poured in under the bathroom door, she instinctively stepped backwards and something snapped under her cowboy boot. As her eyes adjusted to the ambient light, she noiselessly lifted her foot and saw Professor Schmutzig's wire-rimmed eyeglasses winking up at her, one lens smashed under her boot. Grimacing, she turned her head back towards the tub to see what had tripped her. A shoe, a pair of shoes. Opening her eyes wider, staring into the blackness and trying to focus, an ominous prickling anxiety seized her chest and squeezed her lungs in a vice grip. Warm tears streamed down her cheeks even though she wasn't crying, and she had to clap her hands over her mouth to keep from screaming. After what seemed like an eternity in purgatory, the light in the office blinked off, the door banged, and the sounds of the security guard's walkie-talkie receded down the hallway. She strained to hear him leave the building but didn't move a muscle until the heavy front door of Brentano Hall slammed shut.

She took a big breath of putrid air to steel her nerves, and then pulled back the bathtub shower curtain. With all the lights off again, it was too dark to see anything. She took out her cell phone, turned it on, and pointed it towards the tub. She gasped as the outline of a body came into dim focus. Fully clothed, the head and torso slumped inside the tub under the tap, the stockinged feet extending over the side, legs askew, one dangling and the other at attention.

Huddled with Amber in the corner near the toilet, Jack breathed out, "Holy Fuck!" and turned his girlfriend away before she could see the ghastly sight of the bloated blue body in a bathtub. Jessica stifled a scream. Even in the dark, she knew she was staring into the hideous dead eyes of the Wolf.

CHAPTER TWO

A HARSH LAKE MICHIGAN breeze stung his cheeks and smarted his eyes as Dmitry Durchenko hurried toward the university parking garage after working his regular night shift at Brentano Hall. When Dmitry reached the garage, he hesitated at the elevator, trying to remember where he'd parked. He reached into the pocket of his windbreaker, but instead of his parking stub, he found the napkin Vanya had threatened him with the night before at Pavlov's Banquet. Hands shaking, he turned it over and read what was written on the back in thick blocky Russian letters: "Little thieves get shot, but great ones escape." He pushed all of the elevator buttons, figuring he could stick his head out at each floor until he spotted his van. At least he remembered parking it across from the elevator. When the door opened on the fifth floor, he saw a distant glowing ember and the silhouette of a man in the passenger seat of his Toyota minivan. He took a deep breath as he strode toward the van.

All his muscles tightened as he opened the driver's side door and a wall of smoke slammed into his face. Vanya Ivanov may be only *Shestyorka*, the lowest ranking card in the Russian deck, but sometimes the lowball could really mess up a good hand. The wiry little punk was covered in tattoos popular among Russian criminals, the most distinctive on his left shoulder, the face of a cat with crazy eyes and razor fangs. He also had a red rose carved into the back of his right hand, a symbol of acceptance into Bratva, the Brotherhood. Dmitry's stomach sunk thinking about the torture and pain inflicted in the name of "fraternity."

"What do you want, Vanya?" Weak-kneed, Dmitry dropped into the driver's seat. His cousin ignored him and flicked the ash from his cigarette onto the carpet onto a disgusting pile of bent butts on the floor. Black beads had formed on the synthetic fibers where the carpet was charred.

"Could you please quit burning holes in my floor?" He knew he couldn't turn a wall into a door just by pounding on it, but he tried anyway. Dmitry opened the ashtray. "Come on. Use the ashtray or get out of my van."

Vanya dropped his lit cigarette onto the pile, ground it into the carpet with his Italian lace-up, lit another one, then inhaled deeply and blew out a series of concentric smoke rings. "The Pope wants to know why you're keeping secrets from him," he said in Russian, his gold grill reflecting the florescent lights in the otherwise dark parking garage.

"Why would I do that?" Dmitry wondered which secret he meant. Of course he kept secrets from Bratva. Some of them could get him killed.

"Keeping secrets bad for health." Vanya said in broken English, playing with his Porsche titanium lighter, flipping the lid open and shut. Click, Click, Click.

"I'm not in the mood for games. Just get to the point."

"Little birdie told us you give teacher friend something what belongs to the Pope." Vanya continued in English. He grinned and stamped out another cigarette. "The Pope wants them pictures. You better give him pictures if you know what's good for you." Vanya may be his cousin and just an errand boy for Bratva, but that didn't make him less dangerous. If anything, it made him more unpredictable. He had something to prove. Little honey badgers were known to attack big lions.

Dmitry put both hands on the steering wheel to steady himself. The smoke was making his eyes burn. "If you cared about my health, you'd quit smoking so much."

"Just friendly warning, *chuvak*." Vanya's smile had disappeared. "For now, Pope needs you. Not always." He opened the van door, stepped out, and then ducked his head back inside. Slowly the corners of his mouth turned up. "Pope needs you," he said with a sly smile, "but he don't need your bigmouthed teacher." With that, he flicked his lit cigarette at Dmitry and slammed the van door shut.

Dmitry needed to find out what the Pope knew about his father's paintings. He would have to head into the lion's den, but first, he needed to warn the professor. He thought of what his mother always said whenever he cut himself, "Dimka, scars are time's alphabet." If so, his body was covered in poetry, his soul contained an entire encyclopedia of pain and loss, and now that Bratva had found him, the writing was on the wall. It was only a matter of time.

CHAPTER THREE

GASPING FOR AIR, Jessica James burst out of her advisor's fetid bathroom and into his dirty office. Tears blurring her vision, something sharp in the dim mess attacked her left thigh and the stabbing pain winded her. She'd run into the edge of the desk. Grabbing her bruised thigh, she bent over to keep from passing out. Queasy and panting, she melted onto the office floor behind the professor's desk, leaning up against the wall under the one and only window in the room. Tilting her head back against the windowsill, she let the warm tears run down her cheeks. Jack's face was white as parchment as he wiped sweat off his forehead with the back of one hand and led Amber out of the bathroom with the other. He crouched down next to Jessica, pulling his girlfriend down after him. All three of them were puffing and panting.

"What the fuck?" asked Jack. "Schmutzig's dead?"

"We should call the police," Amber said, reeling in the gigantic purse she'd left in the corner with the half-eaten chocolate bar. She fished around inside it with both hands then pulled out a cell phone.

"What are you doing? We can't call the cops." Jessica snatched the phone from Amber's hands. "How are we going to explain why we're in here?"

Jessica heard footfall on the stairs. *Oh Shit, not again*! The security guard was coming back. Peeking around the desk, she shuddered when she saw a large shadow through the opaque glass of the office door. She heard a loud knocking and clasped both hands over her mouth again, trying to remember the calming breathing techniques she'd learned in yoga. Make your out-breath longer than your in-breath. It wasn't working. She was suffocating.

She huddled close to her friends, hoping they wouldn't be spending the night squatting behind this desk only a few feet away from her advisor's rotting corpse. Amber was shivering, and a tangy, acrid organic odor was emanating from her naked body, the smell of fear. Jessica's legs were numb from squatting, so she leaned forward onto her hands. Listening to more noises from the hall, she kicked into full panic mode and scurried under the desk. If she could have chewed off her paw to escape, she would have.

"Professor Schmutzig, you there?" a man's voice asked. Jessica recognized the strong Russian accent, the janitor, Dmitry Durchenko. With his shaggy brown hair and boyish good looks, he'd always reminded her of a thirty-something Chekov from *Star Trek*, the original series--sexy accent, devilish smile, and piercing eyes.

Keys started rattling, then a click in the doorknob, but the door didn't open. The shadow on the other side of the opaque glass vanished, and the footfall receded down the hall. More jangling and another door opened. Dmitry must be in the janitor's closet down the hall. She thought he'd left almost an hour ago. Why was he back?

Riiiing. Startled when the office phone started ringing, Jessica reared back out from under the desk and fell on top of Amber, who yelped and scrambled even further into the corner. When Jack reached up and lifted the handset off the receiver, then dropped it again. She narrowed her eyes and mouthed, "What are you doing?" The sound of footsteps was getting closer again, approaching the office door. More clattering, another knock on the door, and then in the same thick accent, "Professor. It's me, Dmitry." The janitor's large silhouette was smashed up against the glass. Hands on either side of a darkened face, the shadow turned into a giant bear's, then disappeared again.

Amber's nightgown was moving on the floor. Must be the dope kicking in as it was climbing up the doorframe swaying to some groovy psychedelic beat. Maybe it was the Wolf's ghost come back to haunt them from his bathtub grave. The janitor pushed something under the door, followed by a full five minutes of eerie silence.

Finally, Jessica heard footsteps descending the stairs. She listened in silence, muscles taut, ready to bolt. When the office phone started ringing again, she stood up behind the desk and stared down at it. Who the hell was calling Schmutzig in the middle of the night? This time Jessica picked up the receiver and put it back down. The steps stopped, followed by another long silence. She froze in place, holding her breath. After another few seconds, the clomping on the hardwood stairs started up again, then the footfalls faded until she heard the front door squeak open and then slam shut. She fell back against the radiator in relief, and blew at her bangs. "Whew."

Jack crawled across the office floor and over to the window, then peeked up over the ledge. "Dmitry's crossing the lawn towards the street. He's getting into his minivan." His nervous laughter came out high-pitched. "That was close, dude. I think I pissed myself."

"Let's skedaddle NOW," Jessica whisper-yelled. As she tossed Amber her nightgown, the envelope Dmitry had slid under the door went flying too. She hesitated before bending over to pick it up, then she stood up and turned on her cellphone light so she could find her way out through the disaster area. That's when she saw it: her master's thesis in its brand new blue binder sitting on top of a pile of papers.

"What the…" Jessica stood staring at the binder. That liar said he'd read it over the summer, but he didn't even take it with him! She thought of her last meeting with her advisor, just a few days before, when she'd asked him for feedback on her thesis.

"In that yoga outfit," Wolf had said with a slimy smile. "You'd tempt even Francis of Assisi." Eyes ablaze behind his dirty glasses, wiry grey hair sticking out in all directions, he'd looked crazed.

"Have you been drinking your lunch again?" she'd replied (knowing full well Wolf was a teetotaler). He'd had her thesis for over two months already but still hadn't read it, and he obviously didn't plan to until the end of the summer, another three months away. So why had Wolf left her thesis behind?

Lifting the blue binder, she grasped the cover of her thesis between her thumb and forefinger and opened it as if it might bite her. Tucked inside was a letter addressed to her, typed on university stationery. As she read it, her mouth dropped open. Coughing, she glanced up at Jack.

"What is it?" he asked, scooting to her side.

"What's the matter?" echoed Amber. The three of them huddled around the binder while she slowly read the letter out loud.

Dear Miss James,

I have read your thesis, and I regret to inform you that I find it lacking. Given that you have not been able to write a thesis that meets my standards, I am sorry that I will not be able to continue as your advisor. I suggest that you leave the Ph.D. program. Hopefully another life will suit you better than the life of a scholar.

Sincerely,

Baldrick Wolfgang Schmutzig

Distinguished Professor of Philosophy

"What the fuck?" asked Jack. "It's dated three months from now!"

Breathing hard, the blood drained from her face and she doubled over, holding onto her knees for support. The letter was postdated September 15th.

CHAPTER FOUR

AS DMITRY DURCHENKO turned onto Gross Point Road, the fine hair on his arms tingled like antennae signaling danger. On another day, the colorful banners fluttering in the streetlights in Skokie might have lifted his spirits, but today, the blocky Russian letters only shackled him to a family drama he hadn't chosen. He parked his van across the street from the restaurant. As he strode up to the front door, he gripped his keys so tightly they dug into his calloused palm.

Vladimir "the Pope" Popov leased Pavlov's Banquet and lived in the penthouse above the restaurant. Outside, the place was an ugly rectangular brick warehouse on an even uglier block, but inside it was a Russian fun-house crammed with *bezdelushki* nesting dolls, silver samovars, Gzhel ceramic teapots, and paneled icons with dazzling Madonnas. One particularly haunting icon depicted a decapitated Christ's head with dreadlocks, a fumanchu mustache, and beady eyes that followed Dmitry across the room as the bodyguards escorted him to the back. The Pope was just finishing a late dinner in his private dining room. Decorative *Zhostovo* platters piled with succulent meat and tender vegetables reminded Dmitry that he hadn't eaten since breakfast. His stomach growled.

"Vodka, Dima?" the Pope asked through a mouthful of *Syrniki* smothered in applesauce, "Or do you prefer tea?" He gestured to one of his bodyguards. "Pour the man some tea." With a greasy swollen finger he pointed to the platter of fried curd fritters, "Help yourself to *Syrniki*. They're delicious."

"No, thank you. I've already eaten." Dmitry didn't want to share food with this man, but didn't turn down the cup of tea poured from a silver samovar by a burly bodyguard. Maybe the strong Russian tea would help him focus.

"It's been too long Dima. I haven't seen you since you were a scrawny teenager. You've grown into a fine looking man, and I hear you have a beautiful wife and lovely daughter." The Pope wiped his mouth on an embroidered napkin and grinned. Dmitry flinched.

"This reunion calls for a celebration. Sasha, bring us some champagne." The Pope snapped his fat fingers.

The waiter returned with a bottle of *Abrau Durso* Brut, a label Dmitry hadn't seen since he'd left Russia. He'd always found it amusing that Stalin had reopened the vineyard with the slogan "*Sovetskoye Shampanskoye*," "Champagne for every citizen." Only in Russia would the state decree that there be wine for all--the world's worst wine.

"To what do we owe the honor of a visit from the son of the Oxford Don?" The Pope's mouth widened into a yellowed coun- terfeit smile, and with great ceremony, he lifted his champagne glass and took a sip.

Dmitry winced at the mention of his father. His father's henchmen called him "the Oxford Don" because he had gotten a degree in economics from there; his father was a regular Nobel Laureate of crime. Palms sweating, Dmitry twisted a fancy nap- kin under the table, took another sip of bitter tea, then cleared his throat. "I had a visit from that smoke-stack errand boy of yours this afternoon. He was using my van as an ashtray."

"Yes, he leaves his dirty butts everywhere." The Pope's belly shook like *jeleinyi* tort when he laughed.

"I want to know why," Dmitry said with more force than he felt.

"You do, do you?" The fat man laughed again. "You want something from me. I want something from you."

The Pope snapped his fingers. "Bring out the dessert tray." A man with biceps the size of melons brought out a tray of dainty pastries. "Have some sweets, Dima." He gestured towards the tray with his sweaty head.

"Maybe you should put your cur on a leash. I don't want him coming around threatening me anymore." Dmitry forced himself to make eye contact then, glancing around, took note of the nearest exit and any potential weapons within reach.

"Maybe you're the one who needs the leash." The Pope carefully picked out several pastries and put them on his dainty rose-rimmed china plate. He licked each of his bejeweled fingers. "We've heard that you've given your professor friend the Oxford Don's missing paintings, the ones you stole. Is that true?"

"I didn't steal any paintings." It was true; his mother had stolen them. Dmitry put his hands on the table, ready to make a break for it. "The professor has nothing to do with this. Do you think I'm stupid?"

"Maybe you're too smart for your own good. Hanging around that university makes you think you're a wise guy." He threw his napkin on the table and stopped eating. "What if your professor is a stoolpigeon? Or maybe you're the rat."

"Look Vladimir, calm down. No one is a rat. The professor is clueless."

"Maybe you're the one who's clueless. Too much book learning, like your old man. Me, I've got street smarts. You can't learn that in school. It's time to teach you a lesson, one you can't learn in school." He took a slow sip from a dainty teacup. "You're going to tell us why you gave the professor that painting. And then you're going to tell us where to find the other one. Otherwise, we'll donate your body to the Old Country. In installments."

"I told you, the professor has nothing to do with this."

The Pope's massive body shook with rage. "Where are those paintings? You'd better hand them over if you expect me to keep my mouth shut," he shouted. "Or would you prefer I tell your father I've found his thieving son and his priceless paintings? I'm going to get those paintings one way or another. Then we'll see who's got brains." He signaled to his snarling bodyguards.

The two thugs charged, and Dmitry's reflexes kicked in. He just slipped out of their grasp, and headed for the nearest exit, flinging himself through the swinging metal doors so hard pots and pans rattled as he burst into the kitchen. Running full force, he bounced off the cupboards, and then threw himself through another set of doors on the other side of the room. The bulls were still on his heels, breathing down his neck.

Dmitry went careening down several flights of stairs before he realized he was clueless. He'd eaten in the restaurant before, but he'd never come up through the back stairs. Echoes of several sets of shoes ricocheted through the stairwell. The Pope's enforcers were on his heels. Nowhere else to go, he kept heading down. Taking a gamble on another unfamiliar door, he exited the stairwell. He didn't want to get trapped in the basement, cornered by the Pope's *Kryshi*. He stumbled through the door into a hallway but still didn't recognize anything. In the few seconds it took to get his bearings, the thugs came crashing through the door and lunged at him. He dove for the floor. Bad move. Both bulls tackled him.

The thugs dragged him back upstairs by his legs. He tried to catch hold of something--the railing, their pants, his pants--but he couldn't get any leverage. Every time he reared up to try to grab hold of something, the force of his exertion doubled on the way back down. His head bounced hard on each concrete stair, and by the time they reached the dining room again, he was nearly unconscious. An enforcer presented him to the Pope like a pet cat bringing back a live mouse for its master. The blows to his head must be making him hallucinate because the professor's favorite student was sitting with the Pope at the table. The last thing he heard before he passed out was the Pope yelling, "Get him out of here. He's bleeding all over my favorite rug."

CHAPTER FIVE

SITTING CROSS-LEGGED ON the lone attic desk, Jessica James could hear birds singing through their early morning ablutions. The shock of Wolfgang Schmutzig's corpse had sobered her up some, but the dope was making it hard to concentrate as she drifted in and out of a tingly haze. The smell of death mingling with skunkweed still burned her nostrils. She'd been up for almost twenty-four hours and more than anything her body craved sleep, but needles of anxiety pricked at her skin, making sleep impossible. She'd just seen a dead body for the first time and she couldn't tell anyone. Breaking and entering, illegal drugs... Talk about self-incrimination! She slid her hands under her tailbone to keep them from trembling.

She was nauseous thinking of the Wolf, fully clothed, lying downstairs dead in his bathtub. And her thesis was in his office with a post-dated letter in effect kicking her out of graduate school. If anyone found that damning letter.... *Oh shit!* She'd left the letter in the office. She had to go back down and get it. She slid off the desk, tiptoed out of the attic, and headed back down the stairs towards 24B. Standing in front of the door, she took a deep breath and turned the doorknob. It was locked. She turned and ran back upstairs to fetch her wallet. Rummaging around in her backpack, she found her bi-fold containing the "emergency" credit card. Her mom reminded her repeatedly that it was only for "dire emergencies." Saving her graduate career counted as dire. She ran back downstairs, and hands shaking, struggled to pull the card from the slot in the wallet. Holding the wallet between her teeth, she slid the card between the door and its frame. The card struck something and wouldn't budge. She pulled it out and pushed it back into another spot between the lock and doorframe. No luck. She angled the card and pressed it against the locking mechanism as hard as she could. It was no use. She couldn't get the door open. She stuffed her card back into its slot and clomped back upstairs to her attic hovel.

Shutting herself into the dark and musty alcove, she climbed back on top of the desk, pulling a navy cardigan along with her, and curled up into a fetal position. Tears streamed down both sides of her face, soaking into the dirty sweater she was using as a pillow. She should have listened to Michael when he said, "Your advisor is supposed to keep you afloat, not sink you."

The tear-soaked cardigan belonged to him. When his spicy mossy scent appeared as if on cue, it overwhelmed her with longing. She wanted him to hold her, comfort her, and tell her everything would be okay. Since the break-up three days ago, she'd been trying not to think about Michael. He'd opened up a whole new world for her, one that took her far from the one she'd known as a naïve Montana girl who'd never even seen a foreign film or eaten Thai food before, not to mention sex.

She got up from the desk, tipped the trashcan upside down, and sorted through the candy wrappers and used Kleenex until she found the discarded photograph. Staring into Michael's beautiful lopsided face, for the millionth time she chastised herself. If only she hadn't read his journal, they might still be together. Of course, if she hadn't read his journal, she would never have known he was cheating on her with an actress from his community theater. She crawled back onto the desk, buried her face in his sweater, and cried herself to sleep.

Professor Schmutzig was pounding on the door yelling, "This is how to philosophize with a hammer!" Thud, Thud. Thud. The banging got louder. "Go away!" Jessica yelled as the door splintered and wood exploded into the room. When she woke up sweating from her nightmare, someone really was knocking at the door. Holding her breath, she waited for the banging to stop, hoping it would be soon because she really needed to get downstairs to pee. She heard the scraping of a chair on the floor. Then silence. Someone was waiting in the hall. *Crap!*

Jessica wiped the drool off her chin with Michael's sweater, hopped off the desk, then fished a Chinese take-out container from the trash, squatted, and did her best to empty her bladder without peeing all over her jeans. The balancing act reminded her of Goddess pose in yoga. *Peeing Goddess.* Once she disposed of the leaky evidence, she tugged on the butt of her jeans to pull her damp underwear back into place and then attacked her hair with a brush. She inhaled deeply, opened the door a crack, and peeked out into the hallway.

Alexander Le Blanc was sitting in the hallway wearing a pink polo shirt, khaki pants, and Dockers. His concave chest, his nonexistent butt, and a nose long enough to hang an ornament from it, suggested he wasn't yet full grown. Alexander was one of hundreds of weird angst-filled boys who came out of the woodwork to take Professor Schmutzig's Existentialism course every year. Nietzsche's *Beyond Good and Evil* became their sacred scroll. They were seriously mental. They emulated Dostoevsky's Underground Man, for God's sake! Maybe it was just a phase some adolescent boys passed through on their way to becoming investment bankers. Jessica wondered where these guys came from, and where they went after college.

"Alexander, what are you doing here?"

"Mrs. Bush told me you were up here," Alexander said with his unidentifiable accent, probably an expensive accent.

"What do you want?" Jessica blew on her bangs. "I mean, can I help you with something, Alexander?"

"I want my final paper."

"The semester ended a week ago, Alexander. You got an A in the class?" She sensed her cheeks getting hot. She had to get rid of him and get the hell out of Brentano Hall before someone found the professor's body... and her thesis.

"I got an A-minus. And I want my paper back so I can read Professor Schmutzig's comments."

Oh no, he's going to start grade grubbing. Shit! Jessica hadn't actually read the papers yet. She'd had a hundred papers to grade for that class in just 48 hours, so she'd only glanced at the papers and assigned grades. She'd planned to write comments later but hadn't had time. It was always the ones with A-minuses who came around to argue about their grades.

"Um. Let me see." Jessica pretended to look around the room. "I wonder where I put them."

Alexander peered into the attic, and she tried to block his view as he stared down at the dirty sweater bunched up on the floor.

"I need to get your paper from Professor Schmutzig's office. But I'm late for an appointment." She really was supposed to meet Amber at the café in twenty minutes. "Can you come back tomorrow?"

"Can't you go get it now?" he demanded.

"No, Alexander. I can't. I have to wait until tomorrow to get the key from Donnette." *Jeez.* Sometimes these privileged

Northwestern students were so demanding. "I'll have it for you tomorrow. Okay?"

"Did the professor like it?"

"Like what? Oh, he didn't read it. I graded it." She was careful to say, "graded it" instead of "read it."

"YOU graded it? Didn't the professor read it?" He was wringing his hands.

Jessica rolled her mind's eye. These rich kids didn't understand. Their professors were too busy publishing or perishing to read their exams. Instead, poor underpaid grad students read hundreds of exams at a time for less than minimum wage. That way the university could cycle through thousands of tuition paying trust fund brats.

"I was writing it especially for Professor Schmutzig. Based on his last lecture on Dostoevsky." Alexander was even paler than usual.

Jessica was starting to feel sorry for the kid. "Maybe I can send it to him in New Jersey if it's that important to you." She couldn't tell him that Professor Schumtzig would never read his paper, or anyone else's for that matter, since he was lying downstairs dead in his bathtub. She shuddered remembering the grisly scene.

"It's too late for that." Alexander was getting agitated, even a little scary. "I need to get it back now!"

"Tomorrow. Okay?" Jessica ducked back inside her attic cell, shutting the door in his acne-blotched face. She threw her keys, phone, and wallet into her book bag and slung it over her shoulder. Almost to the door, she stopped, dashed back to her toiletries basket, grabbed a bottle of body mist and sprayed herself all over trying to camouflage the smells of the night before, ode to cannabis with a large dash of terror. In a cloud of vanilla spice, she yanked the door open and rushed out.

Alexander Le Blanc was waiting for her in the hall. "So what did YOU think of my paper?" he asked, his voice squeaking.

She lurched back and slammed into the door. Now she'd have another wicked bruise on her thigh. "You scared me." *You Little Shit.*

"Did you like it?" His nose was twitching.

"Oh right. Yes. I liked it very much. It was well written as always. And your argument was clear." She hoped that the paper contained an argument. She had to get away from him as soon as possible. Her head hurt; her jeans clung to her bruised thighs like she'd slept in them; and most importantly, she had to figure out how to get her thesis out of Wolf's office before anyone found it.

"What did you think of my argument that Raskolnikov is an example of Nietzsche's Übermensch?" He was waving *Crime and Punishment* under her nose. Now, the little twerp was threatening her with Russian Existentialism.

"Very clever. Yes, very convincing." As she galloped down the stairs to escape his probing questions about the paper she hadn't read, she slipped on the landing and caught herself just in time to avoid diving head first down the next set of stairs.

Alexander looked confused. "So you agree that he had a right to do what he did because he is a superior sort of man?"

"Um. Sure. I really have to run. Sorry. See you tomorrow." She gathered her thick blonde hair into a ponytail so she could see to get out of the building without running into anything else or falling down the stairs. Outside, Alexander was scurrying to keep up, trying to block her path. She swerved right and rushed towards the back parking lot. Surely, he wouldn't follow her to her car.

Three campus police cars with their lights flashing were pulling up behind Brentano Hall. She froze, staring at them as they approached. When Alexander caught up to her, she blocked his body with the driver's side door, dove into her car, slammed the door, turned the key in the ignition, put it in drive, and stepped on the gas. The crappy old Impala groaned and complained but wouldn't start. *Great!* She tried again. Now she'd probably flooded it. Alexander approached the car like he might try to get in. *For heaven's sakes, what is with this kid?* He rapped on the window. She mouthed "TOMORROW." Finally, the car started, and she took off, leaving him gulping in her exhaust.

CHAPTER SIX

WHEN DMITRY DURCHENKO came to in the dimly lit room, the first thing he noticed was a distinctive floral scent of smoky sweet apple, reminiscent of the chamomile growing wild throughout Russia. As his eyes adjusted to the darkness, he tried to lift his hands to his aching head, but they were tied together behind his back. His feet were bound too, and he was lying on his side in a puddle of something sticky. He wriggled himself up against a wall and into an upright position, leaning his shoulders against the wall. Light flickered in through the thick glass from a window above him. He must be in a basement with high windows onto the street. As his senses sharpened, the sweet chamomile scent turned to sickly mildew rot. His shirt stuck to his back, whether from the dank room or a cold sweat, he didn't know. He twisted his arms so that his hands were above his back right pocket, and patted to see if it was there in its place, the carbide-tipped pocket-scraper he used for woodworking in Brentano Hall. He worked the scraper out of his pocket and then leveraged the tip between the ropes and the wall and rhythmically moved his wrists back and forth to cut the cord.

He had been at it long enough that his hands were cramping when he heard footsteps in the distance. Frantic, he pressed the ropes against the carbide tip. Just as he heard keys jangling in the lock on the other side of the door, his hands broke free. He didn't have time to cut through the ropes binding his ankles, so he scooted back into the middle of the puddle of blood from his cut lip, and pushed his body over into the fetal position he had found himself in earlier. Squinting, he saw the shadow of a large man approaching, backlit by florescent lights from the hallway. The man was pointing a small revolver at him. He willed himself not to open his eyes any further. The man stood over him and kicked at Dmitry's feet. "You alive?" Holding his breath, he fought the urge to move, and after waiting for his target to move into range, took his chance.

When the gangster bent down, Dmitry jack-knifed his knees up so the heels of his shoes landed full force on the man's chin. The brute fell backwards, his gun clattering to the floor and Dmitry lunged for it. The bull moaned, rolled towards him, and, with his arms outstretched, managed to grab Dmitry's left foot. But by then, Dmitry had the thug's revolver in both hands. He kicked his foot free, sprung up off the floor, swung around, and cold-cocked the mobster on the back of the head with the butt of the pistol. The bodyguard slumped, face down, into the coagulating pool of blood.

Surveying the room to make sure he didn't have any more company, Dmitry used his scraper to saw at the thick ropes around his ankles, then used those ropes to hogtie the wrists and ankles of the unconscious gangster, then sneaked out into the bright hallway. At first the florescent lights were blinding, and he stumbled into a wall, banging his already hurting head. As his eyes adjusted, he was relieved to see he was alone, at least for now. But he had no idea where he was, or where he might be going. Following illuminated red exit signs, he staggered outside into an alley. He realized it wouldn't be long before the Pope's *Krysha* were after him again.

As he rounded the corner, the building became a sail waving in the wind, then the street started heaving. He slid along the back of the building clinging to the shadows on the wall, a sailor hugging slippery rigging. When he reached the side of the building, he realized where he was. Gross Point Road was directly in front of him. If he could make it to the corner of the building, he might be able to spot his minivan across the street, provided it was still there.

As he started around the corner, he heard voices and ducked into a doorway. His heart pounding in his chest like a ship in a hurricane, sea sick from the motion of the street, he staggered along holding onto the building. When the voices receded into the distance, he stumbled out into Gross Point Road, dodging an oncoming car that honked as it passed him. He spotted his van parked across the street, and started running full tilt, breathlessly swaying from side to side. Swimming against the current, he finally reached the van. He pulled his keys from his pocket, pressed the unlock button, and dove inside, head first. His right hand was shaking so badly he could hardly get the key into the ignition.

An ear-splitting crash, and the glass of the driver's side window shattered right onto him, and then a huge fist walloped the side of his head. One of the *Krysha* had broken the window and his monster arms were reaching inside the van to grab Dmitry by the throat.

"The Pope says you have 48 hours to deliver the money and the paintings, or *accidents* will happen to your family. Two days or you'll live only long enough to hear them cry for mercy, *súka*," the gangster threatened.

As soon as the bull released his neck, Dmitry gunned the accelerator and swerved onto Gross Point Road right into oncoming traffic. He pulled hard on the steering wheel and the van veered left, just missing a truck. He was being pulled into an undertow;

the street was sucking him down. The blood running into his right eye was blurring his vision, but he didn't dare release the wheel to wipe it off. The whites of his knuckles stood out against the dark steering wheel and he willed himself to focus. *Concentrate. Stay awake dammit.* As headlights blurred by, his mind drifted back to his father and the horrifying night he had fled for his life. His father must have put out a *Bratva* A.P.B. on the two missing paintings, but there was no way the Pope could know where they were hidden. Not even Sabina knew.

CHAPTER SEVEN

WHEN JESSICA JAMES got to the café, Amber was already there waiting at their regular booth. Over the past forty years, customers at The Blind Faith Café had gone from slurping grainy diner coffee out of chipped white mugs to sipping cosmopolitans out of frosted martini glasses. Amber's evolution had followed a similar path, but in a condensed period of time. Hers was human time relative to the café's geological time, and made Amber seem both younger and older than her twenty-five years on planet earth.

Jessica tossed her satchel onto the seat and plopped down in the booth across from Amber. "Whew, sorry I'm late." The cool plastic was sticky against her hot back. "Where's Jack?"

"Jesse-girl, take this to counteract last night." Rummaging through her monster purse, Amber pulled out a baggie full of brown bark. "It's Borotutu bark for cleansing the liver."

Jessica glanced around to make sure no one was watching and snatched up the illicit baggy and slipped it into her jacket pocket.

"I need caffeine," she said. "I'm still in shock from last night. I can't believe we found…"

Amber interrupted, "Caffeine is bad for you. When insects eat a caffeinated plant, they're paralyzed instantly and die." She bobbed her head back and forth as if to some imaginary funky music in her head. She was in surprisingly good spirits for someone who'd discovered a dead body the night before.

"At least I won't have any bugs in my gut then. But if it will make you happy, I'll order Witch's Brew tea instead." Jessica scanned the familiar menu, but she wasn't hungry. Overwhelmed, she slouched over the table and put her head in her hands. Amber slid into the booth beside her, and putting both hands on top of Jessica's head, started tapping.

"Take a deep breath and hold it," she said.

People were turning to stare, and that was saying something given the clientele at Blind Faith Vegetarian Café. But she submitted to the tapping rather than hurt Amber's feelings.

"The energetic circuit of your kidney meridian is blocked. Envision your kidneys bathed in a healing golden light, honey nourishing your organs."

After drinking a whole pot of Witch's Brew, she couldn't help thinking about her kidneys. "Amber, I have to pee." She pulled out from under the drumming fingers and pushed her friend out of the booth so she could escape to the bathroom.

"Good. That means the EFT treatment is working." Amber smiled and nodded.

When Jessica got back from the bathroom, Amber was on the phone. While she waited for her friend to get off the phone, she pulled her own phone from the pocket of her fringe jacket, and as she did, a sharp paper corner poked her finger. Her eyes widened as she pulled the envelope from her pocket, turned it over, and then opened it. Between the dope and the shock of Wolf's dead body (not to mention that messed-up post-dated letter she'd found with her thesis), she'd completely forgotten about Dmitry's note.

"What's going on?" Amber asked in alarm.

When she passed the note across the table to Amber, she noticed the brownish fingerprints staining the edge of the paper.

"This is the note Dmitry slipped under the door last night," Jessica whispered.

"What does it mean? 'You are not safe here'." Amber may be spacey, but a threatening note from the Russian janitor brought her back to earth. "Wow. I see why you're freaked out about this note, but why were you so upset about that letter you found last night?"

"Let's see, could it be because Wolf, may he rest in peace, dated it three months from now, and he said my thesis sucks and I'm stupid," Jessica said. "I'm upset because it means I wrote an entire thesis that took me a whole year, and I still can't get my degree. And unless I can find another advisor, I'll probably get kicked out of the program." She started sobbing. The shock of last night and weeks of uncertainty and heartbreak ran down her face. She wiped her nose on her sleeve, then headed towards the all-gender bathroom marked "For Humans Only," slouched into a stall, and unwound wads of toilet paper to dry her eyes and blow her nose.

When she returned from the bathroom this time, Jack was sitting in the booth next to Amber. "We can't tell anyone we broke into Bald-Dick's office or we'll all go to jail." He looked worse than Jessica felt.

"I saw cop cars pulling up to Brentano when I was leaving," she said. "Someone must have found him." She shuddered. "I hope they don't check fingerprints or anything. What are we going to do? I have to get my thesis back somehow. If anyone reads that letter, they'll know Wolf wanted to kick me out."

"That post-dated letter doesn't mean shit," Jack said with his mouth full. "It only proves that asshole was trying to sabotage you." He was eating off of Amber's plate.

"When I was at the Ashram, he gave a lecture on Existentialism and Zen, and our Guru called him a genius." Amber was trying to pry dirt out from under her fingernails using the ends of her snaky hair. "So he can't be that bad." She started tapping on her own head.

"A genius?" Jack scoffed. "Did your Guru have 'Wolf' tattooed on her ass or something?"

"How can you joke about him now that he's dead?" The note was sticking to Jessica's clammy fingers. She peeled it off and slid it across the table. "Jack, look at this."

He read it and thrust it back at her. "What the fuck? What is it?" He stared into her eyes waiting for an answer.

"Dmitry," she whispered.

Amber's crescent eyes had closed and she was swaying from side to side, drumming her favorite RatDog tune or sending Morse code signals to her own nervous system through her wacky cranium. Whatever it was, she was clearly enjoying her "self-treatment." Amber stopped tapping and opened her eyes. Jessica's whole body jolted and she stared at the table where Jack's phone and hers were buzzing in unison. Jack picked up his phone

"Urgent Message from The University," he said tapping on his phone. "Holy Shit. They found him."

"What the…" Jessica dropped her phone. "Drug overdose?"

CHAPTER EIGHT

DMITRY DURCHENKO WAS relieved when he awoke in his own bed. He surveyed the familiar room with its modest furnishings. Whoever said you couldn't make a silk purse from a sow's ear didn't know Sabina. She'd transformed their cramped stone house into a cozy nest. If it weren't for his throbbing ribs and pounding headache, he'd have been comfortable tucked into their soft cotton sheets and warm down duvet. The scent of Sabina's night cream still lingered on her pillowcase next to him. Soon, he would be trying to conjure that creamy rose petal smell to get the stench of burning plastic out of his nostrils.

His daughter was sitting in a chair next to the bed reading. "Why aren't you at school, *kotyonok?*" He tried to sit up. "You don't want them to take that fancy scholarship away, do you?"

"Don't call me *kitten.*" Lolita glanced up from her book. "I'm not a little girl anymore."

"Sorry, *lyubov moya.* Or can I call you *my love?* Do you hate that too now, *milyi,* darling?"

His lovely daughter was the antidote to his nightmares. When he reached over and patted her manicured hand, he noticed her blood-red fingernails, as she gazed at him, her steely grey eyes piercing straight through his heart. Every time he saw his daughter, he was struck by the discord between those sharp eyes and her soft face, his wife's face. Sabina's lovely features were transformed into something otherworldly on Lolita's face. Her mother was pretty, but Lolita was stunning. At twenty-one, his daughter had many admirers. Whether in response to a gentleman's kiss or a cad's groping, Lolita could land a blow to wound them body and soul and still not kill their ardor. It was probably his fault. He'd taught his daughter to fight like a *voin*, a Russian warrior. *Better voin than vor.* His heart ached to keep her safe, but now that Bratva had found him, he realized it would be impossible.

"Rest, *Papochka*. Can I bring you some tea or soup?" Lolita kissed him on the forehead. He tried to pry himself off the bed, but a stabbing pain in his head forced him back down, so he closed his eyes and tried to sleep in self-defense against the throbbing pain in his right eye. As he rode the waves of slumber, Lolita was singing a Russian lullaby his mother had sung to him as a child. "Sleep-sleep-sleep. Don't lie close to the bedside, otherwise a grey wolf will come and bite you."

The lullaby transported him back to the platform, the last time he had seen his mother. He was only nineteen-years-old, and his breath froze in the night air as he'd whispered, "Mama, *lyublyu tebya*. I love you." His mother had been wearing a full-length blue fox coat and matching hat, her elegant face caressed by perfectly styled auburn hair. She'd handed him a leather wallet. "Dimka, here are the documents you'll need to leave the country. Take this train to Riga. Change there for Warsaw. That way you don't go through Belarus. We didn't have time to make visas for Belarus."

With blood pounding in his head, Dmitry could hardly hear her. He felt like his brain might burst, and with shaking hands he reached for the wallet. Wearing only a woolen dress and hat, Sabina huddled close to him for warmth. Neither of them had traveled out of Russia before, and now they were going halfway across the world. Silent tears streamed down his face as he hugged his mother for the last time.

"This is for you." When his mother handed him a large brown valise with gold locks, he stared blankly at her, unable to speak.

"Dimka. Pay attention. Do you understand me?"

"When will I see you again mother?" His voice cracked. He could no longer cry in silence, and wiping his nose on his suit sleeve, he wept openly.

"Everything changes, *moya lyubov*," she said. "Nothing disappears." With both hands, she'd wiped the tears from his cheeks, and then gave him her monogrammed handkerchief. The potent smell of her French perfume made him dizzy.

A voice came over the loudspeaker: "All aboard for Riga. Track number 7. Anyone with a ticket to Riga should be on board. The train is ready to depart the station." Prodded into action by the announcement, he clung to Sabina as she led him by the arm onto the train destined for an unknown future.

Now decades later, he'd had been so busy looking over his shoulder, he'd ran head-on into his past. He wished he could have left his past on the train platform where he had waved goodbye to his mother twenty-one years ago. But as his mother would say, "the past is not a suitcase you can leave behind. Some baggage you are destined to carry for the rest of your life."

CHAPTER NINE

WHEN JESSICA JAMES returned from the café, five police cars were parked outside Brentano Hall, lights flashing. A chill snaked down her spine as she remembered the gristly scene from last night. What if they'd found her thesis and turned it over to the department chair? She may have resented Wolf's advances, but she respected his opinion when it came to philosophy. Why had he written that damning letter? And who'd killed him? She was determined to find out if it was the last thing she did.

She sneaked around to the back entrance, and then edged along the hallway until she reached the voices coming from inside the main office. When she peeked through the door crack, she saw two police officers interviewing the secretary, Donnette Bush. Poor Donnette. Rivulets of mascara were running down her cheeks through pancake makeup, making her look ghoulish, a zombie Dolly Parton with glistening red orbs, a cockeyed bouffant, and smeared lipstick. Jessica wished she could run in to give her a hug.

Donnette Bush was her only ally in the department, and the "Texas Glue" holding the place together. Today, as always, Donnette sported full make-up, stockings, high-heels, one of her extensive assortment of twin sets and skirts mixed and matched with brash accessories and costume jewelry. She'd obviously just had her bouffant done up at the "beauty parlor," along with fake acrylic fingernails. This afternoon the theme was cotton candy pink.

"Far be it for me to question God's will, but why would He take Wolfie in this way?" Donnette asked the two officers, her voice breaking. "Just lying there in the bathtub. Blue lips. Gray skin. Oh Jesus save me! What a horrible sight." She broke down sobbing. Jessica knew just how she felt.

One of the officers handed Donnette a tissue. "Ms. Bush, I know it's difficult, but it's important that you tell us every detail of how you found Professor Schmutzig."

"The door was open and I didn't see Wolfie, I mean Professor Schmutzig, in his office. So I went in and knocked on his bathroom door. I just had an odd feeling that something wasn't right." Donnette dabbed at the corner of her eyes.

"What do you mean 'wasn't right'?" the other officer asked in a sonorous bass.

"I can't say for sure. I just had a feeling. Maybe God was telling me to open that door. " She started bawling again. Opening her mouth slightly to steady her face, she wiped mascara from under her eyes with a tissue. When she spotted Jessica standing in the hallway, she gave her a pleading "Help me!" look. Jessica shrugged and stretched her lips into an exaggerated frown. Two of the only women in the department, they had to stick together. Standing in the doorway, Jessica tried to look encouraging.

When the cute officer followed Donnette's gaze and spotted Jessica, he walked toward the door. His cocoa-colored skin was smooth, and in spite of herself, she wanted to touch his arm as it reached for the doorknob. His amber eyes locked onto her, "Excuse me, Miss," the detective said in a buttery baritone, as he shut the door in her face.

She darted up the stairs but didn't get far before she saw a swarm of activity around Schmutzig's office. Cops wearing gloves were going in and out collecting "evidence" in Ziploc bags. They were even taking out pizza boxes and going through the wastebasket. *Shit.* What did Jack do with that foil pipe? She hid in a vestibule off the hallway and tried to see what was happening. Every time one of the officers came towards her, she flattened herself against the wall and ducked out of sight.

A burly uniformed officer came down the hallway and stopped right in front of her. "I'm afraid you can't come up here, Miss." She noticed his latex-gloved fingers pinched a baggie containing one large faded pink button. *Oh my god.* She recognized the tatty button from Amber's nightgown dress. Every muscle in her body tightened. "Is there a problem, Miss?" the cop asked. "No sir," she answered, then turned and skipped down the stairs, her heart skipping faster. She ducked into the women's bathroom. The few women in the department knew you could hear nearly everything going on in 24B from the ladies' room next to Schmutzig's office. Through a vent in the wall, she listened to a detective describing the scene. "Judging by rigor mortis, the subject died within the last 24 hours. The needle found in his right arm suggests a possible heroin overdose." She couldn't believe it. No way The Wolf was a junkie. Pepsi was his drug of choice. "There are no signs of a struggle or forced entry, further evidence that most likely the victim died by his own hand." *Suicide?* Her advisor had been too arrogant to off himself. A woman's voice said, "I've found a brownish substance on the wall in the northwest corner. It may be blood. I'm collecting a sample."

Jessica snuck back downstairs and into the department library to wait for the cops to leave so she could go back up and retrieve her thesis. Maybe she could convince Donnette to give her a key or call Jack to bring his credit card. One way or another, she had to get her thesis out of that office before someone found it along with the damning letter attached to it. An odd thought popped into her head, and she wondered if there could be any relation between that post-dated letter and the Wolf's death. Certainly, her thesis couldn't have anything to do with his death. What a weird idea.

The smell of ancient dust and German philosophy filled her nostrils. Surrounded by wooden shelves crammed with hardback books, a round carved wooden table occupied the center of the library chamber. The stacks formed a labyrinth spiraling around it, a vortex of two thousand years of philosophy. She thought of the beautiful Ariadne leading Theseus out of the maze after he had slain the Minotaur…her skein of thread the clew (or clue) that saved his life. She needed a lifeline now her advisor was dead and her thesis was still sitting up there in his office labeled reject.

Jessica slid into one of the smooth wooden chairs and sat her satchel on another. With their high backs, curved arms, and clawed feet, the chairs were thrones for philosopher kings. She pulled a Kindle out of her backpack and pretended to read. Peering over the Kindle, she saw two uniformed men lift a stretcher carrying a body bag. She watched as they maneuvered the stretcher out the narrow front door, trying not to bang it into the molding as they went, then loaded the stretcher into an ambulance, and shut its double back doors. In the twilight, there was something peaceful about the scene. The graceful movements of the cops who'd obviously done this many times before, the silhouette of the ambulance against the pink-orange clouds, the way Wolf's body had floated into the vehicle, seemingly levitating. The mist rising off the asphalt swirled around the stretcher, spirits escaping the black body bag, one more ghost to trouble her sleepless nights in the attic.

The door to the main office opened and the two officers who had been grilling Donnette were heading toward the hallway and the library. Heart racing, Jessica ducked under the table. Peering up from a crouching position, she saw the library swing shut. When the lock clicked, her heart hurtled into her throat. Now, she was locked in. She banged her head as she scooted out from under the table. She crawled over to the door, sat down, and listened. She caught a rustling across the hall and then the distinctive sound of Donnette's high-heels clicking on the hardwoods. She pounded on the door, "Donnette, let me out!" The clicking got louder and then stopped. A torrent of Chanel No. 5 blew up from under the door, and she heard a key turn in the lock.

"What are you doing, honey?" Donnette asked, staring down at her with puffy eyes. When Jessica sprung up and gave her a hug, Donnette started crying again. It was contagious, and Jessica locked onto her, sniveling and choking back tears. Even though she'd often imagined killing him herself, Jessica lamented Wolf's death, and even worse, she hated to see her one ally so distraught.

Donnette pulled away from their embrace, wiping tears off her cheeks with the backs of her hands. "I'm sorry. I have to get myself together. God help me." Jessica dug in her satchel, pulled out a packet of Kleenex, and handed one to her.

"Thanks honey."

"How did it happen?" Jessica asked, and then added in a whisper, grimacing, "You found him?"

"Mr. Bush and I went out to the movies last night." Donnette always called her husband Mr. Bush. "The special 75th anniversary showing of *Gone with the Wind*. Have you seen it?"

"Yeah, it's 75 years old. Who hasn't seen it?"

"Don't take that tone with me young lady." Tears were welling in her swollen eyes.

"I'm sorry, Donnette. We're all under a lot of stress." Jessica took her hand. "So you went to the movie, and then what?"

"Well, when Mr. Bush and I got home from the movie, there was a message on the answering machine from Zelda, Wolf's mother. She was asking if I knew where Wolf was." She picked at the polish on one of her nails and shifted her weight from one foot to the other. Rumor had it that years ago Donnette and Wolf had had a fling, back when he was a lonely assistant professor locked up in his office writing his masterwork and she was a newly arrived Texas beauty-queen. She baked him pies, cakes, and cookies, and he devoured them faster than the latest issues of *Philosophy Today*.

"I called Zelda back first thing this morning," Donnette said, a little shiver reverberating through her plump body. "Of course, I didn't realize Wolfie was, was…had passed away. Wolf was a good son. He always called Zelda if he was going to be late." She was wringing her hands.

"Yes, poor Zelda. She must be heartbroken." Jessica struggled to think of consoling words, the sorts of things you are supposed to say when someone died. She didn't know what to say, not because she didn't care, but because she didn't have a lot of experience with death, except for her father's when she was ten…. But that was more like the end of the world than a matter of etiquette.

"Zelda said the strangest thing. She kept calling Wolf's office all night and someone kept picking up the phone and hanging up on her." Donnette raised her eyebrows. "She wanted me to go to the office right away to check on Wolfie. She thought he might be up to something." She straightened her skirt and pulled her blouse down over the folds of her ample torso.

"That's odd," Jessica said, avoiding eye contact.

"Yes, very. If Wolf was….if he'd already passed away, like the police say, then who picked up the phone?" Donnette put her hands on her hips as if expecting Jessica to answer.

"I don't know." Jessica blushed.

"Well I do." When Donnette narrowed her eyes they disappeared into smears of black mascara.

"You do?" Jessica's voice cracked, and she felt Donnette's omniscient eyes drilling into her very soul.

"Yes, I do, Missy," said the Goddess of Brentano Hall.

"Who? Did you tell the police?" At least in prison she would have a bed and food, and if they let her have a computer, she could write her dissertation.

"Not exactly." Donnette tugged again at her blouse that kept riding up on her bosom.

"You lied to the police?" Maybe she and Donnette could share a cell in prison. She imagined Donnette wielding a butcher knife in the prison kitchen and topping her famous pecan pie with whipped spit when someone crossed her.

"I didn't say that." She wagged her finger at Jessica.

"I heard you tell the police you didn't use the master key. How did you get into Wolf's office?"

Donnette narrowed her eyes and straightened her skirt. "I used the key that Wolfgang gave me. Anyway, what were you doing spying on us? I never should have given you the key to the attic and allowed you to stay there."

"Wolf gave you a key?" Jessica regretted asking as soon as the words escaped her mouth. "Could I borrow it? I left something in his office the other day"

"Of course you can't. The police have his office taped off. They told me no one is to enter until they finish their investigation." Even though they were alone in the building, Donnette glanced around, then whispered, "Wolfie told me someone broke into his office." She squinted and jerked her cotton candy crowned head to one side.

"Who?"

"That cursed Russian, the janitor, Mr. Dmitry Durchenko."

"He was trying to get into Wolf's office last night. Ah, that's why his keys wouldn't work…" Jessica's eyes widened when she realized what she'd just said. *Ooops!*

"How do you know that?" Donnette raised her hands skyward in a supplication, as if Jessica discerned it through divine intervention.

She couldn't tell the secretary the truth about her weed-induced caper with Jackass and Amber. Donnette wouldn't be at all happy to find out her only kid was a pot-head, not to mention breaking and entering, illegal drugs, a post-dated letter, the ominous note, and Wolf's dead body.

"Ummmm. I was sleeping in the attic when I heard him in the middle of the night." Jessica stared down at her Converse All-Stars to avoid facing Donnette's lie-detecting eyes.

"Aha! I knew it. That cursed Russian did it." Donnette triumphantly poked at her big light pink hair with a big light pink fingernail.

"What?" Jessica asked. "You think Dmitry murdered Wolf?"

CHAPTER TEN

WHEN SOMEONE TOUCHED his wrist, Dmitry Durchenko woke with a start and sat up in bed. The stabbing pain in his ribs forced him back down.

"It's just me, *moya lyubov.*" Sabina caressed his face. "You need to eat." His wife pointed to a tray with strong tea, cabbage soup, and homemade black bread. She may have been only a teenager when they left Russia, but his lovely wife could cook like his Russian grandmother. His stomach grumbled when he realized it had probably been days since he'd eaten, and the aroma of the freshly baked bread nourished him even before he took a bite.

"Who did this to you, *milyi?*" his wife asked.

"I fell down the stairs at work," he slurped a spoon full of soup and looked away.

"You fell down the stairs and no one took you to the hospital?" She shook her head and brushed the hair out of his eyes.

As he attacked the bread, he noticed his daughter sitting in the corner of the room with her book. "More English poetry, *kotyonok*? Why aren't you at the University?"

Lolita stood up and walked to his bedside. "Dad, something has happened at Brentano Hall." She took her father's hand.

"Professor Schmutzig was found dead in his office. Apparently, he overdosed on heroin."

Dmitry dropped the bread and moved the tray to the other side of the bed. If the professor was dead, *Bratva* must have killed him. The Pope's thugs were probably looking for the paintings when they ran into the professor. Dmitry never should have hidden them under the floorboards in the professor's office. If he hadn't, the professor would still be alive.

"Sabina, Lolita, we're not safe here." He threw back the covers and swung his feet out over the edge of the bed. "We need to leave. Now." When he tried to stand, shooting pain brought him to his knees. He crawled over to the dresser and used it to pull himself upright. His wife and daughter both got up and dashed to him, and hoisting him from under his arms, they steered him to a chair. Bunin appeared in the bedroom barking like he'd gone insane, nose pointed skyward, his blue eyes blazing, and his black and white fur standing on end. He ran back and forth between the bedroom and the hallway, barking so much the sound turned into one loud howl. Except for the time he had wrestled a giant raccoon out of the house through his dog door, the middle-aged Siberian Husky was usually mellow. He'd never acted like this before.

"What in Heaven's name?" Sabina asked, following the dog out of the room. The scream knocked Dmitry off his chair. He scrambled to his feet and jolted toward the screams. He smelled it before he saw it, the acrid stench of burning plastic, and billows of black smoke assaulted him when he reached the hallway.

"Run! Get out of the house," he yelled. Trying to find Sabina, he staggered into the living room and found her dashing around the room snatching up family photos and pulling paintings off the wall as she went. Smoke was enveloping the living room, so he pulled his t-shirt over his mouth and nose. Just as he reached Sabina and pulled at her arm, a monstrous boom threw him across the room. The explosion temporarily blinded him, and by the time he came to his senses, Lolita was pulling him out the front door. Once outside, frantic, he searched for Sabina, but realized she must still be inside the burning house.

"Sabina!" Standing on the front lawn, Dmitry was squinting into the smoke, choking on fumes.

"Mama, Mama, where are you?" Lolita was screeching at the top of her lungs, as she sprinted back toward the house. His ribs burned as he caught his daughter, held her with all of his might, and then hauled her into the minivan on the strength of sheer adrenaline. The van was parked on the street only fifty feet from the front door. He opened the van door and pushed his daughter inside. Minutes before he could barely walk, but now his family was in danger, he had the strength of taiga wolverine.

"Don't you dare leave this van! Do you hear me?" he yelled, and then sprinted back towards the house. But it was too late. The house was engulfed in flames shooting fifty feet into the air and a cloud of toxic smoke mushroomed overhead. Dmitry collapsed on the sidewalk as his whole world collapsed around him.

CHAPTER ELEVEN

"THOSE RICH GUYS make me itch. I think I'm allergic to them." Jessica James shifted her cell phone from her right hand to her left. "Anyway, I need to prepare for my meeting with Professor Van Dyke tomorrow. I'm going to ask her to be my new advisor. I guess no one's found my reject thesis yet, so I'm going to quit before I get fired."

"You're not going to be fired! Don't even say that. Look, Jessica, you've got to help me," Lolita pleaded over the phone. "My dad's laid up and I can't host the game tonight."

"Why can't you just cancel?" Jessica asked, even though she knew the answer. High stakes games like Lolita's took years to develop. She'd cultivated these guys. With her jet-black mane, alabaster skin, sage-green eyes, along with those angular bangs accenting her high-bones, topped off by purring Russian terms of endearment, and Lolita had the city's rich and famous sitting up begging for more as she fleeced them. She may not be much of a poker player, but Lolita understood how to make rich men feel cherished and adventurous.

"I'm not the only game in town so if I cancel at the last minute, I'll lose these guys to another game. And I need to keep this game to pay my tuition." Lolita lowered her voice. "*Milaya*, darling, you won't refuse me, will you, *lyubjmaya*?"

Jessica blew at her bangs. Nobody could refuse Lolita when she whispered in Russian. "Okay. I'll try. Who's on the list for tonight?" She was acquainted with the regulars who played every week, but there were always a few new players. The regulars liked to feed off of fresh blood, so Lolita recruited marks from the city's hottest parties and clubs. She made sure they were flush with cash, a little bit star-struck but not too much, and not good enough poker players to piss off the regulars. The Russian beauty had a nose for men who had the gambling itch and she knew just how to scratch it.

"Who's dealing?" asked Jessica.

There was a pause on the other end of the phone. "Bad news, my usual dealer, Raul, called in sick, so we need to find someone else to deal. Remember $5000 buy-in, $100 big blinds, $50 little blinds."

Jessica heard Bunin barking in the background. "How am I supposed to find a dealer in the next five hours?" She barked louder than Bunin.

"Call Jack or Michael. If they can't do it, you'll have to deal." Lolita was all business. "Get there early to set up. Jimmy is on security as usual." Jimmy was a security guard at Northwestern University who had a serious crush on Lolita, but he still took her "tip" money for standing watch all night. He'd been on guard at Brentano Hall every night since Schmutzig's death anyway.

"Thanks Jessica, you're a life saver. Call if anything comes up that you can't handle." Then she added, "I know what you're like when you're nervous. Whatever you do, don't drink."

"But, what if…" Jessica said to the dial tone. Lolita had already hung up.

Sigh. Now she had five hours to find a dealer and get herself ready. She couldn't bear calling her ex, Michael. She hadn't seen him or spoken to him since he'd smashed her heart into mush.

She remembered how the first line of his journal had made her want to retch: "Amy and I made love in the boat house." She'd dropped the journal back onto his desk and ran out of his apartment, tears streaming down her cheeks. When Michael finally appeared at her place later that afternoon, she'd suggested taking a walk to avoid being captive in her tiny apartment if things got ugly.

"Last night I dreamt about you," she'd said as she stepped outside the apartment building. "You were at the lake with a tall black-haired woman named Amy."

"What?" Michael ran his hand through his hair. "You dreamt that? Look JJ, I don't know if you're a witch or what, but there's something I need to tell you." He stopped and turned her to face him. "That girl from the community theater, Amy, we might have fooled around, but it didn't mean anything. Really."

She pulled away from him and started walking again. She couldn't bear to see his face.

"Come on Jessica. For Christ's sake, stop."

She stopped on command. When he put his arms around her, she went rigid, arms straight at her sides, staring down at a crack in the sidewalk.

"I'll make it up to you. I promise."

Silent tears were streaming down her cheeks, but she didn't respond.

"What?" he asked desperately. "Do you want to get married?" She glanced up at him. *Was that a proposal or a threat?* When he held her at arm's length and tried to look into her face again, she averted his gaze.

"No, of course not." If it was a proposal, she'd just turned him down. He'd hugged her stiff body goodbye outside her apartment door and that was the last time she'd seen him.

Obviously, she couldn't call that lying-sack-of-shit Michael, so she called Jackass to fill in as dealer. Anyway, Jack owed her big time after the herb-smoking caper in her advisor's office. She cringed, wondering if the police had found any other evidence of their break-in, besides Amber's button. She had to find a way to smuggle her thesis out. But with the police barricade and round the clock security, it was proving impossible.

"Jess, are you insane? I'd rather have a colonoscopy than deal for a bunch of rich assholes." Jack sounded adamant.

"Please, Jackie. I'll do anything you want. Do it for Lolita." She figured like everyone else, he had a crush on the feline Russian.

"Anything?" he asked, his voice lightening. "Never mind. I'll do it for you, because I love you."

She did a victory dance waving her phone in the air. Dealer. Check. Next on the to-do list, transform herself into a supermodel poker hostess. She bounded down to the bathroom on the second floor. Staring at her reflection in the cracked mirror, she realized she hadn't washed her dishwater blonde hair in days, so it was a thick mess. Who came up with dishwater to describe a hair color anyway? She had hardly slept, so purple bags the size of ripe Italian plums hung under her swollen blue eyes. And her best dress, a vintage turquoise Queen Anne with sweat stains in the armpits, was crammed into the corner of a moldy cardboard box.

And even if Jessica could solve the face problem, the hair problem, and the dress problem, there was still the shoe problem. She owned two pairs of shoes: classic cream Converse high-tops and scuffed black cowboy boots. Luckily she and Lolita wore the same size, so she usually just borrowed some strappy designer numbers when she needed to dress up. But that would mean facing Lolita's emo roommate, always a contact downer. She decided to deal with the hair and dress problems first and face the depressive Igor later.

Jessica lined up the things she needed to do and took aim. She had just enough time to stop at Nordstrom's to buy a Little Black Dress on Lolita's account. Although usually she did her shopping at Goodwill, speed shopping was one of her specialties. She ran red lights getting to the mall, squealed into a parking space, and dashed across the asphalt into the department store. Once inside, she ran down the escalator to the evening-wear department, scanned a rack of dresses, pulled out half a dozen, and chose a flattering black embroidered lace sheath she hoped would make her boobs look bigger and her butt look smaller. For added ammunition, she seized a strapless Miracle Bra and some Spanx on her way out of the store. Only two hours until show time and she still had to get the shoes, shower, change, and help Jack set up the poker table and bar in Brentano's basement.

When Emo answered the door of Lolita's dorm room, Jessica ignored her, made a beeline to the closet, and snatched up a pair of open-toed Guccis with thin Mary Jane straps and cute little gold buckles that probably cost as much as her monthly stipend. She slithered into the sheath dress, wedged her feet into the 5-inch heels, and then stuffed her old high-tops, jeans, and t-shirt into a grocery bag. Rummaging around the bathroom, she found mascara and eye shadow and did her best imitation of Lolita's smoky look. She even used the flat iron she found in a cupboard to straighten her hair.

"Thanks," she said in Emo's direction as she flew out the door. She left her crappy Impala parked at the dorm, knowing it would be quicker to walk to Brentano than drive around the maze of campus dead-end streets.

One last stop to get through the long night ahead. Walking as fast as she could on the towering heels, she headed straight for

Starbucks. When she opened the front door, threw back her slick hair, and strode through the café, she could almost hear Mustang Sally playing in the background as she flaunted her new look.

"What can I get for you, gorgeous?" asked the hipster barista.

She ordered her usual warm weather drink, Cinnamon Dolce Frappuccino. "Make it a double," she added. Then she ordered a double dirty chai tea for Jack.

Rushing out the door, she wedged the hot beverages between one arm and her chest as she pulled on the door handle with her other hand. She almost got through the door when in a split second one of her spike heels slid out from under her, the lids popped off both drinks, and she was showered in double dirty Cinnamon Dolce Frappuccino as her hip bounced off the metal doorframe. A coffee-coated bruise started forming on her bare thigh. *Shit.* She should have worn black stockings. As she lay on the sidewalk just outside the door, a swarm of customers came at her, some gawking, and some extending hands. She picked herself up, and with both hands, dusted off her dress and her pride. The embroidered lace fabric absorbed the sticky liquid like a sponge and one of the straps had broken on Lolita's right shoe. Only a half-hour until game time, she had no choice but to hightail her soggy ass straight to Brentano.

CHAPTER TWELVE

A PRESENCE CAME INTO focus, a pulsating glow in the corner of the room. Dmitry Durchenko tried to speak, but the tube down his throat made it impossible. He swatted at the tubes and tape fastening him in place. Now he was sure of it, someone was sitting in the corner of the room. He screamed, but it was as if he were under water; he couldn't make a sound or take a breath. His surroundings were going in and out of focus. *Had Bratva drugged him? Was he being tortured?* A soft voice emerged out of nowhere. "There, there, my son. Mama's here now. Everything will be okay as long as Vassily and Natalia are safe." *Vassily? Natalia?* The paintings. "Mother?" he mouthed, lips opening and closing around the hard tube.

In the sterile darkness, two red lights next to the bed glowed like the menacing eyes of a demon. A clamp pinched his index finger, and a machine hooked up to his feet rhythmically squeezed. His entire body hurt. His eyes burned, so did his throat. He tried to sit up, but he could barely move. Again, he forced his stinging eyes to scan the chamber. That's when he realized he was in a hospital. Desperate to escape, he clawed at the bedding, but even if he could loosen the bindings and hoses from his arms and feet, he was too dizzy to sit, let alone stand.

The terror of the abandoned Hospital and the gruesome image of his brother's face flashed up from darkness. Dmitry flinched. He had seen too many men broken by *Bratva* at the Hospital. Some pleaded for their lives, some cried like babies, some prayed to God, while others spit in the face of death. Dmitry wasn't the type to spit, but he wasn't a crier either. He would face death if it meant keeping his family safe. Except his brother. It was too late for Sergei. At least he wasn't the one who'd pulled the trigger. If he had, he might be living a life of luxury in Russia now instead of being tied to a hospital bed awaiting god-knows-what.

The florescent lights flickered on, shocking him into full consciousness. Stunned, he surveyed the room. A cheerful nurse's aide with a nose ring, pink hair, and matching Hello Kitty scrubs said, "Morning, Mr. D." Even her rubber clogs were pink. Soon the room was alive with white lab coats and blue nurse's scrubs moving into his field of vision and back out again.

"Mr. Durchenko, are you ready to breathe on your own?" a doctor asked. Apparently, not expecting an answer, the doctor ripped the tape from his face. Each breath clawed at his scorched lungs, but as soon as he could, he whispered "my family." His voice was hoarse and weak.

"Relax, Mr. Durchenko," the doctor said.. "Your daughter is fine. Right now you need to concentrate on breathing. In and out. That's right," the doctor encouraged him. If the Pope had really wanted him dead, he wouldn't be on life support.

"All in good time, Mr. Durchenko. All in good time," the doctor said, as if he could read his mind, and then disappeared.

Hello Kitty said, "You have a visitor, Mr. D. There she is, our lucky Miss D."

"Daddy." He heard her before he saw her.

"We'll leave you two to visit. But don't stay too long sweetie," the nurse said as she pulled a brown curtain across the doorway as she left.

His throat hurt from the intubation, and his face stung where the doctor had ripped off the tape without any warning. A sadistic streak must be a prerequisite for doctors. For his daughter's sake, he hoped he didn't look as bad as he felt. He was afraid to ask about Sabina, so he tried to read his daughter's face. Her sage-colored eyes were swollen and red, and her beautiful pale skin seemed sunburnt. She was wearing a hospital gown over sweat pants, a telltale plastic bracelet around her wrist.

"So they've got you in here, too." His voice broke. She bent down to hug him, but there were too many gadgets in the way, so she took his hand instead. "I'm fine. I'm being discharged later this morning." At least his daughter was safe, but what about his wife?

As he did so often, he wondered what happened to his mother. She'd risked her life to help him escape with a million dollars worth of rubles of his father's money. *Damn.* The money. Hidden behind the false back of the dresser in his burned up bedroom, now it was nothing but ash. He hoped the paintings were safe. A tremor of guilt and longing seized him. How could he think about the paintings when he didn't even know if his beloved Sabina was dead or alive? Hot tears rolled across his temples onto the plastic pillowcase. How could he go on without her? He couldn't move his arms to wipe away the tears, or get the hellish smell of smoke out of his nostrils.

He must have dozed off. It was dark again and he was alone with the beeping and blinking machines. He stared into the darkness waiting for his eyes to adjust, and then scanned the room again. He was fully conscious this time, but he still sensed the presence. He slid up on the bed so he could get a better look around. He saw it again, the pulsating glow from the corner of the room.

Maybe the smoke smell was the remnant of the fire. No, someone was sitting in the corner of his hospital room smoking a cigarette.

"Who's there?" He tried to sit up, but got tangled in the tubes and wires. He recognized the earthy, robust smell of the strong Russian cigarettes. "Vanya is that you, you smokestack sonofabitch? What the hell are you doing here?"

"Dima, I'm so sorry," Vanya said in Russian, moving into the chair next to the bed, his boney knees vibrating up and down as he fidgeted in the chair.

"Vanya. You can't smoke in here. Put that damn thing out for God's sake." He couldn't believe the little punk had the nerve to come to the hospital.

"I'm so sorry, Cousin." His voice broke, and he almost sounded like he would cry. "I didn't mean it, *chuvak*."

"Didn't mean what?" Dmitry asked, narrowing his brows.

"Didn't mean to burn your house down." Vanya was flicking his lighter as fast as he could, a berserk metronome. Click... Click...Click...Click...Click.

"YOU burned my house down?" Dmitry jerked so hard he ripped out his IV line and the damned machine started sounding a steady alarm. Beep. Beep. Beep.

"Why? Why, Vanya?" He began tearing at tape, wires, and tubes to free himself from his bed. He was lunging toward Vanya when a stout nurse whipped open the curtain and marched into the room.

"What's going on Mr. Durchenko?" For a large woman, she moved fast as she marched over to his bedside and stood over him glowering. "What are you doing out of bed?" She asked and then grabbed him by the arm and practically threw him back into the bed. Up close, he saw that her stern upper lip sported a downy mustache. "Do I smell smoke? Have you been smoking? No smoking in the hospital." She scowled and shook her head as she jabbed the IV back into his arm. He let out a yelp. "Don't leave your bed again," she barked. "I'm going to check with the doctor about authorization to sedate you just to make sure." As she stomped out the door, her large backside eclipsed the light from the hallway.

"Vanya, get your ass out here." When the gangster popped out of the bathroom, Dmitry hissed, "You're going to tell me what the hell is going on, why the hell you burned down my house and killed my wife."

"Right, Cousin. I'll take you to Sabina." Vanya peeked around the curtain, out into the hallway, and then pulled a wheelchair from the corner up to the side of the bed. "The coast is clear, *chuvak*. Get in the wheelie-chair and we'll blow this bitch."

"I'm not going anywhere until you answer me. Sabina? Is she...."

"Yes! Now get in the chair before that fat Siberian boar comes back."

Naked under his hospital gown, and barely able to stand, let alone walk, Dmitry had no choice but to comply. Once he was in the wheelchair, Vanya sped through the corridors so fast Dmitry wished he had a helmet, or at least shoes. His cousin showed no concern for his toes as they rounded corners or crashed through swinging doors. Dmitry chuckled. They must have looked a sight, a wiry tattooed gangster racing a battered patient through the hospital. A few nurses and aides glanced up as they zipped by, but none of them seemed fazed. No doubt they had seen stranger things in a city this size. Vanya sailed the chair into the elevator just before the doors closed. A well-dressed woman gave them a dirty look as they rolled onto the ground floor. As the wheelchair broke through the emergency room doors and emerged into the mild night air, Dmitry heard the mustachioed nurse yelling after them.

Vanya put the brakes on the chair and helped him into the

passenger seat of his black SUV, and then maneuvered the wheel-chair into the back of the Cadillac Escalade as if he'd done it a million times before. "My granny's in a wheelie chair," he explained. "I take her to Dairy Queen on Sunday after church." He knew his cousin wasn't as tough as he looked, but he had no idea he was such a softie. Dmitry buckled his seatbelt and braced himself. If Vanya drove the SUV like he steered the "wheelie-chair," he was in for a rough ride.

A familiar tongue licked his cheek. "Bunin! *Sobaka*, what are you doing here?" The Husky was wagging his tail and stroking Dmitry's arm with his paw. Dmitry smiled at his cousin. "Ironic that I named Bunin for a harsh Realist who depicted peasant life as brutal, violent, and stupid, the very opposite of this sweet, docile, smart, pup." At the sound of his name, Bunin wagged and licked so hard it shook the car.

His cousin shrugged, flashed his golden grin, revved the powerful engine, and swerved onto Central Road.

After reaching between the seats to give Bunin a big hug, Dmitry asked, "What's going on, Vanya? Where did you find my dog? Why did you burn my house?" But he didn't ask the one question he most wanted to ask, "Is Sabina okay?"

"*Chuvak*, I told you. It was an accident," Vanya said in Russian. With one hand, he took a packet of cigarettes from his shirt pocket, tapped one out, put it between his lips, replaced the pack, flipped open his lighter, and lit the cigarette, all in one graceful movement.

"The Pope asked me to follow you. I was just watching from your back porch. I guess there was a gas leak or something. Flames and then boom." Vanya waved his arms around, and then glanced at his cigarette and stamped it out in the already overflowing ashtray.

"I saved your life, Cousin. I convinced the Pope not to tell the Oxford Don we found you." Vanya's hands were shaking as he lit another cigarette. "I had to promise to get those pictures in exchange."

Dmitry pulled his hair as hard as he could to keep from screaming. "You burnt my damned house. *And* told the Pope about the paintings. Why?"

"Look, I'm sticking my neck out for you, Cousin, but I don't want to get my head chopped off. You've got to give them pictures to the Pope if you want to live. Come on Dima, they're just stupid pictures. "

"Those paintings are worth millions, you idiot." Dmitry shook his head. "Where are you going? Brentano Hall is the other way."

"Me and Bunin got a surprise, Cousin," he said with a flash of gold.

"Tell me what's up. I'm not in the mood for surprises."

Vanya pulled into the parking lot at University Hospital and slid the mammoth Escalade into a spot marked FOR COMPACT CARS ONLY.

"OK, party-poop, chill out." He tapped another cigarette out of his pack, lit it, and blew out a perfect ring of smoke. "Bunin pulled Sabina out of his doggie-door and we brought her here." At the sound of his name, Bunin wriggled between the seats and licked Vanya's face.

CHAPTER THIRTEEN

WHEN JESSICA JAMES arrived at Brentano Hall, she found Jack waiting for her outside the backdoor, smoking a joint.

"Whoa. Holy Hollywood makeover, Batman. You look amazing." He grinned as he passed her the blunt. "Is it true what Nietzsche says, vanity keeps the well-dressed woman warm?"

"Try hot," Jessica said as she pinched the roach.... Just one drag to calm her nerves. She wished she could give him a makeover, but it was too late for that. They'd have to take him as is.

She fixed the broken Gucci strap with duck-tape, and sloshed around the basement getting everything set up for the big game, unfolding tables and covering them with green felt cloths, cutting limes and lemons to garnish the drinks, counting out stacks of poker chips, and making sure she had the guy's preferred liquors. As she worked, she thought of family poker games back home when her grandfather would stake her ten dollars and she'd mix his Mac and Coke. She'd been weaned on Canadian whiskey and poker. Her mom claimed Jessica's first words were "straight flush."

As a kid, she'd loved staying up past her bedtime to play cards, and hang out with the grownups, especially her grandfather. She had been only seven or eight, but he'd treated her like an adult, talking to her about the great chain of being, the elusive meaning of life, and the doubtful existence of God. Even though he had only a grade-school education, she'd known for a long time he was the first real philosopher she'd ever met.

When everything was ready for the big game, Jessica paced back and forth in front of the bar, tempted to throw back a shot of whiskey to calm her nerves. She'd just picked up the bottle of Jack Daniels and was about to pour, when the actor, Vance Hamm, arrived. He was tiny, much smaller in person than he looked on the big screen. As usual, he brought his $15K Shuffle Master because he didn't trust any human being to shuffle the cards. She juiced his carrot juice, added some lime and two ice cubes. As the rest of the guys sauntered in, she mixed drinks, served snacks, and did whatever else they asked her to do. If one of them had asked her to wipe his butt, she might have done it, anything not to mess up Lolita's big poker game.

She folded bills into neat piles and exchanged money for colorful chips, not the cheap plastic numbers she'd grown up with, but heavy duty compressed clay like they used in the casinos. Nine guys sat around the table smoking cigars, drinking booze, and stacking their chips. The air was tense as they waited for the last newbies to arrive, Northwestern University's star quarterback, Kurt Willis. He'd been the number two NFL draft pick a few weeks before. Lolita had told her that he liked to drink screwdrivers because beer slowed him down and the orange juice provided vitamin-C. Vance was pacing around the table, chopping at the bit, probably eager to take the quarterback's signing bonus. She tried to distract him by asking about his latest film, but that was the last thing he wanted to talk about. He was firing up the Shuffle Master when Kurt finally showed up.

The stocky quarterback had scrawny Alexander Le Banc in

tow, a Pit Bull with a Chihuahua. She intercepted them before they reached the table.

"I'm sorry, Kurt, but the game is by invitation only," she whispered, nodding towards Alexander then glancing over her shoulder at Vance. He was chewing on his straw, glaring back at her.

"Look, Hottie," Kurt said, lapping her up with his eyes, "Zander's my personal assistant. He's not here to play." Then he winked at her and added, "Baby after this game, how 'bout you and me play a hand at my place?"

"You may be undefeated in regular season, but you're not going to complete this pass." Reevaluating how far she was willing to go to make these idiots happy, she tugged at the wet sheath sticking to her butt. *Talk about a tight end.*

"Okay. Please take a seat." She gestured toward the open chair, forcing a smile. "Screwdriver, right?"

"Make it a slow-screw-up-against-the-wall," Kurt winked again and high-fived "Zander."

"Screw yourself," she said under her breath. "Alexander, could you come with me to the bar?" When they were out of earshot, she grabbed him by the arm and asked, "What are you doing here?"

"Kurt told you." He looked smug. "I'm his assistant."

"And what exactly do you assist him with?" she shot back. "His homework?"

"Not exactly." He smirked. "Not that Alley-Oop doesn't need help. Let's just say I fill his prescriptions." Alexander laughed his annoying high-pitched snicker. "I don't suppose you've got my paper hidden under that dress?" She rolled her eyes and wished she could wipe the shit-eating grin off the arrogant little weasel's face.

"You didn't read it, did you?" He sneered at her.

"Excuse me miss, could you be a sweetheart and pour me a couple of fingers of Lagavulin?" Distracted, she'd forgotten to give Mr. Schilling his drink.

"Of course, I'll be right there." Nicholas Schilling III was the only son of some billionaire Manhattan media mogul. He'd just moved to town and liked to drink expensive single-malt scotch, neat, of course. Lolita had instructed her to be especially attentive to him so she could cultivate him for one of the regular slots.

"Yeah, sweetheart," Jack said, "how about you pour me a whole hand?"

She tottered from the bar to the table, a drink in each hand, trying not to fall off the Gucci's. Handing Jack a water glass full of scotch, she said, "Here, that should last you a while." He nodded and smiled.

As she bent to set Schilling's drink on the table, her heel slipped, and she grabbed his shoulder to steady herself. "Excuse me, Mr. Schilling," she said trying to balance on the five-inch platforms.

"Please call me Nick," he said, turning to flash a billion-dollar smile. "You aren't Lolita."

"Are you always so observant Mr. Schilling?" She couldn't help herself. She was wearing a sticky black dress balancing on chop-sticks, she hadn't eaten anything all day except a slice of leftover pizza for breakfast, and this rich bastard was treating her like a waitress.

"Only when it comes to the obvious. What's your name?" Nick grinned. "And what's that perfume? You smell delicious."

"Jessica James." She white-knuckled the back of his chair for support. "Cinnamon Dolce Frappuccino."

"Jessica James, Cinnamon Dolce, glad to meet you." He extended his hand.

When she released the chair to take his hand, she fell forward right into Nick's arms. "Spicy and sweet," he said as he stood to set her back on her feet, "my favorite." Another strap popped off Lolita's platforms as she stumbled backward, until grabbing onto one of Nick's arms, she steadied herself, and he pulled her toward him. Confronted head on, his handsome features startled her. His blue eyes were framed by long dark lashes and arched brows, and his angular chin sported just enough stubble to offset his prettiness. Cheeks burning, she fought a nearly irresistible urge to touch his wavy chestnut hair. It looked so soft. His scent, citrus and juniper mixed with expensive single malt, made her light-headed, and she thought she might vomit. He was still holding onto each of her arms, looking directly into her eyes, when Vance's voice broke through the haze.

"Hey Romeo, you gonna play cards or play paddy-cake?"

"Hey, sweet and salty," Jack said, with a sly smile, "how about some snacks over here? Stacking the deck makes me hungry." She would have kicked him under the table if she could have balanced on one spiked heel.

Vance shot him a dirty look. "You better not be stacking the deck, friend."

The room had gotten too hot and Jessica needed a drink. She hobbled back to the bar and made a strong whiskey and Coke with plenty of ice. She was enjoying her first mouthful when Charles Henrotin, the richest and most important man in the game, asked for another cocktail. He was the Head of the Stock Exchange, a tall man with a neat mustache. She made him a Manhattan just the way he liked it, shaken in a cocktail shaker, Peychaud's Bitters and a dash of Maraschino cherry juice to "sweeten the pot." She smiled politely at the old man's joke. After she had refreshed everyone's cocktails, she returned to her own. Ah, nothing like a Jack-n-Coke to take the edge of a nerve-wrecking evening.

Alexander was hovering around the bar, and when she tried to swat him away, he started grilling her again her about his final paper. As if on cue, Nick called her over to the table. "Sit next to me for luck, Cinnamon Dolce."

"Lolita doesn't allow..." she stammered unsure of what made her more nervous, Alexander's grade-grubbing or Nick's icy-blues.

"As we've already established," Nick interrupted, "she isn't here. Sit down. I won't bite, I promise." He leaned back, reached for the extra chair, and dragged it over to the table next to him.

She staggered to his side, wondering why he'd mentioned biting her. Thankfully, the Frappuccino had made her skintight dress more forgiving as she levered herself into the chair next to him. With one hand, he moved the chair closer until her bare arm brushed against his burgundy wool blazer.

The quarterback and the actor were going head to head over a monster pot, when actor Vance Hamm went all in. "Since you're new, I'll give you a break," he said. "I've got the nuts on this one, pal. So you probably want to fold."

Kurt looked dubious. "How do I know you're not bluffing?"

"I swear to God, kid. I swear on my mother's grave that you don't want to call this hand," Vance chuckled and rubbed his hands together. "Unless you want to lose that hefty signing bonus."

When Kurt shrugged and threw his cards into the middle of the table, Vance laughed demonically and flipped his hole cards over to show a measly pair of threes. Kurt easily had him beat with two pair. She'd seen Vance pull this bluff off before. He was an actor for Christ's sake. Kurt lunged over the table. "Why you little fucker!"

"Dinner will be delivered soon." Jessica tried to distract the agitated players. "Would you guys like to take a break?"

"Hell no! We're just getting started." Vance danced away from the table to avoid the quarterback's grasp.

Jessica downed the rest of her Jack-and-Coke. "Anybody wannaother," she drawled. The slur in her words caught her off guard. She'd only had one drink, so she couldn't be drunk, but when she stood up to get more cocktails, she was queasy. She tried to hold onto the chair, but brought it down on top of herself as she crashed to the floor. She scrambled to get up, but the room was spinning. Lolita would be furious. She'd ruined the game.

Kurt the quarterback rushed over to her and sliding his thick arms under her back, scooped her up off the floor in one smooth movement. "She's drunk. I'll see little miss gets home okay." He headed towards the door cradling her in his arms, and Alexander trailed behind. Struggling, she tried to free herself from his grip, but everything was hazy as if she were looking through a thick cloud of her mom's cigarette smoke back home sitting at the red Formica kitchen table in the rundown trailer park.

"What the fuck? Are we playing poker or not?" Vance threw his cards on the table.

"I think the game is over for tonight," Nick said, stepping between Kurt and the door. "I'll take Miss James home."

"I've got it covered, pal."

"I don't think so, *pal*." Nick pulled a tiny gun from the inside pocket of his jacket.

"Okay, dude. She's all yours," Kurt said as he dropped her. She hit the floor with a hard thud. The impact should have hurt, except it didn't. Like a spectator watching a movie, nothing was actually happening to her but to someone else, someone who only looked like her from above.

"In my book, the man with the gun, no matter how small, always gets the girl," Jack said, throwing the rest of the deck into the middle of the table.

The last thing Jessica heard before she passed out was Vance yelling. "This fuckin' takes the cake. I'm calling the poker Tsarina right now. She's got some explaining to do." Then, everything went black.

CHAPTER FOURTEEN

DMITRY DURCHENKO KNEW he was a dead man if he mentioned *Bratva* to the cops. The Russian Brotherhood didn't take kindly to narcs. They didn't tolerate betrayal. The key to surviving this police interrogation was to say as little as possible. To his surprise, the two uniformed officers never asked the important questions, the ones he dreaded. He never asked about Dmitry's father or his brother. He never asked about the money or the paintings. He didn't even ask about his house burning down. All he wanted to know was why Dmitry had a bag of Professor Schmutzig's laundry in the back of his minivan. No wonder the Pope ran this city like its mayor.

Vanya was waiting in his Escalade outside the police station to take him to fetch Sabina from the hospital. Since the "accident," his smokestack cousin had been chauffeuring him around town, calling him "boss." Maybe Dmitry was following in his father's footsteps after all. He had one little mobster where the shoe pinched. It was a good thing too. He needed help. The Pope's men had broken so many of his ribs, he was tottering like an old man.

He glanced at his watch. Sabina might have been discharged by now. Remembering the second degree burns on the side of her beautiful face made him wince. She'd been so brave and stoic last night at the hospital and he couldn't wait to take her out of that horrible place and bring her home. Except they had no home, and now he'd be lucky to keep his job after the police showed up and hauled him off in front of that Texan *Baba Yaga* and the chair of the department.

"Got some place to go Mr. Durchenko?" the officer asked.

"My wife is being discharged from the hospital today, sir. I have to pick her up."

"It won't be much longer. Detective Cormier would like to ask you a few questions before you go," the policeman said. He left Dmitry alone in the small cubical room.

A few minutes later, a handsome African-American man in a suit sailed into the room and extended his hand to Dmitry. "Detective Harvey Cormier," he said, giving Dmitry an extra firm handshake. After a few pleasantries, and offering him a much-appreciated cup of coffee, Detective Cormier took a seat behind the desk, asked his permission, and then turned on a tape recorder. Perhaps he had misjudged the police force. Obviously the uniformed cop was just the warm-up act. The bag of clothes in the back of his van didn't bother this cop. The black detective must think it normal for a rich white professor to have a poor Russian janitor do his laundry. Detective Cormier was digging at a different hole.

"How well did you know Professor Schumtzig?" he asked.

"I'm the janitor. I see him everyday."

"Why did Professor Schmutzig change the lock on his door?" Cormier asked.

"I don't know," he replied, his hands folded in his lap. His practiced stoicism, essential to surviving his childhood, served him well. He possessed such self-control he could pass a lie detector test if necessary. The trick was paranoia. Passing a lie detector test while lying just required building up the requisite level of anxiety for the simple questions. *What is your name?* had to provoke the same emotional response as *Is your father the most wanted crime boss in the world?* No automatically reeling off your address. No letting your guard down. Every answer must feel forced and fearful inside, but sound natural and calm outside.

"Donnette Bush told us he changed the lock last week because you broke into his office. Why would she say that?" Detective Cormier stared at him.

That big-mouthed Texan Baba Yaga doesn't know anything. "I don't know, sir," he said in a steady voice. "I'm the janitor. Why would I break in to an office I clean every day?" For the next hour, the detective asked the same question over and over again in different ways, waiting for him to crack. He didn't know Dmitry.

The second hour of interrogation, things got ticklish.

"I hear you're an artist Mr. Durchenko," Detective Cormier said.

"I paint as a hobby, yes, sir." Dmitry tried to conceal his surprise.

"What do you paint, Mr. Durchenko?"

What could he say? That he painted the same painting over and over again. "Mostly abstract paintings," he mumbled.

"Do you ever copy other artists' work?" The detective's pensive stare bored into his skull.

"Yes, sir," he said. "That's the way all artists learn the craft."

"Which artists have you copied?"

"Russian artists."

"Which ones?" Detective Cormier was typing something into his computer.

"Kandinsky mostly." Dmitry wiped his brow with his handkerchief.

"Any others?"

"No."

"Why only Kandinsky?" he asked.

"He is my favorite," Dmitry lied. His palms were sweating. He caught himself worrying the corner of his handkerchief between his fingers. He had to stay focused. He couldn't afford to betray himself with little tells.

The detective turned the computer screen toward him. "You paint only this picture, isn't that true Mr. Durchenko?"

When he saw the image of Kandinsky's *Composition VII*, his heart jolted at the sight of the familiar forms: The conversion of matter into energy, the fusion of body and soul. Even the computer screen couldn't flatten the spirit of Kandinsky's masterpiece. He made up half-truths about the painting being his childhood favorite after he'd seen it on a school field trip to Moscow. It was true, *Composition VII* was housed in the Tretyakov Gallery. But Dmitry's painting was *Fragment Number 2 for Composition VII*, a small study Kandinsky had made for the larger painting.

After over two hours of questioning, Detective Cormier finally asked, "Have you ever sold your paintings?"

"Of course not," Dmitry replied. "Sir," he added less forcefully.

"Did you give one of your paintings to Professor Schmutzig?"

"Yes, sir," he answered.

"What did he do with it?"

"He hung it on his office wall, sir."

"Where is it now?" Cormier asked.

"I told you sir, it's on his office wall."

"What if I told you it's not on his office wall?"

Dmitry had no idea why the painting would be missing from the professor's office.

"One last question Mr. Durchenko. How did you get those bruises on your face?"

Dmitry took a breath and looked him straight in the eye. "I fell down the stairs at Brentano Hall, sir. I wasn't looking where I was going." After nearly three hours of questioning, the detective finally let him go. Dmitry was exhausted from the exertion of holding his tongue. His entire being ached. In the last 48 hours, he'd been beaten, burned, intubated, interrogated, and stabbed with needles by an evil nurse. The money his mother had risked her life to give him had turned to ash, and now the paintings may be missing. If the paintings went on the auction block, his father's *Kryshi* would find him for sure, and then Dmitry was a dead man.

CHAPTER FIFTEEN

WHEN JESSICA JAMES came to, she was in a soft bed--her first clue something was wrong. The second was she was wearing large men's pajamas. Third, and most disturbing, she had no idea where she was, but it looked like a museum with a bed in the middle. To top it off, her mouth tasted like she'd licked a bar floor after a rodeo. She groaned and leaned her head over the side of the bed.

"Good morning, Cinnamon Dolce," a man's voice said. "There's a wastebasket next to the bed. Please use it." She took his advice then rolled back into bed. "Where am I?" she asked. "What day is it?" She put her hands over her eyes to block the blinding light burning into her skull.

"You're in my apartment, Dolce." She peeked through her fingers and saw Nick Schilling sitting in a carved wooden chair across the room. "It's Tuesday."

"How did I get here?" she asked. *Kill me now, please.*

"I'll tell you over breakfast when you're well enough," he said.

"Give me a few minutes," she said stalling to figure out what to do next. She was afraid to get up for fear she'd throw up again, but she wanted to get out of Nick's apartment as soon as possible.

"Okay, Dolce. Come down whenever you're ready." Somehow Nick's voice both calmed and stirred.

When Jessica was sure she could move without fainting, she stalked the circumference of the room, taking it in. The floor to ceiling windows with a view of the Chicago skyline to the right and Lake Michigan to the left made her feel like she was standing on a cloud. She'd never seen such a posh apartment. As she surveyed the room, she was drawn to a canvas smeared with thick blue, red and green paint, an abstract landscape with a giant blue tree covered in candy red dots at its center. An original Kandinsky? "The more frightening the world becomes," Kandinsky had said, "the more art becomes abstract." Her world was certainly frightening, but the art on every wall was just making it weirder. Growing up in Montana, Jesus-prints pasted onto slices of wood along with a few Western landscapes were all she'd known of art.

She hoped the door straight ahead led to a bathroom. She had to pee, and she wanted the sick taste out of her mouth, so she took the risk and padded down the hall. The bathroom was bigger than any apartment she'd ever rented. With its marble floors, walk-in stone steam-shower, and art on the walls, even the bathroom could have been a museum gallery. Her favorite painting so far was one in the foyer to the bathroom. A gorgeous Chagall with a woman holding a bouquet and a man dressed in green flying over to kiss her. Everything in the room was off kilter and the woman was tipping forward like she might fall into an awaiting cake on the table in front of her. When Jessica saw the cake, she realized she was starving. Yesterday's breakfast was long gone.

A plush robe folded across a heated stand, a new toothbrush still in its box next to the sink, and her dress and underwear from the night before cleaned and hanging behind the door, made her wonder if she'd been kidnapped and her blackout at the poker party was somehow expected or even premeditated. She locked the bathroom door, then turned on the water as hot as she could stand it, and stood under the shower. After a few minutes scalding herself under the hot water to combat her hangover, she coated her skin in rich lather from a decorative bar of perfumed Hermes soap. The orange scent was rejuvenating, and her hangover was melting under the hot water.

Pulling on the sheath dress-of-shame first thing in the morning--*or was it afternoon?*—was a chore. It brought back memories of last night's fiasco, starting with the backfired Frappuccino. Whatever time it was, it was way too early for Lolita's high-heels. She descended the spiral staircase barefoot. Is that Munch's original Scream? She stared at the sunken cheeks, bulging eyes, and silent scream. When she saw Nick waiting for her at the bottom of the stairs, his cheeks bronzed and eyes sparkling, she let out a silent scream. "Without art we would die of truth." She hoped Nietzsche was right and all this art would protect her from the dreaded truth about how she'd ended up in some friggin' billionaire's penthouse wearing his pajamas.

"You look refreshed." Nick handed her a fluted glass of fresh squeezed juice. "Would you like some orange juice?"

"How did I get here? And why was I wearing your pajamas?" Jessica gazed over the rim of her glass at him. "Did we…."

"No. God no. I'm not a sexual predator."

She was relieved. But what did he mean, "God no" as in No never, not in your wildest dreams? Her face must have betrayed her thoughts because he added, "Don't get me wrong. Under better circumstances, I wouldn't rule it out."

"Rule it out?" she asked, "Like a normal chest x-ray doesn't rule out lung cancer?" She chugged the rest of her juice. "Sorry, that's what the doctor always told my dad."

"Your dad has lung cancer?" Nick asked, concerned.

"He smoked a pack of Marlboros a day for decades. But that's not what killed him. His generosity did."

When Nick wordlessly gazed at her and then wrapped his arms around her, she buried her face so he wouldn't see her puffy bloodshot eyes. "Dolce," he whispered in her ear, "I'm here for you now." In spite of herself, she sunk into his arms and clung onto him, a little girl desperately in need of a hug. Just as he moved in for a kiss, the doorbell rang, followed by a pounding that sounded like it might splinter the door. She pulled away from him, and Nick went to the door and opened it. Two hulking men towered over him.

"Nicholas Schilling III?" asked one of the charmers.

"Yes, can I help you? How did you get past the security guard?"

The one with the pockmarked face flashed a badge. "We're looking for Jessica James."

PART TWO

CHAPTER SIXTEEN

P ALMS SWEATING, JESSICA James gripped the edge of the vinyl seat in the back of an unmarked black Interceptor. The seat was cold against her bare thighs, and she longed for pants instead of the skimpy dress from the poker game the night before. Rigid, she sat in silence and watched buildings and cars fly by outside the tinted windows. She didn't know if she was being questioned for breaking into Schmutzig's office, or worse.

The Chicago Police Headquarters on Michigan Avenue was housed in a concrete building with four floors of rectangular windows. From the back parking lot, the L-shaped building with small blocky windows looked like a prison. A uniformed officer led her through the parking lot to the backdoor. Inside the air was chilly, and she was glad Nick had insisted she wear his wool jacket. She rolled the edge of the jacket's piping back and forth between her right thumb and fingers, inhaling the faint reassuring scent of Nick's cologne.

A pot-bellied cop led her past a line of messy desks stacked with papers, computer, clipboards, and coffee cups. When they reached the end of a long corridor, he dropped her off in a tidy office and closed the door behind her. Everything on the desk was just so, as if whoever put things there had used a ruler to measure the distances between the computer, the keyboard, and a cup of pens and pencils. When she noticed photographs on the wall, she tiptoed over to take a closer look at them. They all featured the same handsome young detective she'd seen questioning Donnette at Brentano Hall. The athletic man with cocoa skin and amber eyes was accepting awards, grinning broadly, shaking hands with various officials in suits. She heard the door open behind her, and took a step back away from the photos. The man from the pictures said, "Take a seat Ms. James. I'm Detective Harvey Cormier. I'd like you to answer some questions."

She was on autopilot, answering his questions. "Name?"

"Jessica James."

"Age?"

"21."

"Occupation?"

"Graduate student." But probably not for much longer once they found out about her breaking and entering and illegal drug use.

When Detective Cormier started asking her about her dead advisor, she sat on the edge of the chair, feet firmly planted on the floor.

"How well did you know Professor Schmutzig?" he asked.

"For the last year, he was my thesis advisor and I was his teaching assistant." She shifted in her chair, shivering from the cool air blowing down on her from the vent over her head.

"Ms. James, have you ever known Professor Schmutzig to use drugs?" he continued.

"I don't think he was a drug addict, if that's what you're asking. Switching from Pepsi to Coke was hardcore for Wolf. " The detective's gaze was so intense she had to look away, but not before she noticed the golden flecks of light in his amber irises.

"We found your fingerprints in Professor Schmutzig's office."

"I'm his teaching assistant, so I was in there a lot." Jessica's face was on fire.

"Even in his bathroom? When was the last time you were in his office?"

"The last time," she repeated, choking on the words. The detective left the office to get her some water, and returned a few seconds later with a paper cup, and handed it to her. Her eyes were tearing up from coughing, so she reached into her jacket pocket for a Kleenex. Her pockets were always full of tissues, especially in June, the height of allergy season. But this wasn't her jacket. Her right hand recoiled from Nick's pocket as if a snake had bitten it. She stared down at the offending pocket.

"Is something wrong, Ms. James?" the detective asked.

"No, I'm fine officer," she said, sitting bolt upright.

"Would you like a cup of tea or coffee?" he asked.

"Yes, a cup of tea would be nice," she said to get him out of the room again. When he was gone, Jessica put her hand back into the pocket and carefully pulled the little revolver up to the edge of the opening. She glanced around the room for hidden cameras, but didn't see any, so she slid the gun out onto her lap to examine it. Its size made it look like a toy, but the heft of the black steel, and the rough pattern on its handle, left no doubt that it was real. Before she could get the pistol back into her pocket, the detective had returned with her tea. She opened her legs and swallowed the gun into her little black dress. Pressing her thighs together, ankles crossed, she took the cup of lukewarm tea in both hands.

"Did you notice anything different about the decorations on his walls the last time you were in his office?" the detective asked as he sat back down behind his desk.

"Decorations on his walls?" she repeated.

"Yes, the posters or prints on his walls."

"Posters or prints?"

"That's right. Did you notice anything different about his walls, Ms. James?"

She liked the way he said "Ms. James," pronouncing the final s as z, producing a pleasant buzzing sound. Mzzzz. James. She thought of those adorable furry yellow and black bumblebees in the lilac bushes back home, the ones she used to catch in a jar, then regret it and let them go. But what if the detective was more like a detestable yellow jacket, sporting a nasty stinger lying in wait in the bushes? Best not to find out.

"His walls?" *For Christ's sake Jesse, quit repeating everything the man says.*

"I think he had one of Dmitry's painting on his wall," she finally managed to say.

"Dmitry Durchenko? The janitor? Are you sure, Ms. James?"

"Dmitry was an art student back in Russia. He paints when he's on break. Recently he gave one of his paintings to Wolf." She wondered where this was going.

"Describe the painting please."

"If I can borrow your computer, I can show you," Jessica said, forgetting the pistol hidden in her lap. "It's a Kandinsky knock-off, Russian Expressionism."

"Please explain."

She tried to remember the lectures on Expressionism she'd slept through as a hung-over undergraduate at the University of Montana. "Russian expressionists tried to capture the emotional and spiritual levels of existence rather than the material or physical levels."

"No, explain what you mean by knock-off. Is Mr. Durchenko selling forgeries?"

"Forgeries?" She'd never thought of Dmitry as a forger. He painted as a hobby, not to make money or swindle people with fake art. Dmitry wasn't a crook. Then she remembered the note he'd left under the professor's door. "YOU ARE NOT SAFE HERE." Was it a warning or a threat?

"Just because an artist copies a painting, does that make him a forger?"

"Depends, does he sign these copies?" the detective asked.

Jessica shut her eyes to conjure one of Dmitry's paintings.

It was lunchtime by the time Detective Cormier extended his hand, and said, "Call me if you have any more information, Mzz. Jamezz." Detective Cormier was holding the door open. "Would you like me to escort you out, Ms. James?" He gestured for her to exit. He'd been pensive during the interview, but his parting smile lit up the room. The gun was still between her thighs, so she couldn't get up from her chair without it falling onto the floor. Hiding a weapon between your legs in a police station had to be a crime.

"Could I get another cup of tea first?" she asked, even though the first cup was still almost full.

"We'll get it on the way out." He waved his hand toward the hallway.

"I'm feeling a little lightheaded. Maybe you could get me some water instead?" Jessica put on her damsel in distress smile.

"Hold on. I'll be right back with some more water." Sure enough, the detective was not immune to her charms. She turned her head to watch him walk out of the office to the water fountain, and then glancing around, slipped the tiny gun back into her pocket, and stood up to go.

The detective was back in a few seconds with another cup of water.

"I only have one more question, Ms. James," he said, staring straight at the offending pocket.

CHAPTER SEVENTEEN

EVEN THOUGH IT had been just a few days, it seemed like a month since Dmitry Durchenko had set foot in Brentano Hall. Bunin whimpered as he locked him in the Escalade, and he could still hear the dog crying as he and Vanya sneaked into the building through the back door using his master key. Except for a faint glow floating into the hallway from the front porch light, the place was dark. Dmitry glanced around for signs of life in the dead house. Loneliness emanated from the antique wood, and he sensed no one was there. A house sounded, smelled, and felt different when someone, or something, was living in it.

Dmitry led his cousin up the stairs. This was going to be a delicate operation. Since his keys no longer worked, he needed Vanya to pick the professor's lock, but then he needed him to go away so he could retrieve the paintings from beneath the floorboards without being seen. Vassily Kandinsky's *Fragment Number 2 for Composition VII*, and Natalia Goncharova's *Gathering Apples*. He'd always wondered why his mother had chosen those paintings when his father owned dozens of Russian masterpieces. Why these two in particular? She must have been trying to tell him something.

For the last two decades, he'd copied Kandinsky's masterpiece over and over again, trying to decipher his mother's secret message.

In honor of his mother, he always painted a miniature Tiger Lily, just a wisp of orange with the tiniest of black freckles, in the corner of each of his copies. In his mind, he'd clawed at Kandinsky's canvas, picked off the paint, scoured every millimeter of cloth, traced and retraced its intractable forms. He even studied Kandinsky's writings looking for clues. "The eye is the hammer. The soul is the piano with its many chords. The artist is the hand that, by touching the keys, sets the soul vibrating." Every time he gazed at the painting, he sensed Kandinsky's masterful hand playing a concerto on his soul.

Every day, sitting alone in his janitor's closet, he'd studied the colors in the painting until he saw them recreated on his eyelids at night. He listened to the sounds of the colors and sniffed their individual scents. He waited to be touched by their discrete wavelengths, to feel their singular vibrations. One day, he even licked the very corner of the painting to see if the taste of Kandinsky's burnt orange might solve the mystery.

Now he prayed his beloved Kandinsky was still hidden under the floorboards in the professor's office. Adrenaline racing through his veins, he bounded up the stairs, stopped in front of 24B, and removed the police tape, careful to preserve its glue so he could reattach it later.

"Did you bring your tools?" he asked his cousin.

"Sure, Coz." Vanya took a small black pouch from his back pocket.

"Can you pick this lock?"

Vanya examined the lock, and then put the pouch back in his pocket.

"What's wrong? Don't you have the right tool?"

"Sure. Give me your wallet, Boss." Vanya's gold grill reflected the ambient light.

Dmitry frowned, then glanced around and lowered his voice,

"Don't forget. You owe me big little cousin. You burned down my damned house."

"How many times do I have to tell you? That was an accident." Vanya shook his head. "Hand over your wallet, *chuvak*."

Dmitry handed him the wallet, thick with fringes of receipts and scraps of paper sticking out.

"Watch and learn, *chuvak*. Watch and learn." Vanya pulled out one of the credit cards, slid it in between the lock and the frame, and the door popped open. It was ridiculous. The professor had his locks changed from the standard university security lock to this flimsy doorknob piece of crap. He may have been a brilliant scholar, but he didn't have much common sense.

Dmitry pushed through the door, and then turned to his cousin, "Wait here and stand guard. I'll just be a minute." Once inside the office, he headed for the spot where he'd hidden the canister. Unfortunately, Vanya followed him in and closed the door behind them. Dmitry was half way across the room when a knocking sound stopped him. When he motioned for his cousin to get behind the desk, Vanya ducked down to hide just as a skinny campus cop in a brown uniform pushed the office door open. When he saw Dmitry, the jumpy fellow pulled out his side arm and shouted, "Freeze! Hands above your head."

Dmitry held his hands over his head and kept his eyes locked on the security guard to avoid giving away his cousin crouched right next to him behind the desk.

"What's going on?" the guard asked, pointing his gun at Dmitry.

"I'm the janitor at Brentano," he answered.

"Your name?"

"Durchenko."

"Oh, Mr. Durchenko. Apologies," the campus cop said. "I'm so sorry. I didn't know it was you." The guard was so flustered he couldn't get his gun back in its holster. He was still fumbling with his pistol when he introduced himself.

"I'm Jimmy, a friend of your daughter Lolita." When he was finished fumbling with his sidearm, the confused cop extended his hand, and Dmitry scooted around the desk to shake his hand. He sensed Lolita had something on this guy. Maybe like so many others, he was just another casualty to her beauty. "Do you need any help Mr. Durchenko? How's Lolita?" the cop asked.

"We're all fine. I'll just finish up cleaning in here and then I'll be out of your way."

"Give Lolita my best." The gangly guard shook his hand again and turned to go. "I'll just wait downstairs in case you need me."

"That won't be necessary." As soon as the security guard left the room, Vanya sprang up from behind the desk, switchblade in hand.

"Calm down Vanya. He's not a real cop."

"Real enough, Boss." His cousin tapped a cigarette out of the pack in his pocket, flipped it into his mouth, and lit it with his titanium lighter.

Scowling, Dmitry grabbed the cigarette out of his cousin's mouth, pinched it out between his fingers, and stuffed it back into Vanya's pocket.

"We'd better get out of here before that knuckle-head starts to wonder why I'm cleaning in the middle of the night."

Kneeling on the floor, Dmitry pried up a floorboard with his life-saving carbide-tipped scraper. Groping around under the boards first with his right hand and then with his left, he cursed, "*Blyad!*"

"What's wrong, Cousin?" Vanya asked.

"The canister is gone."

Chapter Eighteen

TO HER RELIEF, the cute detective's final question had been, "Do you need a ride home?" Shaken from the interrogation, Jessica James waited outside the police station for Lolita to pick her up. The reflection of the setting sun off the steel tower across the street pierced her right temple and made her head hurt. In the saturated minutes she waited, the sky smoldered from a dusty violet and ignited into singed ocher. The skyline transformed from a shining technological wonder shimmering on the horizon into a two-dimensional black façade pasted onto blood stained parchment paper. On another day, she would have walked down to the lake and back. Now, she stood in the same spot for what seemed like hours wondering if her mother was right when she said, "The city is full of big stack bullies either buying the blinds or giving air, who turn every decent hand into a bad beat." Maybe her mother was right, she would be better off in Whitefish. If her mom had her way, Jessica would have been married by now with a beer-bellied husband, two kids and another on the way, living in a tin can next door in Alpine Vista trailer park.

Jessica thought of her last trip home almost a year ago. Her mom had gone into a tailspin, staying in bed for a week playing poker online, and gambling away money she didn't have. Jessica had to force her to drink broth and tea to stay hydrated. She blamed her dad. Her mother hadn't been the same since his death. If only he hadn't given those hitchhikers a ride across Marias Pass during a blizzard.... She shuddered thinking about her dad's mangled truck and all those kids on that burning bus. She fished in her pocket for Kleenex to wipe her tears, but all she found was the cold, hard gun.

Lolita pulled up with a thunderous roar, skidded to a stop, and then thrust a helmet at her.

"Here, put this on." It looked more like a mixing bowl than protective headgear.

Glad she hadn't gone commando, Jessica hiked up her dress and trying not to burn her calf on the exhaust pipe, carefully stretched a bare leg over the vibrating bike. She'd been burned too many times in the past.

"What the hell happened at the game?" Lolita yelled over the motorcycle's rumbling. "Jack said you fainted. I told you not to drink, dammit."

"I'm sorry Lol. I only had one." Jessica's voice was trembling as she fought back tears. "Then I blacked out."

"You only had one drink?"

"I swear, only one. It was strange. I got dizzy all of a sudden and felt paralyzed, like I'd swallowed hemlock, and then I blacked out. I'm really sorry. I don't know what happened."

"Well, we're going to find out. A Montana girl weaned on whiskey doesn't pass out after one drink. Especially you! Maybe you were drugged."

"Drugged? Why?"

The engine revved and Jessica reached out for her friend's motorcycle jacket, grabbing onto one of its side-straps just in time to stop herself falling off the back of the bike. She wrapped her arms around Lolita's slender waist and held on tight as her speed-demon friend weaved in and out of traffic across Lake Shore Drive. By the time they pulled up in front of The Rape Crisis Center, Jessica was as woozy as a ropin' calf at a rodeo.

"Are you volunteering today? Can't you take me home first," Jessica whined. "Back to Brentano?"

"Come on." Lolita hopped off the bike, and then pulled her off by the arm. "We're going to see the SANE."

"The who?"

"The Sexual Assault Nurse Examiner."

"Why?" Too tired to resist, she staggered along as her friend led her inside.

Her friend greeted everyone by name as she dragged Jessica down the narrow hallway. The stench of bleach and mold made her even dizzier, so she counted the cracks in the blistered linoleum floor to keep from fainting. Lolita by passed the check in window and pulled her through the vestibule and down another hallway into an examination room. When she pointed to a chair, Jessica collapsed into it. Then her friend opened a drawer, pulled out a paper gown, and said, "Put this on and sit down. I'll be right back."

She did as she was told. Why, she didn't know. Wearing only the flimsy gown, she sat on the examination table shivering, waiting for god knows what. In a few minutes, her friend returned with a middle-aged woman in scrubs. "I think someone slipped her a mickey last night. Can you check her urine for rape drugs? And do a rape kit. She might have been sexually assaulted."

Jessica's face was on fire. "What? I wasn't raped. I just drank too much." A single tear sprouted from each eye. She'd messed up everything.

"Since when do you pass out after one drink? I told you to watch out for Kurt Willis. He has a reputation for what's now called "nonconsensual sex," in other words, rape." Lolita glowered at her.

As hard as she tried to stop from crying, what was just a trickle became a stream of tears running down her cheeks. Her friend sat down next to her and put her arm around her.

"Sweetie, I'm sorry. I should have known better than to let that quarterback asshole into the game." She got up to get some tissues from the wall dispenser. "It's not your fault," she said, and then added under her breath, "but I told you not to drink."

"What makes you think Kurt slipped me something?"

"First your symptoms. Second his reputation as a rapist. Third he's the only one who didn't text to ask about you. Even that megalomaniac Vance asked if you were okay." She was counting each point on her fingers for emphasis as she went through the list.

The nurse finished the exam and then used a test-strip to check her urine. "The good news is there's no sign of forced intercourse," the nurse said. "The bad news is your urine tested positive for gamma-Hydroxybutyric acid, or GHB. The best news is you're still alive. Large amounts of GHB can be fatal."

"What's GHB?" Jessica asked.

"Its street names are G, Georgia Home Boy, Goop, Liquid G," the nurse said. "Along with Rohypnol or Roofies and Ketamine it's a popular rape drug. GHB leaves the body quickly, so you're lucky you came in when you did."

"How did I get it?"

"It's not a disease," Lolita said. "Someone drugged you."

"Did anyone offer you a drink? Was your drink in your possession at all times?" the nurse asked. "Did your drink taste salty?"

"I made my own drink. I might have left it on the bar while I was making everyone else's cocktails. But all the guys were playing poker." She wanted to sleep, even if it meant going back to the desk at Brentano Hall. She was so exhausted she could have slept propped up in a corner.

"What about Kurt? Could he have spiked your drink when you weren't looking?" Lolita asked.

"No. He was playing cards." She squinted and brought her hand to her mouth. "Unless…"

"Unless, what?" the women asked in unison.

"Unless it was Alexander? He was the only one not at the card table. But why would he do that?" Her head was spinning.

"Alexander who?" the nurse asked.

"Alexander Le Blanc. He's friends with Kurt. I can't believe he'd drug me. I'm his T.A. Why would he do that?"

"We're going to find out. Come on." Lolita tossed Jessica her little black dress. "Right after we get you some real clothes."

"And some food and sleep," she begged.

"You got it sweetie. Let's go."

Jessica recognized that steely glint in her friend's sage eyes. She was about to embark on some feminist revenge scheme, and there was no stopping her when she got the bit between her teeth.

"Hurry up," Lolita barked over her shoulder as she pushed open the double doors with both hands and exited the clinic. Stumbling over her own sluggish feet trying to catch up, Jessica tripped and fell in the parking lot and skidded across the asphalt, arms outstretched in front of her. By the time she rolled over and sat up, both knees were red and oozing from a bad case of road-rash. Her knees stung like heck, and wiping tears from her face with the backs of her dirty hands, she wondered how she'd landed in this mess. Before she could finish picking the tiny rocks out of her palms, her friend grabbed her beneath each arm, lifted her up, set her back on her wobbly feet, and then half-carried her to the motorbike.

"Food, sleep, and a plan for revenge. Not necessarily in that order." Lolita threw her long leg over the Harley. "Hold on."

CHAPTER NINETEEN

ALTHOUGH IT WAS a cool evening, people were sitting outside under the giant sunflower above the blue awning of the Blind Faith Café, enjoying the first hint of summer. The bistro tables were full of shivering hipsters drinking cocktails, huddled in excited conversations over the noise of the busy street. Jessica James reckoned she was safe in the familiar surroundings. Colorful frosted cupcakes in the bakery case were harbor beacons beckoning her to shore. Whatever the ailment, these deceptively pretty pastries were the cure, from Calming Carrot Cupcakes spiked with St. John's Wort, to Brainy Brownies containing Ginkgo Biloba, or Honey Heart Cookies laced with Horny Goat Weed. Combined with a steaming pot of Darjeeling tea, those treats were the antidote to even the worst nightmare.

Sitting in a booth across from her friend, Jessica devoured the comforting banana pancakes, her Blind Faith usual. The hot pot of Organic Darjeeling was the perfect counterpoint to the tepid tea at the police station. She closed her eyes, savoring the sweet sensation on her tongue. She remembered her grandmother's homemade waffles with strawberries and whipped cream, and for the first time in a year, wished she were back home in Montana. A wave of homesickness washed over her and she stopped eating.

In her daze, she'd barely registered Jack and Jimmy the security guard sitting on the other side of the booth ordering mountains of vegetarian grub and fancy cocktails. Amber sat attached to Jack like a tick, removing little vials from her big purse, and lining them up on the table. At least she'd traded her dirty nightgown for some full-length tie-dyed sarong number wrapped around her yoga pants, crowned, of course, by her Uggs.

Jessica concentrated on finishing her pot of strong tea. The English were on to something with this rejuvenating beverage. On her second pot, she was feeling alive again and her head had finally quit hurting.

"I forgot to ask about your parents and the fire. Are they okay?" she asked Lolita.

"My parents are fine. They're staying at the Residence Inn with Bunin." Lolita sipped espresso from a tiny demitasse. "One step at a time, comrades. We don't have to see the top in order to start climbing the stairs, but don't be surprised if these steps lead us all the way to the top."

"What do you mean?" asked Jessica.

"I have a plan to take down those rapists. We'll start with those frat boys and footballers who think rape is a spectator sport. You know the ones who text trophy photos of themselves committing felony crimes?" The Poker Tsarina was on a roll. "We're going to take them down on their home turf." She took another sip. "Jessica, you could have been the next victim if Nick hadn't intervened."

"I really don't think Kurt put something in my drink," she said, picking up her fork again. "He was playing the whole time." She stuffed her mouth with the last bite of pancakes, closed her eyes, and concentrated on chewing.

"But he could have had Alexander do it for him. He said he fills his prescriptions, right?" Lolita took out her iPad. "We're going to turn the tables on those fuckers. Jack, can you get your hands on Rohypnol, Ketamine, or GHB?"

Jack dropped his veggie burger. "I don't need drugs to get action. Action being the operative word. I prefer sex with animated women."

"What about the handcuffs, Jackie?" Amber asked innocently. "And that time when you tied me…"

Jessica burst out laughing. "Yeah, what about the handcuffs, Jackie?" she asked, spitting tea onto the table.

"Ah, yes," he wiped his mouth on a napkin and then handed it across the table to Jessica. "Playful resistance and tension incite passion. Sex with the unconscious is more like necrophilia. Rapists aren't interested in sex so much as power."

"I suppose they teach you that in your criminal psychiatry classes," Jessica said. "And what about the connections between sex and power? Perhaps we could use your handcuffs as exhibit A?"

"Stop bickering, kids." Lolita ordered. "Can you get the drugs from the hospital where you work or not?" Jack was interning at Northwestern University Hospital as part of his medical training.

"I suppose so," he said with a mouth full of sandwich. "Why?"

"Taste of their own medicine." Lolita barely glanced up from her device.

"I can get Ketamine," he said. "It is used as an anesthetic in cases where respiratory function is compromised. It's also a dissociative hallucinogenic that will put your frat boys through the psychedelic K-hole."

"The K-hole for the A-holes," Amber said.

"Those rape drugs all over campus don't appear by magic. We need to get to the source. That's our first flight of stairs. We're going to start our revenge operation at the Tau Kappa Epsilon Red X party tomorrow night. It's graduation week, so the fuckers will be in rare form." Lolita tipped her cup and swallowed the dregs of her coffee, then barked out orders to her lieutenants, "Jack, meet us tomorrow night at Brentano at nine pm. Bring the drugs. Jimmy, I want you outside the party in your cruiser, out of sight. I'll call you on your cell when we're ready for you to pick up the trash."

Mouth full, Jimmy looked up from his plate and nodded blandly. Lolita had him on such a short leash, he'd do anything for her. His affable nature was at odds with his tall, toned body and his pocked-marked face. Like the saltines next to his bowl of chicken soup, he was good to have around for an upset stomach, but easy to pass up otherwise.

When she'd finished outlining the plan, Lolita paid the check with a crisp Ben Franklin. "Everyone got it? Remember, courage stays one step ahead of fear." As always, heads turned as the Russian beauty rose to her full five feet ten inches, and waved her black hair back and forth before stuffing it into her helmet.

"If I'm right," Lolita said picking up her saddlebags, "we're going to double down on this game."

CHAPTER TWENTY

B Y THE TIME Dmitry Durchenko got to the hospital to fetch Sabina, it was the dead of night and the clinic was nearly empty. As he took the elevator to the second floor, the silence weighed on him. Exiting the lift, disoriented, he stared at the room numbers trying to figure out which direction to his wife's room. He walked towards the nurse's station, a bright island in a dark sea. The nurse didn't even look up as he walked past. He continued down a long corridor, past door after door, all the same, sealing in the sickness within. The punishing florescent lights were giving way to shadowy dread, and he stopped to catch his breath. Haunted by the nocturnal stillness in this liminal place of both healing and death, he was transported back to his last night in Russia.

Following his father's instructions, he'd driven an hour out-side Moscow to The Hospital. "Dima," his father had said. "Do this one thing for me and you're a made man, a *vor*. I'll even make you my *Sovietnik*." In spite of himself, Dmitry had been proud his father would promote him to his right-hand-man over his older brother. Whether out of fear or love, he obeyed his father.

He'd gotten to The Hospital early to make sure it wasn't a set-up. Trembling, he'd crossed the threshold of the abandoned building and crept along its dark corridors. The turquoise plaster walls were peeling like the sunburned skin from some exotic alien creature and reminded him of all the times he played nearby as *Bratva* "extracted information" or got rid of stoolpigeons, moles, and rats. Illuminated only by rays from a full moon, he'd drifted down the hallway to the "operating room," an abandoned maternity ward. Passing lab coats hanging from hooks in closets with doors falling off hinges, vials of medicines in rusted cabinets below diagrams of pregnant bellies covered in plaster dust, and surgical instruments laying at the ready in dilapidated surgery bays, he wondered if one day everyone had simply disappeared.

He hid in the shadows and was watching out a window when Yuri pulled into the parking lot. He gazed out at two of his father's *Kryshi* dragging a limp hooded man out of the trunk of a black sedan and lugging him into the building. Speculating on who might be under the hood, ears pricked, he listened to the scuffle as the *Kryshi* approached with their mark.

His father had said, "Meet Yuri at The Hospital and dispose of a *Kassir* who's stealing from me. I don't tolerate disloyalty from anyone. Is that clear Dima? This *Kassir* carries fire in one hand and water in the other. We can't allow such dishonesty." Until now, his father had never asked him to dispose of anyone. He shuddered. He'd never wanted to be part of the "family business." All he'd ever wanted was to paint and study art.

When the clamor reached the "operating room," Dmitry stepped out into the light. "Hello, Yuri. My father said you have an assignment for me."

"This is your assignment." Yuri pointed to the hooded figure suspended between the burly arms of the two bulls.

As Dmitry helped the *Kyrshi* tie the mark to one of the red chairs with stirrups, he noticed the *Kassir's* starched white shirt was splattered with fresh blood and his camelhair suit was soaked.

The bulls pushed the battered mark into a chair, rebound his arms around the back of the chair, and tied his feet to the stirrups. When Dmitry bent over the target to secure the rope around the chair, the unmistakable scent of bergamot, oak moss, and sweat punched him in the gut.

He leaned over and whispered "Sergei?" When he pulled the hood off the slouching figure, Dmitry was shocked to see his brother's face so distorted, swollen, and raw.

"For God's sake, don't just stand there, Dima. Kill him," Yuri yelled. "He's a traitor!"

Dmitry righted himself, realized he was still holding the bloody hood, and flung it across the room. "But he's also my older brother."

"I don't care who the hell he is, the boss wants him dead, so he's already a dead man whether you pull that trigger or not." Yuri drew his Makarov pistol and pointed across the birthing chair at Dmitry. "But the Oxford Don insists you do it."

Shaking, Dmitry reached into his pocket for his gun, and keeping his eyes locked on Yuri, removed it. Small and silent, the MSS-VUL, or "Wool," was his favorite hand-held.

Sergei raised his head and opened the one eye not swollen shut. He glared straight up at Dmitry and said, "Poor little Dimochka, pissing your pants. What are you waiting for *Súchka*? Little Bitch. Are you afraid of guns?" Pink spittle sprayed from his mouth.

Dmitry was used to his brother's abuse. Sergei had always been unpredictable, even cruel. As he graduated from slingshots and knifes to pistols and daggers, he progressed from squirrels and rodents to dogs and cats. Sergei, or "Sly" as the Brotherhood called him, was strong and sneaky, but not so clever. As their mother would say, "A liar should have a good memory," and his brother should have taken that to heart. How could he steal from their father and expect to live? It was true, Sergei was a dead man whether he pulled the trigger or not. He hated his brother more in that moment than he ever had before.

With both hands, Dmitry held out his pistol, and looked his brother straight in the eyes and pointed it at him, but Sergei only scoffed.

"Pull the trigger *Súka*," his brother taunted, blinking his one good eye. Dmitry's hands shook as he extended his arms, holding the gun just inches from his brother's face. He closed his eyes, opened his hands, and dropped the gun. The echoes of steel striking concrete followed him out into the night. As he walked away from The Hospital, he heard two shots, sounds that still haunted him to this day.

"Can I help you?" asked a perky young woman wearing stained blue scrubs and a messy ponytail.

Startled, Dmitry gaped at her, and then continued down the hall to his wife's room.

CHAPTER TWENTY-ONE

DMITRY DURCHENKO DEPOSITED his wife and dog in the pet-friendly room at The Residence Inn, a small one-bedroom with a kitchenette and televisions in every room. Sabina was like a kid on vacation, looking in every cupboard and closet. It reminded him of their honeymoon at the Ritz in Moscow when they were teenagers. He thought of the first time he saw her dabbing Prussian Blue paint out of a tube onto a pallet and then mixing it with yellow ocher to make a green as vibrant as her eyes. He'd watched her from the hallway to the painting studio, transfixed by her graceful brush-strokes and pensive gaze. At that moment he knew his life had meaning so long as she would marry him. They spent two heavenly months painting together in Gorky Park, taking long walks along the Moskva River, and visiting Tretyakov Gallery, before he proposed on one knee in Neskuchny Gardens. On Sabina's eighteen birthday, in the Church of the Archangel Michael at the former Andronikov Monastery, he swore to honor and cherish her for the rest of his life.

Now, Dmitry waited for his wife to get into bed so he could sneak out to look for his paintings. Once his wife was asleep spooning Bunin in the giant king-sized bed, he whistled for the dog. When the husky hopped off the bed, Sabina only rolled over and groaned.

Vanya was waiting downstairs in the Escalade. When Dmitry got to the parking lot, his cousin was dumping his overflowing ashtray into the hedge while lighting up another cigarette. By now, Dmitry knew better than to say anything. After what happened last time, he wasn't eager to return to Pavlov's Banquet and confront the Pope. His side hurt just thinking about it.

"We've got to go back to campus and find Alexander, the scrawny kid that works for *Bratva*," Dmitry said. "He's always hanging around the professor's office and I suspect he knows something about my missing paintings."

"You mean the skinny dude with an attitude?" Vanya asked.

"That's him. He deals for *Bratva* on campus."

"Alex, the Pharmacist," his cousin smiled his golden grin. "I know where to find him. Good thing you're with me, *chuvak*."

"Indeed. Let's go find him."

Alex the Pharmacist lived in a rundown rental near campus. The patchwork house suffered from years of shoddy repairs and mismatched paint. Dmitry took the front entrance and instructed Vanya to climb the fence and circle around back just in case Alexander decided to bolt. He walked up the cracked sidewalk to the rotting front porch, and stepping over several broken beer bottles and a melted stovetop espresso maker, knocked on the dented front door. He stared at the stuffing escaping from a ratty recliner on the dirty porch, as Bunin scavenged the littered wrappers from every fast-food joint in town. Bunin would have continued cleaning up the crumbs if Dmitry hadn't yanked on his leash. It was the wee hours of the morning on a weeknight, so any respectable honor student should be in bed, or at least cramming for an exam. But, as his mother would say, "even the barber knew" Alex the Pharmacist was not respectable.

Alexander Le Blanc answered the door wearing a terrycloth bathrobe with more bald spots than threads. Thin nose twitching and black eyes shining, he asked, "Dmitry, what do you want at this ungodly hour?"

When Vanya busted through the back door, Bunin started barking.

"What's going on here?" Alexander's head jerked towards the back of the house as Vanya and Bunin crashed through the kitchen and into the living room.

Dmitry heard rattling from upstairs, and a light came on in one of the rooms. By the looks of the place, several other guys must live in this dilapidated rat hole.

"Can we talk in private?" Dmitry asked. Alexander just stood there blinking at him across the threshold, as if he were speaking a foreign language. Maybe he had asked in Russian.

"Is there some place we can talk alone?" he asked again.

Vanya moved in behind the kid and hissed, "Ya deaf or something, *súka*?"

"No need to get techy, gentlemen. We can converse in my bed-chamber. With your racket, I fear you've woken my housemates. Gerard is an especially light sleeper." Alexander waved them into a small bedroom directly off the living room. Unlike the rest of the house, his room was tidy. The sparse aesthetic was a welcome change, as well as the waning of the unsavory smells emanating from the other rooms. The small space contained only four pieces of furniture: a twin bed, a wooden desk and chair, and a bookcase loaded with tattered paperbacks by Dostoevsky. A banker's lamp and sleek titanium laptop sat neatly on the desk next to a copy of Nietzsche's *Beyond Good and Evil*. Alexander scurried to make his bed so his "guests" could sit down, but neither did.

Pacing the tiny room, Dmitry noticed one other object in the corner, a plastic cart on wheels with eight drawers, each labeled with a color-coded tab marked in black block letters, MJ, GHB, K, R, H, C, and X. The top drawer was marked RECEIPTS. He could only guess what the others contained. He stopped in the middle of the room and stared at Alexander. Lit only by the desk lamp, he was a mere child. *He's just a messed up kid.* "Why are you mixed up with drugs?" Dmitry asked. "For a smart kid, you sure are stupid."

"The idiots who buy the drugs are the stupid ones," Alexander said. "Those hedonists care only for what their small minds can conceive of as fun."

"If you sell them the drugs, you're worse than they are. Maybe they don't know any better, but you do."

"That's where you're wrong. I'm better than they are," Alexander said. "I prove it every time those dullards purchase and consume this poison. I'm superior to those fat-head frat boys and air-head sorority sisters because I can control them using drugs."

Vanya pointed to the cart and asked, "Hey Alex, got good Boris blow?"

"Sure, if you've got the cash," Alexander replied, heading towards the cart.

"Taste first?"

Dmitry glowered at his cousin.

Alexander removed a small white box from the drawer marked C. The box had a picture of the cartoon characters Boris and Natasha stamped on it. He reached in and pulled out a tiny packet with a tiny version of the same stamp. Vanya extended his hand to take the packet, but the kid yanked it back. "Pay in advance," he said with a smirk.

Dmitry shook his head. "We don't have time for this. We came to ask about my paintings."

"What paintings?" Alexander took a step away from him.

"What did you tell the Pope?" He moved in on Alexander.

"Nothing." Alexander glanced around the room, as fidgety as a Siberian vole. "Why do you ask?"

"Look kid, you know damned well why I ask."

Vanya snapped open his switchblade. "Want me cut him, Boss?"

"Whoa, look here gentlemen," Alexander tightened the belt on his robe and stepped backwards. "No need for violence."

"Put that thing away," Dmitry said. "At least for now," he added, looking straight at the teenage drug dealer. Maybe he and Vanya could intimidate the kid with some good cop, bad cop.

"Alexander, be reasonable. The Pope is dangerous. Tell us what you told him and we can protect you," Dmitry said, realizing his good cop was coming off patronizing.

"I know full well what Vladimir is capable of. That is precisely why I'm not telling you anything."

Dmitry took out his wallet. Maybe he'd have better luck with a carrot instead of the stick. He took out a hundred-dollar bill. "Answer one question and we'll go. Do you have my paintings?"

Alexander held out his hand palm up.

"Answer the question first," Dmitry said, holding the edge of the bill just out of the kid's reach.

"No," he said, snatching the money.

"Answer one more question. Did you take my paintings?"

Alexander opened his palm and held it out. Dmitry emptied his wallet and placed the contents, eighty-two dollars on the kid's sweaty palm.

"I did you a favor, Dmitry." The kid stuffed the bills into the pocket of his oversized robe. "The Pope thought that forgery you made for Professor Schmutzig was the real deal, so I got him what he wanted. And I got what I wanted." He pointed to the cart. "In fact," he said grinning. "He may have sold your fake to some gullible collector by now."

Dmitry resisted the urge to shake the stupid kid until his teeth fell out. "You little idiot. You're in way over your head."

"What do you know?" Alexander asked. "Vladimir and I are like this." He crossed his fingers.

"Sure you are, kid." Dmitry whistled and Bunin appeared at his side.

"Come on Vanya. We're going to Pavlov's Banquet for breakfast."

"But Boss," his cousin said, following him out of the dumpy house, "Banquet doesn't serve breakfast."

"Don't worry, we'll be doing the serving." Dmitry said as he marched to the car. "I plan to serve the Pope his own deep-fried sins."

CHAPTER TWENTY-TWO

"THE POPE DON'T like prying," his cousin said, getting behind the wheel of the Escalade.

"It's not just about the Pope anymore." Dmitry Durchenko buckled his seatbelt, and then scratched Bunin behind the ears. "If my father learns about the paintings, I'm a dead man. I have to find out if the Pope has Kandinsky's masterpiece or my lousy copy. Whatever he has, we need to get it back before he sells it, or worse."

"What do you mean, Cousin?" Vanya asked, lighting a cigarette.

"I mean, if the Pope tries to move those paintings in an art house or on the black market, my father will find out and then he'll find me." Dmitry rolled down the window to get some fresh air. "Whatever the Pope does, Kandinsky's *Fragment*, real or fake, is going to get attention. You can't hide an anvil in a sack." He was trying to calm himself by stroking Bunin's head.

"Real or Fake? I don't get it."

"I hid the two masterpieces together in the same canister, so if the Pope has the real Kandinsky, then he's got the real Goncharova too. Those two paintings are worth millions of dollars."

"Whew." Vanya whistled through his grill.

"Whew, indeed. If the Pope has the original paintings, word will get back to my father faster than a Siberian lynx." Dmitry took out his handkerchief and wiped his brow.

"If it's fake?"

"If it's fake, then according to that detective, I'm a forger and my father would still find out." He dabbed his forehead. "If it's fake, then at least the Blue Riders won't be on the auction block or headed back to Moscow and we'll still have a chance to find the real ones. Either way, we need to get my paintings back from the Pope."

"Blue Riders?" Vanya asked.

"Vassily Kandinsky and Natalia Goncharova were both members of The Blue Riders, a group of artists, mostly Russian and German, known for figurative expressionism and abstract compositions."

"Figurative what?"

"Never mind."

As they pulled up in front of Pavlov's Banquet, remembering his last visit, Dmitry winced. He sent Vanya to the front door, and a burly thug answered it. From the Escalade, Dmitry watched his cousin bounce from foot to foot talking to the bull. When the front door shut, Vanya turned towards the SUV, gave an exaggerated shrug, then lit a cigarette, and stood under the awning smoking.

When Dmitry rolled down the window, the cool, damp, dawn air reminded him of why sunrise was his favorite time of day. At dawn, there was always still the chance that today would be better than yesterday. When he glanced towards the Banquet, he saw that the brawny bull was back. His cousin waved, so Dmitry got out of the SUV, and walked up to the entrance.

Red-eyed, the *Byk* motioned for them to follow, and then lumbered up the stairs, dragging one size 12 boot after the other. When they reached the top floor, Dmitry put his hands on his knees and bent over, trying to catch his breath. His cousin was coughing so hard he dropped his lit cigarette onto the carpet. When the breathless bull scowled at him, Vanya stomped on the smoldering butt with one of his fancy Italian lace-ups. Dmitry smiled.

The Pope's man led them into a parlor with weighty dark-burgundy curtains, dark leather, overstuffed chairs, and substantial wooden side-tables with thick legs, and then instructed them to sit and wait. A uniformed maid appeared with a tray and offered them strong Russian coffee and *Vatrushka*. Vanya noisily attacked the thick pastry, smacking his lips and licking the sweet cheese filling off his fingers. He grinned at Dmitry as he took a second slice. After twenty minutes of waiting, Dmitry lost his resolve and helped himself to the *Vatrushka*. After all, he needed to keep his strength up. The bitter coffee and hearty pastry were a match made in *Rayu*.

Finally, the Pope appeared, freshly showered and shaved, wearing a formal green smoking-jacket with dark velvet lapels attached to its glimmering sharkskin fabric. Dmitry thought of Kandinsky's description of the color green, "a fat cow, capable only of ruminating and contemplating the world through its stupid, inexpressive eyes." The Pope's round body, blunt pink nose, and narrow-set black eyes, along with the fact that he was constantly chewing, added to the bovine effect. Close behind the Pope, a man in a butler's formal black tails wheeled a cart loaded with Russian delicacies. Vanya rubbed his palms together and flashed his gold grill.

"Serve our guests and bring me a plate too," the Pope said to the butler.

Cheeks bulging, Vanya was making obscene noises as he wolfed the rest of the pastry. Dmitry narrowed his eyes.

"Whaa?" his cousin said, *Vatrushka* shoveled into his open mouth. "Can't a man enjoy good food?"

"Glad you are enjoying it," the Pope said. "I trust a man with a hearty appetite." The contrast between his dainty movements and his giant fingers was unsettling. "To what do I owe the pleasure?"

"Vladimir, we've heard that you recently acquired some art works," Dmitry said, glancing around the room.

"You did, did you?" The Pope laughed and wiped his mouth on his embroidered napkin.

"Yes, Alexander, uh, Alex the Pharmacist, told us that you might have a painting for sale."

"He did, did he?" Those delicate motions must be efficient because the Pope finished his plate and demanded another. "Our little birdie has a big mouth."

"What are your plans?" Dmitry asked, looking up over his coffee cup.

"My plans? Yes, well, I haven't decided yet. I'm thinking that the Oxford Don would pay a pretty penny if I sent it to him and that you would pay pretty if I didn't." The Pope laughed. "Am I right, or am I right?"

"If you allow me to see it, I'll let you know." *So the Pope only had one of the paintings.*

Still chewing, Vanya smiled and nodded his head.

When the Pope ordered his bodyguard to fetch the painting, Dmitry's pulse quickened. "It's true, my father would go to great lengths to retrieve his painting. But once he knows you have it, you can be sure he'll find a way to take it from you." Dmitry watched for his reaction. "As you know, his methods can be brutal. Of course, with your formidable knowhow, I'm sure you can keep it out of his hands if you want to."

"I can do what I want because it is mine." He licked each fat finger one by one.

"Yes, you've succeeded where my father couldn't."

"Your father thinks he is so smart with his Oxford degree. But who has the painting? Him or me?" The Pope chuckled. "I've got street smarts."

"As you say, you have the painting. And, as long as my father doesn't, you are the wiser man." He continued down the path he hoped would lead the Pope away from his father.

"Is that so?" The Pope paused. "Perhaps you would like to buy it back then? Am I right?"

"You would be right, of course, if I had any money," he said. "But, as you know someone burned my nest and my nest egg along with it." He glared at Vanya.

"I did hear about that. Unfortunate accident." The Pope folded his fat hands over his rotund belly and sat back in his chair.

When the bodyguard returned with the canvas and unrolled it on the table, Dmitry leapt to his feet, put on his glasses, and inspected the painting. Even if it was his copy and not the master-work, he had to get the painting back before the Pope did something stupid with it. As he examined it, he couldn't conceal the smile stretching across his face. There it was, his tiny Tiger Lily. Then, it dawned on him, and a shadow fell over his glee. If the Pope didn't have the original, who did?

CHAPTER TWENTY-THREE

J ESSICA JAMES FIDGETED in the wooden chair as she waited in the hallway. Her future was riding on this meeting. But distracted by thoughts of her advisor's dead body, her rejected thesis still in his office, and the plan to crash a frat party later tonight, she had a hard time concentrating on the spiel she'd prepared to give Professor Cynthia Van Dyke about her thesis. Van Dyke was her last chance to stay in the Ph.D. program. For the zillionth time, she repeated her Nietzschean mantra: "Everything decisive in life comes against the greatest obstacles." So far, graduate school had been one long series of obstacles: seminars that flew over her head, professors ignoring her hand raised in class, or worse, calling on her just to humiliate her, and then criticizing her in front of the pedigreed boys. In that stable full of pure-bred geldings (stallions they weren't), she was one mangy filly, the only girl in the Ph.D. program and the only kid grown and raised in a trailer park--in the backwoods of Montana no less. Looking down their snooty noses, the geeky boys in the program alternately insulted her (calling her "air-head" and "pussy-galore"), or hit on her, drinking too much at parties and then declaring their undying love.

One day in her first semester, she was walking down the hall when she overheard two advanced graduate students talking to one of their professors in his office. The professor asked them, "Who's that blonde girl sitting in the back of the class sulking?" Heart racing, she stopped, held her breath, and listened from the hallway.

"That's Jessica James," one of the stuck-up bluebloods responded.

"Oh, right, the fellowship girl we had to admit because the Dean was on our case to accept more women. I remember now. We got double points for her, both female and *underprivileged*."

"Trailer trash air-head. And what's with her clothes? Western grandma with red boots?" the other arse-hole said, and the professor laughed.

Jessica ducked into the bathroom, locked the door, and then spooling toilet paper by the handfuls, dried her silent tears. No way she'd let those bastards see her cry. Their insults just made her more determined. She'd get the damned degree just to spite those elitist horse turds. Success would be the best revenge. Ever since she could remember, boys had been trying to tell her what she could and couldn't do. In fact right before her very first rodeo competition when she was only eight years old, little Jimmy Dalton told her, "My dad says girls shouldn't ride horses coz then they can't have babies no more." She'd glared at him. When her name was called to race, she gripped the reins with her right hand, clutched the saddle horn with her left, and gave her grade horse the spurs. Spirits flying as high as her legs and arms rounding the third barrel, she'd decided then and there she'd take horses over babies any day. She'd show Jimmy Dalton she was no ordinary girl.

Now, sitting on a rickety chair alone in the hallway, rejected by one advisor and waiting to make her appeal to another, she was beginning to wonder. Maybe she was an ordinary girl. Maybe she should give up her dreams of becoming a professor, move back home to Whitefish, and have babies like the girls she'd hung out with in high school. Maybe Wolf was right and she wasn't Ph.D. material.

She stared down at her cowboy boots. She'd painted them blood-red with model paint to cheer herself up before her meeting with Van Dyke. She'd also put her unruly hair into French braids that wound around her face, and worn her great-grandmother's cobalt-blue calf-length gingham dress with black velvet embroidery. It still held a whiff of mothball tinged with early 20th Century perspiration, and she was hoping it would impart some of her great-grand mother's grit along with her sweat. She tried to imagine her great-grand mother wearing that fancy dress back in Montana: Saturday night dances at the Eagles or the Elks Clubs, and picnics on Whitefish Lake; she knew it wasn't to church, since apart from her own wedding, her great-grand mother proudly proclaimed she'd never set foot in a "holy meeting-house full of hypocrites." Her great-grandmother had obviously taken better care of her dresses than Jessica did. Then again, they probably weren't made for climbing over fences, playing flag football, or leaping onto elevated trains.

Jessica's breath caught when the door to the office opened and a short stout woman in her early thirties stepped out, and said, "Sorry to keep you waiting," gesturing for her to enter the office. Before today, Jessica had only exchanged pleasantries with the junior professor at holiday parties and departmental functions. Now, sitting in her office, Jessica grasped the weight of the diplomas hanging on her wall. Surrounded by shelves of books the junior professor had undoubtedly read, bitter bile rose in her throat as it always did when she was expected to sound smart. She noticed Van Dyke staring at her cowboy boots and blushed. As she stammered to explain her thesis project, the professor sat upright on the edge of her chair, eyes wide, nodding. Either she liked what she heard, or she was in a hurry for Jessica to finish and get out.

"Nietzsche's influence on Russian art, I like it," Van Dyke said with a smile. "Have you considered a feminist angle? Nietzsche has some interesting, *ahem,* things to say about women."

"'When you go to woman, don't forget your whip'. Or, 'Women make the highs higher and the lows more frequent'. That sort of thing?" Jessica was trying to remember more of Nietzsche's spicy tidbits about women. She stifled a laugh.

"Does Nietzsche ever talk about men strew ation?" Van Dyke asked.

"Excuse me?" She frantically tried to understand the question. *Did he talk about what? What in the hell was men strew ation?*

"Menstruation, he might have something to say about it." Van Dyke's fuzzy brown hair sat on top of her round head, dried moss on a boulder.

Jessica's cheeks turned as red as her boots. "Oh, uhm, not that I know of, but I can look into it."

"Yes, that might be interesting. Say, have you met the new art history professor? Professor Charis? He specializes in 20th century Russian art. He just moved into his office next door." Van Dyke picked up her telephone. "We should add him to your committee." She looked up his number on her computer, dialed, and then chatted amiably to someone on the other end about Jessica's project.

"He can see you this afternoon if you have time to go over to his office. It's just next door, Rockwell, third floor," she said with satisfaction as she hung up the phone.

"Okay." Jessica shifted in her chair. She was ready to do whatever Van Dyke asked if it meant getting the damned degree.

"Do you know if any of these artists actually read Nietzsche?" Van Dyke asked.

"Kandinsky mentions Nietzsche in *On the Spiritual in Art* and supposedly the artists involved in The Blue Rider's Almanac were reading Nietzsche aloud to each other." Jessica tightened her lips to keep from laughing imagining a bunch of painters consulting Nietzsche's *Gay Science* as a sacred text. "It's on Nietzsche's influence on Russian Expressionism."

"Interesting. It might be worth thinking about the gender politics in The Blue Riders. The women always get short shrift," Van Dyke said.

"Okay. If you think it best." Jessica picked at the velvet on her dress. "I mean if you're willing to direct my thesis."

"Of course, I'll be happy to direct your thesis," Van Dyke announced as she stood up and extended her hand to Jessica. Relieved, she bounced up and hugged her new advisor. They both laughed to release the awkward tension, two women swimming upstream in a river full of men.

"I'll see you at the memorial this afternoon." Professor Van Dyke said as she waved goodbye.

Skipping out of the office door, Jessica rammed her hip into the doorknob, but she didn't care even if it meant another giant bruise. With tears in her eyes from pain and happiness, she bounded upstairs to her attic nest to find a black dress for Schmutzig's memorial. No, not that one. She chose another of her great-grandmother's, a long black gabardine frock with a black cord bow at the collar. Between her black Converse All-Stars and red cowboy boots, she decided the latter were more formal. And besides, they added a big dollop of fun to her ensemble. She smiled. She was too happy to be going to a funeral. Now she just had to get the meeting with the new art professor out of the way.

When she stepped outside, clouds were suffocating the brilliant June sunshine, so she trotted back upstairs to fetch her umbrella. She smiled as she thought of the wacky French philosopher who wrote a whole book about Nietzsche making a marginal note about forgetting his umbrella. She was glad she'd grabbed

Nick's jacket on the way out. Just a hint of his cologne had reached her slightly crooked nose as she put it on, and she'd lowered her head to breathe in its spicy scent. She hoped her oversized woolen armor would keep her safe.

As she walked across the lawn, she noticed branches brown and dead just weeks ago, now bursting with blossoms, Azaleas bordered by Tiger Lilies. Brentano Hall was surrounded by a moat of burning orange. After months of constriction, the world was expanding again. The grass was wet, but luckily the thick red model paint she'd used on them had made them waterproof. She did a leprechaun kick, slipped on the grass, and landed on her butt. She laughed, picked herself up, brushed off her damp bottom, and continued on her way to meet the new art professor.

If Professor Charis agreed to be on her thesis committee, Jessica just might get her Ph.D. after all. She'd had to work hard enough to catch up to her stuck-up, prep-school peers. She went to Northwestern to study with Wolf Schmutzig, and then she'd put up with his inappropriate comments and oblique advances for months, only to find out he'd sabotaged her in the end anyway. She shook her head and sighed. She still didn't know why, but she was going to find out.

Jessica shook off her umbrella as she buzzed into Rockwell Hall. She'd never been inside before. Like Brentano, it was a converted Victorian mansion, but unlike the dumpy and dusty old Philosophy Department, the Art Department was stylishly decorated in black, gray and white tones. Jessica gawked at the huge black and white photographs of Chicago street scenes on the walls. As she ran her fingers across a sleek glass table in the entryway, she saw her unruly reflection. Her braids were coming undone, hair escaping every which way, and Nick's baggy jacket made her look like a bag lady. She used the sleeve to wipe water droplets off the table as they fell from her wet hair.

She took the stairs up to the third floor and walked down the hallway scanning the nameplates of the Art Department faculty offices until she found Professor Nicholas Charis. She took a deep breath, blew it out, and knocked on the door. When the office door opened, she fell back and her eyes widened. Nicholas Schilling III stood before her wearing a tailored cashmere jacket, starched white shirt, and faded blue jeans.

"Cinnamon Dolce, we meet again." Nick flashed his heart-stopping smile.

Her cheeks did their 'Scarlet Begonia'. *What the hell?* In the eventful twenty-four hours since she'd last seen him, she'd forgotten how handsome he was. But what was Nick doing in Professor Charis's office? Mortified and excited at the same time, blood rushed to her head, making her tipsy. She froze at the threshold, pointing her dripping umbrella at him.

"What are you doing here?" she finally found her voice.

"Come in and have a seat," he said taking her arm and gently guiding her into the office. He offered her a wooden chair, and instead of sitting behind his desk, he sat on its front edge, his knee almost touching Jessica's.

"Nice jacket," Nick said with a wink. "You look lovely, but I must say, I prefer your other black dress."

Flustered, she took off the jacket and handed it back to him.

"No, you keep it," he said. "I wouldn't want to be responsible for your catching cold."

"What are you doing here?" Readying her wet umbrella to strike, she repeated her question.

"This is my new office. I just started work here." Nick was clearly amused. "I've been unpacking books." She gazed at the boxes and half-filled bookshelves.

"But, Professor Charis…" she stammered.

"I am Professor Charis," he said, reaching for her hand.

Stunned, she let him take it. The warmth of his touch traveled through her fingers, up her arm, and, as if flowing through her pulsating arteries, coursed straight into her heart.

Still lightheaded, she retracted her hand. "Why? How is that possible?"

"At the university my father's name is just as likely to close doors as open them. Anyway I want to succeed on my own merits," Nick replied. "So, in my academic life I use my mother's maiden name. It's also a way of honoring her. She was one of the first women poet laureates, and she taught me to appreciate art. She's been the most important person in my life… at least until now."

"You tricked me," she blurted out.

"How was I to know the adorable poker hostess was also a brilliant philosopher?" he asked, his glacial-blue eyes sparkling.

"Let's start over." He stood up and extended his hand. "I'm Professor Nicholas Charis. Good to meet you Miss James."

Jessica took his hand and Nick raised it almost to his lips. Their eyes locked in a tight embrace and when he leaned forward, she thought he might kiss her. Instead he stood up, walked behind the desk, and sat down on a high backed leather swivel chair. Heart galloping, she was both relieved and disappointed.

"What can I help you with, Miss James?" he said in a professional tone. "Why are you coming to see me?"

"I was coming to see Professor Charis." Tears were welling in her eyes, and she looked up at the ceiling and back to keep them from escaping down her cheeks. "I was coming to see you, to ask if you would be on my thesis committee," she sputtered, staring down at the floor.

"Yes, I will," he replied.

"But, I haven't told you about my project."

"Well, I'd love to hear about it. Why don't you tell me now."

"It's on Nietzsche influence on Russian Expressionism, especially Kandinsky. My hypothesis is that The Blue Riders were reading Nietzsche and his writings shaped their philosophy of art."

"Brilliant! I know Paul Klee mentions Nietzsche in his diary. I've done some research on Nietzsche's relationship to *Die Brücke*, but I'd never thought of *Der Blaue Reiter*. Do your parents approve of you becoming a philosopher, Miss James?"

"That's a laugh. They don't even know what a philosopher is. Everyone at home thinks I'm studying psychology. While my mom went to church to pray for our souls, my dad went to nature to commune with God. But when my dad died and my mom became an alcoholic, I was left to find the meaning of life all on my own."

"My father thinks I'm wasting my life in libraries and museums, with books and art. He wants me to go into business with him. But that would kill me. Art is what gives my life meaning. Nietzsche is right, without art life would be tragic. Why study philosophy? I bet not many girls from Montana become philosophers."

"Well, I had a biology teacher in high school who'd tell me about night courses he was taking in philosophy where they asked how we know everything we experience isn't just all projections from our own mind." Jessica smiled slightly, shifted in her chair, and then pulled at the butt of her damp dress. "Everything I'd been studying in high school was boring and insignificant compared to questions about the nature of reality. I didn't know it then, but I was already a philosopher. When I got to college and took my first philosophy class, I was hooked." When she glanced back at Nick, his broad smile made her blush. She stared at her red boots and wondered why she'd said so much.

"Anyway, I'm just here to ask you to be on my committee," she said, biting her lip, she reached into her backpack, pulled out a form.

"Your thesis project sounds excellent and I'd love to serve on your committee. Sign me up."

Her heart sank as she handed the form to him to sign. That sealed their fate. Now that he was officially on her committee, he was also officially off limits.

"Now our business is done, would you like to join me for dinner tonight?" he asked.

"Excuse me?"

"Dinner, evening repast," he said.

"Main meal, food consumed after sundown," he said, less sure of himself now.

"I don't think that would be appropriate."

"Why not? You can tell me more about your fascinating research project," he said, standing up and coming around to the front of the desk.

"I have to go to a funeral this evening," she said after a long pause and stood up to go.

"Ah yes, the esteemed Baldrick Wolfgang Schmutzig. Very well. Another time then." Softly pressing his hand against her back, he guided her to the door.

She remembered his jacket and started to take it off again.

"No, you keep it, please, I insist," he said.

"Keep it forever?"

"Forever," Nick said with an exaggerated sigh.

Cheeks flaming, white-knuckling her damp umbrella, she did an about face and marched out the door.

CHAPTER TWENTY-FOUR

JESSICA JAMES STOOD adrift outside Brentano Hall in the drizzling rain waiting for Jack, wondering how the afternoon had become so dreary. Unable to get her bearings, she bent over and leaned on her umbrella for support, but it slid out from under her and she almost did a face-plant on the sidewalk. Light spring rain was running down her cheeks like warm tears. Was she in the same situation she'd been in with the Wolf only Nick was handsome as hell? Maybe she'd merely traded up from one ugly old pervert to a hotter younger one. Rain dripped off of the pleated skirt of her stiff black dress into her cowboy boots. She teetered from one wet foot to the other wishing she'd never met Nick's alter-ego, the sexy billionaire playboy, although the nerdy art history professor was definitely more her type. By the time Jack pulled up in his shitty old Chevy, she was damp and dazed. The beat-up sedan smelled of stale smoke and was cluttered with books and CDs. Amber scooted closer to Jack and Jessica slouched into the front seat next to her. She turned the dial on the dash to crank up the heater and pointed the vent at her skirt to dry off.

"Doesn't work," said Jack. "Looks like you're taking ole' Wolfie's death pretty hard my fair friend." He handed her a joint. "Lest you forget, he intended to sabotage your career." The stereo blasted "We are Young." As they drove across town, Amber sang along at the top of her lungs.

"Give me a second,

I need to get my story straight,

My friends are in the bathroom,

Getting higher than the Empire State."

Their jovial mood was contagious. She joined in the chorus.

Tonight.

We are young.

So let's set the world on fire.

We can burn brighter.

Than the sun.

By the time Jack pulled up in front of a funky contemporary prairie house in the heart of the fashionable Aspen Park suburb, Jessica was beboping to the music and shimming along in the front seat. By contrast, the misty rain shrouded the upscale neighborhood, and the stream of black umbrellas leading to the front door contributed to the somber mood outside. Windows traveled the length of the house creating a layered effect, each thin layer topped a porkpie hat, both elegant and adorable. As mourners blew in, the house came to life, an enigmatic creature with playful bright orbs and a cavernous stone orifice swallowing up the umbrellas one by one.

Once inside, the solemn mist gave way to boisterous festivities. Upbeat jazz filled the airy spaces with good cheer. More Irish wake than Jewish Shiva. Fingal O'Flannery greeted them at the door wearing skintight purple leather pants with a flouncy white shirt, an S&M Mr. Darcy. His thick bottle-brown hair was pulled back in a neat ponytail, a silver halo circling his scalp. Handing Jack a joint, he pulled him into the living room where a butler was serving champagne on a silver tray. The girls trailed behind glancing around the room at flocks of men congregated in clumps throughout the house.

There were two species, easily distinguishable. The drab Worm-Eating Warblers, Gadwalls, and Turkey Vultures from the university and the colorful Vermillion Flycatchers, Flame Tanagers, and Lucifer Hummingbirds fluttering around Fingal and his lover, the flamboyant (and bipolar) poet Harry Orse. Harry was always the life of the party, at least until he stripped off his clothes and ran through the streets yelling obscenities. The cops patrolling the upscale suburb knew him by name, and not for his prose poetry. Usually, they quietly returned Harry home, where Fingal would spoon-feed him Valium until he babbled like a baby.

Although in his sixties, Fingal O'Flannery was a swinger. Decadence was his middle name. He was famous for his parties--lots of food, drink, and drugs--and he took any excuse to throw one, even the death of a colleague. The only heir to a Philadelphia fortune, legend had it Fingal had been considered a boy wonder in his youth. His "genial" Ph.D. thesis had landed him the prestigious job at Northwestern University. That piece of youthful brilliance was still locked in a vault at Yale. Perhaps the world wasn't ready for his radical thesis that geography determined personality. Beyond a couple of essays, well placed by friends, he hadn't published anything for decades. Never promoted beyond Associate Professor, everyone knew Fingal O'Flannery resented Wolfgang Schmutzig's professional success. Whether to compensate for his guilty conscience, or in true celebration of Schmutzig's demise, he was throwing an extravagant bash in his honor.

Jessica was wandering around holding a paper bag filled with chocolate chip cookies she and Amber had baked that morning. After seeing the catered jewels on display, platters of fancy appetizers and petit fours, she dropped the bag in the bedroom where guests were leaving their coats. As she hid the bag under the pile of coats, she noticed Donnette at the corner of the bed fussing with her raincoat, and looking for place to put her dripping pink plastic umbrella. Donnette was talking to herself, her once perky bouffant had gone limp, and her fleshy cheeks were flushed. Even through thick concealer, the dark bags under her puffy eyes were a dead give away she'd been crying. She must be taking Wolf's death pretty hard. When Jessica tried to help her with her coat, she prickled and pulled away, clutching her handbag to her bosom. Under her coat, she was wearing a smart black sweater set with matching skirt, and a string of giant fake pearls. But when Jessica complimented her on her outfit, her painted eyes glazed over, and she only grunted. Something was wrong. Jessica led her to an armchair and coaxed her to sit. Donnette's hands were trembling as she white-knuckled the straps on her purse.

"Want a cookie?" Jessica asked, hoping to cheer her up.

"I took Wolf's diary from his desk before the police came," she said looking up mournfully. "Was that wrong?"

"The Wolf... Wolf, kept a diary? Have you read it?"

Donnette scowled. "It is going with him to his grave. I'm taking it to the burial this evening." She spoke in a strange monotone, as if she'd been hypnotized.

"Can I see it?"

Donnette opened her handbag an inch and Jessica spied a black moleskin notebook just like the journal she kept in her book bag.

"Can I see it?" Jessica repeated.

"You saw it."

"I mean, can I look inside?"

"Of course not! Wolf's secrets are safe with me." Donnette zipped her purse shut and stood up. "God bless his soul, they will be buried with him."

"What secrets?"

"Never you mind, Missy," Donnette said and then marched out of the bedroom.

Jessica had to find a way to get her hands on that diary. Maybe then she'd find out why Wolf wanted to sabotage her career. She was dying to know Schmutzig's secrets. She couldn't even imagine. Maybe Amber was right and he'd secretly been sending his pay check off to an orphanage in Tibet or maybe he'd invested in oil and was a tycoon running some middle eastern country from his desktop computer. More likely, he'd stolen pencils and legal pads from the main office or given As to his favorite boys just because they brought him bagels.

She scanned the crowd for Jack, but he'd been absorbed into the sea of men. She spotted Lolita's elegant silhouette outlined against the kitchen windows. Elbowing through the crowd, she kept her sights on her friend, not wanting to lose her in the throng. Lolita was talking to a group of dweeby philosophy boys who were inhaling her every word. Jessica tapped on her shoulder and whispered in her ear, "Wolf kept a journal, and Donnette nabbed it before the police could. We have to get it out of her purse."

Lolita extricated herself from the gaggle of geeks and followed her to a quiet corner. "What? He kept a journal? Grab Jack and Amber. We have to make a plan. If the professor had a diary, I need to read it. It might have a clue to why my father cares so much about him."

Jessica finally found Jack snorting cocaine off of the latest model iPhone with Fingal in the bedroom. Fingal's face fell as she led Jack out into the hallway. For the next hour, they tailed Donnette around the party as she ate her way through the buffet, cried on shoulders, and drank a bit too much champagne. Just as she was headed towards the coatroom, and Jessica was about to make her move, she heard the sound of someone tapping a spoon against a crystal champagne flute. She was so close on Donnette's heels, when she did an about face, she almost smacked right into her.

"May I have your attention?" said a man's voice. It was Harry Orse. "Please everyone, can I have your attention? I would like to make a toast."

Conversations stopped and faces turned towards Harry. "First, I would like to salute our dear departed friend, Wolfgang Schmutzig. He was taken from us in his prime. In his honor, I recite this poem." He took out a slip of paper and began reading,

"Do not stand by my grave and weep,

For I am here,

In your memories I will keep.

I am scented wind upon your face that blows.

I am moonbeams dancing in dark night's glow.

I am sunlight on ripened grain.

I am droplets in autumn rain.

When you awaken in the morning hush.

I am gentle meadowlark's uplifting rush of joyous flight.

I am sparkling stars that shine at night.

Do not stand at my grave and cry.

I am here,

For as long as you remember me,

I do not die."

Donnette started clapping, but when no one else followed, she looked around, cleared her throat, and fished around in her purse and pulled out a tissue. Crying, black streaks of mascara were carving canyons through her thick pancake foundation. Lolita lit a cigarette. That was the signal. Jack and Jessica moved in behind Donnette, and Amber came at her head on, wrapped her arms around her mother, and held on tight. "Mommy, I love you," she said, "Don't cry." Donnette was thrown off guard. She and Amber had always had a tense relationship.

Trying to catch up, Jessica tripped and her drink flew out of her hands. Its contents rained down on Donnette's already soggy up-do. At the same time, Jack swooped in, lifted the diary from her purse, and dropped Jessica's moleskin journal in its place. The three of them cycloned around their mark and spun off into the crowd. Later, Jessica would insist that she fell on purpose, improvising as she went.

Really, her mind had been miles away, at her dad's memorial service years ago. Folks he'd helped had showed up from all over the state, people she'd never even met. She always wished he'd paid more attention to his own family, but he'd said it was the Christian way to help others. After God repaid his generosity with tragedy, Jessica turned to philosophy for answers, but all she found were more questions.

Jessica turned back and peered through the throng to make sure Donnette was okay. With a dazed expression, Donnette dabbed her face with a napkin and listened to the rest of the speech. Harry ignored the ruckus and resumed his toast. "Next, I would like to salute my best friend and life partner, Fingal O'Flannery, who means more to me than life itself." Waving a half empty bottle, he motioned for the servers to top off champagne glasses. "Congratulations darling." He blew a kiss to Fingal disco-dancing across the room. "My dear friends," Harry continued, "this morning, Fingal sent off a manuscript that he has been working on for the last twenty years. His first book is called *Phenomenology of the Eye and the....*" The sounds of glasses clinking and applause cut him off. When the noise died down, he said, "Wolfgang has big shoes— or should I say sandals—to fill, but, I know he'd be pleased if his Endowed Chair went to Fingal."

Snickers at the joke, followed by murmurs, rippled through the crowd. The colorful birds kept on dancing and drinking while the drab fowl from the university faculty looked at each other in dismay. No way Fingal O'Flannery would be promoted to Distinguished Professor with just one book. Endowed Chairs were reserved for renowned philosophers, not party boys, unless of course they'd published a book a year along with throwing a debauched bash at New Year's. Odd coincidence, Fingal's book manuscript suddenly appearing right after Schmutzig's death. Jessica stared at Fingal dancing and shook her head. No way, she couldn't believe he'd finally written a book.

She followed the trio of pickpockets as they scurried out the front door just as Harry was concluding his toast. Jack had the diary tucked under his wrinkled navy blazer, the only jacket he owned. Jessica broke out ahead, hoofed it to the car, and her friends picked up the pace to catch up.

Jessica knew each one of them had their reasons for wanting to read the diary. Amber wanted to know why this man had always meant so much to her mother. Lolita wanted to know what this man had on her father. Jessica wanted to know why he postdated the letter. And Jack, well Jack, just thought it would be amusing to learn the dickhead's pathetic secrets.

As soon as she slammed the passenger door shut, Jack took off, still holding the diary tight under his right arm, steering with his left. When Jessica reached over Amber and tried to grab the notebook, his hands flew off the steering wheel and the car ran up onto the sidewalk and then bounced back into the street. Amber was riding shotgun and jerked the moleskin out from under his arm. She held it above her head and dove into the back seat. She flipped through the diary to the last entry.

"June 13th, the day of his death," she said.

"Read it out loud," Jessica begged.

Amber's snaky hair bobbed up and down on her head as she read, but when she looked up from the journal, she had a single tear rolling down her cheek, and then her mouth wordlessly opened and closed. Jessica kneeled on the front seat and reached into the back and grabbed the diary away from Amber and began reading out loud.

Friday June 13th

I wish Donny would allow me to pay for Amber's college. Although it was a moment of drunken weakness on my part that brought her into existence, she is still my responsibility.

She glanced at Amber, horrified, and wondered if she should keep reading.

My poor mother wants nothing more than a granddaughter. For Zelda's sake, Donny should permit me to claim the girl as my own. When I get home tomorrow, I resolve to tell mother whether Donny approves or not. She stopped reading when she realized Amber was crying in the back seat. She turned around to see the back of Amber's curly head in Lolita's lap.

Jack stopped the car, parked along side the road, and then reached into the backseat to stroke her curls.

In a small voice, Jessica read the last entry aloud.

Alas, Alex has arrived for our last weekly appointment, so more later. He comes bearing gifts.

"Poisonous gifts," said Lolita.

CHAPTER TWENTY-FIVE

WHEN DMITRY DURCHENKO got back to The Residence Inn, Lolita was waiting for him, tapping her blood red nails on the flimsy hotel dining table.

"Dad, we need to talk."

"Yes, *kotyonok*, when I get back," he said. He'd only stopped by the hotel to check on his wife. Vanya was waiting for him downstairs to continue their search for the missing paintings. Besides the Pope, the only other person who could have taken them was the professor. And he was dead. Dmitry had to find out if the professor had moved the paintings and where. His stomach sank. He had a terrible thought. What if the police had confiscated them and were looking for their owner?

"I keep telling you not to call me *kitten*." Lolita slipped into the flimsy chair, extended her long legs, and crossed her ankles. Her gaze pierced his heart.

"Sorry, *moya lyubov*. Oops." Dmitry grinned.

Lolita gave him the evil eye. When she was a little girl, she'd loved her nickname. She'd purr, meow, and crawl around the house on all fours. He had to face the fact that his little kitten had grown up into a Siberian tiger.

"You're not going anywhere until you answer some questions."

Sitting at the miniature dining room table, her tall frame made the table and chairs look like they belonged in a doll's house.

"Did you say hello to your mother, *milaya*? She's been anxious to see you." Dmitry pointed towards the bedroom where hopefully Sabina was sound asleep.

"Yes, and she won't tell me what's going on either."

"Would you like something to eat? Or some tea maybe?"

"Quit stalling, Dad."

"Well, I'm going to make myself some tea," he said.

"What was going on between you and the professor?"

"What do you mean, darling?" He busied himself in the kitchenette. He put a pot of water on to boil and rummaged around looking for tea bags. Lipton's, courtesy of the Residence Inn. He knew he should have gone shopping.

"What were you doing in his office?" Her voice held the word *doing* between its fingers like a dirty rag.

He put two cups on saucers, filled them with boiling water, and placed a tea bag beside each cup, along with an individually wrapped package of Saltine crackers. He'd pocketed a couple of packets at lunch yesterday because he hadn't had time to shop for food. A pauper's tea compared to the Pope's spread. He put one cup in front of Lolita, and then sat down across from her at the tiny table.

"Well?" Lolita asked. Patience was not one of her virtues.

"That, my dear, was a misunderstanding," he said.

"What were you hiding in the professor's office?" she asked, dunking the tea bag up and down in her cup.

"Hiding?" Dmitry asked, startled.

"In his journal, the professor wrote that he caught you in his office, hiding something," she said.

"The professor kept a journal?" he asked, astonished. The saltine crackers he was tearing open flew out of the package. He pushed the cracker crumbs to the corner of the table, scooped them off into his palm, and then threw them into the sink behind him. Dmitry wondered how much the professor had seen that morning in the office and how much he'd recorded in that journal. What had Lolita read there?

"Dad, I need to know what is going on."

"Okay, *milaya*, okay." He sighed, took a long slow sip of the weak brown liquid that passed for tea, and thought about where to start. "Please try to keep an open mind, *moya lyubov,*" he said, folding his hands and closing his eyes. It occurred to him, someone who didn't know better might have thought he was praying.

"Don't look so worried, Daddy," Lolita put her hand on his and smiled, lightening the mood. He shifted on his teetering chair and drew in a long breath. It was time he told her the truth, the awful truth about her heritage. He didn't know which was worse, the burden of carrying his secrets all of these years, or the burden of revealing them.

"I'm not proud of everything I've done. But I've tried to protect those I love." His eyes glistened. He quickly wiped his eyes with his handkerchief so his daughter wouldn't see him cry. He took another drink of tea to stall until he could speak without his voice cracking.

"You are twenty-one years old, a beautiful, intelligent, young woman," he said, choking back tears. "My little kitten has grown into a tiger. And you have a right to know the truth."

"I'll always be your kitten," she said, eyes watering. She briskly wiped under both eyes with the knuckles of her index fingers.

Sabina appeared from the bedroom in her pink bathrobe and slippers, so lovely with her wavy black hair loose and sleep on her face. "What's going on out here?" She yawned. She pulled up a mini-chair, and sat down on at the mini-table. The three of them were so cramped that their knees were touching. "What happened? Did someone die?" she asked. "Why are you crying?"

"Sabina, *moya lyubov*, our daughter is no longer a little girl," he said. "It's time to tell her the truth about her grandparents."

"No, Dimka. Ignorance keeps her safe," his wife said, eyes wide open. "Please, *moya lyubov*, she can't be hurt by what she doesn't know."

"Mother, I demand to know the truth about my grandparents." Lolita pounded her small fist on the table. The teacups jittered and their saucers filled with brownish water.

"Three things cannot be hidden long: the sun, the moon, and the truth," Dmitry said. For emphasis, he waved his hands over the remaining cracker crumbs and water droplets in front of him, wishing all the messes he'd made could be cleaned so easily. "This might be a good time for that bottle of vodka in the freezer," he said with a heavy sigh.

CHAPTER TWENTY-SIX

DMITRY DURCHENKO WIPED the soggy crackers and puddles of tea off the tabletop, and his wife replaced the teacups with chipped Residence Inn glasses and poured them each a splash of vodka.

"Okay, out with it you guys," Lolita said. "What's the big secret? Am I adopted or something?"

Dmitry chuckled. "You're too much like your grandfather to be adopted. And you're a double of my mother as a young woman." He tried to put on a good face, but his heart was sad. He hadn't seen his mother in decades, and not a day went by when he didn't think of her. Nothing could replace her calming presence.

A pounding on the door startled Dmitry, and he jolted up, sending the tiny table with him and their vodka and glasses flying. The table was lying on its side and the glasses were rolling around on the floor. He went to the door and peeked through the peephole. It was Vanya dancing from foot to foot with a cigarette dangling from his mouth. Dmitry had forgotten that he was waiting for him in the Escalade. When he opened the door, Bunin ran in and jumped on Lolita, tail wagging.

"Hey Dima, where have you been? Bunin and me have been

waiting thirty minutes, Cousin. Where's the toilet?" Dmitry pointed towards the bathroom.

"Who's that unsavory character?" Lolita asked under her breath.

"That, my dear, is your cousin, Vanya," he said.

She wrinkled her nose. "I'm really related to that little creep?"

"Do you still want to know the truth about your family?" Dmitry grinned. "Vanya is just the flower. The berries are yet to come."

When Vanya returned, they moved into the sitting room. Sabina poured more vodka and brought out some mixed nuts. She must have figured they needed a stiff drink to bear the weight of what they were about to hear. Vanya took a comb from his pocket and smoothed his thick greasy hair. He flashed Lolita his golden smile. Dmitry shook his head. *Here we go again.* Vanya didn't take his eyes off of Lolita, and she seemed to be basking in the attention. She stretched her long legs out in front of her and crossed her ankles again. "Cousin Vanya" she purred, "can I bum a cigarette?"

Dmitry exchanged a worried look with his wife.

"'Course, Miss." He did his cigarette trick. The Marlboro magically traveled from the pack to Lolita's lips and was aflame in one single movement. She batted her eyelashes and smiled up at her newfound relative. Dmitry squinted and shot him a warning glance.

"Tell the story, Cousin," Vanya said. At the sound of his voice, Bunin ran to him, wagging, and put his head in his lap.

Dmitry started his story. "Once upon a time in Russia, there was a little boy born into a very wealthy but very corrupt family known as *Bratva*, the brotherhood. His father was Godfather of this organization. Like God, he was feared and obeyed, and like a father, he took care of his children. That is, until they betrayed him with disobedience."

Lolita interrupted. "My grandfather is the *Pakhan* of the Bratva Syndicate?" As she walked across the living room, Vanya's gaze pursued. She returned with two saucers, and handed one to him and flicked her ash into the other.

"Yes, and your uncle was the *Kassir* until he started embezzling," Dmitry said.

"I have an uncle! He's a bookie?" She sat up on the sofa. "What's his name?"

"His name was Sergei," Dmitry said. "But everyone called him Sly."

"Was?" Lolita asked.

"Yes, he died," Dmitry interrupted. He looked away. Only fools and madmen tell the whole truth.

"What are you telling me?" Lolita rose up from the couch, walked back into the kitchenette, filled her glass with vodka and downed it in one gulp, then gasped, whether from the drink or the shock, Dmitry didn't know.

"My father expected me to go into the family business," he said. "He was going to make me *Sovietnik* the night I left Moscow." He grimaced remembering the terrible scene.

"You were going to become the *Consigliere* to the most powerful mob boss in the world!" Lolita exclaimed. "What are you saying? That I'm a daughter of Bratva?"

Dmitry downed the rest of his vodka and held out his glass to Sabina. "Sweetheart, could you pour me another?"

"No. You're our beloved daughter," Sabina said. "That's why we left Russia, for you, *moya lyubov*. So we could have an ordinary life."

"Like many young lads, I didn't want to follow in my father's footsteps," Dmitry continued. "I wanted to take a different path. "He put his chin in his hands. "I wanted to become an artist. You can imagine how that went over with my father." He sipped the cold vodka, careful to avoid the jagged chip in the glass.

"Your grandfather is one mean *súka blyad*," Vanya said. "A year ago, he took my father, his own brother, to the Hospital and shot him. But first, he cut off…"

"We don't need you to paint us a picture, Vanya," Dmitry interrupted. He shuddered to think of the gory dismemberments, brutal torture, and coldblooded assassination his father's Kryshi performed in the operating room.

"Hospital?" Lolita asked.

"An abandoned maternity hospital where the Oxford Don disposed of his trash," Sabina said in a harsh tone.

Lolita raised her eyebrows. "Oxford Don?"

"Your grandfather is known as the Oxford Don because he has an advanced degree in economics from Oxford. See, you come by your brains honestly." Dmitry tried to make a joke.

"How did you get away?" Lolita asked. "I thought the only way anyone left Bratva was in a pine box."

"Or, in Ce-ment overshoes," Vanya added. He stopped chuckling when no one else joined him.

"Aren't they still looking for you? Won't they hunt you down?" Lolita was upset. "How can you be so calm?"

"This is our fate, *milaya*. No one can change fate," Dmitry said with a sigh, leaning on the table with his head in his hands. Lolita came to him and put her hand on his shoulder. "I'm the child of Bratva and there is no changing that."

"Come on, Dad," Lolita said, "Bratva may have formed you, but that doesn't mean it determines who you are." She put her arms around his neck. "Daddy, as you always tell me, a wolf is not beaten for being grey, but for eating a sheep."

"Let's get some Chinese take-out," Sabina said. "I'll call and order it from the place next door."

Once lunch was delivered, he told the rest of his story while they ate. He left out the pain and anguish of his relationship with his father and brother. He didn't mention what he'd seen in the Hospital.

He couldn't describe what had happened to Sergei. The words would only cut his throat. His only brother's gruesome battered face. The smell of bergamot mixed with fear. Sergei shouting at him to kill him, spitting in the face of death. The distinctive crack of Yuri's Makarov pistol ripping through the frigid night. The sound of those two shots ringing in his ears for the rest of his life. Some things are better left unsaid.

He told her about her grandmother, her elegant dress and demeanor, her Russian sayings and sound advice, her love of art and music. He told her about their trip to the Count's estate at Caën, the story of how her grandmother's favorite flower, the Tiger Lily, got its name. Wiping his eyes on a damp napkin, he told her how as a teenager he'd been forced to leave his mother behind forever. For all he knew, his father had killed her for helping Dmitry escape. By the time he told her that she was named after her grandmother, even Vanya had tears in his eyes.

CHAPTER TWENTY-SEVEN

D MITRY DURCHENKO COULDN'T decide how much to tell his daughter about the paintings. He remembered when his father had bought them on a trip to Tajan auction house in Paris. His father stayed behind in the city while he and his older brother and mother visited her favorite cousin's 17th century estate. He and Sergei ran wild through the huge castle and sprawling grounds. That was before Sergei started torturing small animals, before he killed anyone, before he betrayed their father. Now, those idyllic fraternal days in the French countryside seemed like a childhood fantasy, something he'd dreamed, or a story his mother had read to him from a children's book.

Her cousin the Count was a handsome man a few years older than his mother. He had kind eyes and a gentle voice. At the time, concerned only with catching frogs, climbing trees, and trying to keep up with his brother, he hadn't suspected anything romantic between his mother and her "close friend." Now he wondered.

The Count taught him to fly fish on the river running through the estate. Dmitry gazed in wonder as the Count cast his line in a graceful loop expanding into ever larger ovals until he let it loose and then a magical pause hovered overhead at its full back extension, as if time were standing still before it would ricochet forward again. Dmitry especially loved the furry little flies and their funny names, Wooly Bugger, Sofa Pillow, Royal Wulff. He couldn't imagine doing something fun outdoors with his own father. Whenever his father had taught Dmitry anything, it was more like punishment than fun. Whereas the Count was mild-mannered and compassionate, his father was gruff and scary, more Grizzly Wulff than Royal Coachman.

One afternoon, his mother prepared a picnic and joined them on the riverbank. While his brother smashed mushrooms with rocks and poked at moss with sticks, Dmitry and his mother picked wild Tiger Lilies growing along the river. They smelled spicy, of cloves or nutmeg, like his mother's perfume.

"Dimka, those flowers have freckles, just like you," his mother said. "Do you know how Tiger Lilies got their name?" she asked.

He shook his head.

"Once upon a time," she began, "there was a Chinese prince hunting in the forest. He was ten years old, just like you, Dimka," she said.

"I want to go hunting!"

His mother laughed and continued the story. "The prince shot an arrow at a beautiful tiger but only wounded him, and the tiger cried out in pain. The regal animal was suffering, and when the prince pulled out the arrow, the tiger yelped. Ashamed, the prince cried too. The bloody arrow tip fell to the ground along the riverbank, and after the tiger's death, it grew into a Tiger Lily. In his sorrow, one day the prince threw himself in the raging river, and the tiger's spirit paced up and down the river looking for the prince. This is how the flowers spread along the shore." When his mother took his hand, he carried the full weight of the story.

When it was time to rejoin his father in the city, he had mixed feelings. It was the first time he was allowed to accompany his parents to an art auction, and he was in awe when subtle movements, barely noticeable, beckoned to the rare beauties on the block and took them away forever. Dmitry had never seen anything as beautiful as the wild contrasting colors exploding off the canvas of Kandinsky's *Fragment* for his *Composition VII*. Colors as sheer as veils. Bold shapes surrounded by thick black lines, a cockeyed mess that threw him off balance. That is when he decided he wanted to be a painter.

His father bought two paintings that day, Kandinsky's *Fragment* and a Goncharova's *Gathering Apples*. As his mother instructed that last night on the platform, Dmitry had waited until he got to Warsaw to open the valise. He had opened it in a bathroom stall in the Warsaw train station. He'd been stunned to see the suitcase full of rubles. But he'd cried in astonishment when he unrolled the canvas and saw his beloved Kandinsky.

"What other secrets have you been hiding from me?" Lolita's question brought him back to the small table in the Residence Inn.

"How did you get the professor's diary?" Dmitry asked, piling fried rice onto a Styrofoam plate.

"Jessica stole it," Lolita replied, coyly sipping her vodka. She was up to something.

"Did it mention that I gave one of my paintings to the professor just before he died?" he asked. He poked at his eggroll with a chopstick and pushed it around his plate.

"He wrote about it hanging on his wall. And then something about finding something under the floorboards." She peered at him over the rim of her glass.

"What?" He leapt on her words, dropped his chopsticks, and flew up from the table.

"What's wrong, Dad?"

"The real pictures, Boss?" Vanya chimed in. "Or more fakes?"

He was feeding Bunin BBQ pork with mustard sauce, licking off the sauce one piece at a time.

Dmitry shot him a dirty look. "Vanya, take Bunin for a walk."

"What's wrong?" He was pouting.

"Just take Bunin to pee so we can get back to Brentano Hall and find out what the professor did with my paintings."

Chapter Twenty-Eight

A S DMITRY DURCHENKO climbed into the passenger seat of the Escalade, he noticed Lolita running out after him. "Meet you at Brentano," she yelled, as she stuffed her hair into her helmet and hopped on her Harley.

The sky had cleared and the air was fresh after the misty rains of the day before. Opaque hints of summer humidity formed a steamy barrier between the earth and the sun. It was just warm enough that Dmitry turned on the air-conditioning in the SUV. He didn't want to risk Bunin jumping out the window. Lolita sped past them, weaving in and out of traffic. He had never seen her riding her bike on the freeway. He was terrified. She was fearless.

When Dmitry burst into Brentano Hall, from her desk Donnette looked up and glared at him.

"We're just here to visit Jessica," Lolita called to her.

Donnette waved, shooing them away. As he climbed the stairs, Dmitry noticed that the police tape had been removed from the professor's door. He wondered if that meant he should start cleaning the office again. That gave him an idea. Unfortunately, it involved talking to that big-haired Texan *Baba Yaga* at the front desk.

When he got to the third floor, he spied Jessica holed up in the attic reading. She was so pale, he wanted to tell her to go outside and get some sun for a change. Instead, he glanced away as she threw a man's suit jacket over her ripped sundress. Swimming in that jacket, with her blonde hair in pigtails, she looked like a little girl trying on daddy's clothes, although he wondered what kind of daddy would wear a tailored blazer with dirty tennis shoes. He wondered whether dresses and high-tops were a new college fad.

"What's going on?" she asked, staring at Vanya.

"Meet my cousin, Vanya," Lolita said raising her eyebrows. Jessica shook his outstretched hand, and then discretely disinfected with hand sanitizer attached to her backpack.

"Where's the professor's diary?" Lolita asked. "What did it say about my dad's paintings?"

Since there was only a desk in the attic, they all were standing while Jessica sat cross-legged on the desk with her sundress tucked up under her thighs. Dmitry couldn't help but notice that her legs were covered in bruises. He wondered if she was a hemophiliac like the House of Romanov's youngest son. He thought of Rasputin who treated the boy and later was poisoned, shot, and then drowned in the icy Malaya Nevka River with weights attached to his fur coat. The coat sunk, but his body floated to the surface in plain sight.

"The police were asking me about your paintings." Jessica hopped down from the desk and rummaged in her book bag. "The detective said the Kandinsky you painted for the professor was missing from his office."

"Does the professor's diary mention anything else about paintings?" he asked.

"There is a strange entry near the end," she said. "Here, let me find it." She pulled the journal from her bag, and flipped through the pages, scanning them as she went, then stopped and read something to herself.

"What does it say?" Lolita asked.

"It says… " Jessica started reading out loud. *Mr. Durchenko doesn't know I am aware he removed my floorboards. Much to my delight, I found a tube with two wonderful Russian Expressionist works. One by Kandinsky, but the other I don't recognize, signed by someone called Goncharova. Either Mr. Durchenko has outdone himself on these, or they are the originals, in either case, they should not be stored in a tube under the floor. I moved them to a temperature-controlled vault for safekeeping. What will he think when he discovers the empty tube? I wish I could be there to see his face. Over the summer, I will decide what to do with these fabulous paintings. For now, I have rescued them from further damage in their subterranean tomb.*

"Are these the paintings you're looking for?" she asked, closing the journal.

"Yes, my copies of Kandinsky and Goncharova," he replied glancing around the attic. "Does it say which vault?"

"That's all it says." Jessica hopped off the desk and slid the journal back into her pack.

Under his breath, Dmitry said, "I just have to wait for the sack to slip the anvil and float to the surface."

"Float to the surface of what?" Jessica asked.

"We have to find that vault," Lolita said. "There must be a key or a receipt or something somewhere. Maybe in his office, but how can we get in now that your key doesn't work?"

"Got a credit card?" Vanya asked, smiling his golden grin.

Jessica's face turned red and blotchy. "How did you… " her voice trailed off.

"I have a better idea," Dmitry said. "Let me go talk to the witch."

"The witch?" the girls asked in unison.

Dmitry marveled at the difference between the two girls. At 5' 10", with her silky black hair and ivory skin, Lolita could have walked off the pages of Vogue magazine, whereas with her oversized jacket and messy blonde hair, Jessica was a bright-eyed unkempt urchin who'd be adorable if someone would just clean her up.

"Mrs. Bush," he said. "If I'm not back in 15 minutes, come looking for me."

"Don't mention the professor's journal," Jessica whispered after him. "Donnette thinks she threw it in his grave along with her three shovelfuls of dirt."

Dmitry scooted down the hall to fetch his janitor's cart, took it down the elevator to the first floor, wheeled it up the hallway to the main office entrance, and then watched Donnette Bush through the door, steeling himself for the upcoming confrontation. She was standing at a filing cabinet with her back to him. He dreaded asking her for the key to the professor's office, but since his master key no longer worked, he had no choice if he wanted to enter legally. He tiptoed into the main office and came up behind Donnette. When she turned around and saw him, she let out a squeak.

"Heavens to Betsy, Mr. Durchenko, you scared the living daylights out of me. Can I help you?"

"Do you have the key to Professor Schmutzig's office?" he asked.

"Of course I do," she answered.

"May I borrow it so that I can clean his office?" he asked.

"No, you may not." She tugged on her skirt, pursed her lips, and stared at him without blinking.

"How am I supposed to clean the office if I can't get in?" he asked.

"I'll let you in," she said. "But I'm watching you like a hawk, Mister." She turned with a huff.

Wordlessly, staring straight ahead, they shared an awkward elevator ride to the second floor. She led the way and he followed after her with his cart. They stopped in front of 24B. She reached into the pocket of her jacket and pulled out the key, and with much ceremony, unlocked the door.

"Clean away, Mr. Durchenko." When the Baba Yaga waved him into the room, he walked into the office and glanced around, unsure where to look. Plus, she was still standing in the doorway.

"Well, what are you waiting for?" Donnette pulled at her skirt again.

Dmitry moved towards the wastebasket and picked it up, surveying the room at the same time. The basket, of course, was empty, but he went through the motions anyway, carrying the empty basket to his cart, tipping its phantom contents into his black garbage bag. He glanced at Donnette who hadn't budged, and then reached into his cart and pulled out his Liberon Repair, Revive, Renovate Kit. He carefully unrolled it and went over to the wooden desk, pretending to polish it.

"Really, Mr. Durchenko," she said. "What do you think you're up to?"

He realized that he couldn't properly search the room for receipts or safety deposit box keys with the Texan witch hovering over him. He would have to come back later with Vanya. "Thank you Mrs. Bush," he said. "I'm finished." He left the office and closed the door behind him. She removed the key from her pocket and relocked the door.

"You will never get this key, Mr. Durchenko," she said. "Do you hear me, never." Donnette held up the key in front of his face.

That's when Dmitry saw it. On the ring with the key to the professor's office door was another much smaller key, the key to a safety deposit box.

CHAPTER TWENTY-NINE

J ESSICA JAMES STUMBLED backwards. She was expecting Lolita, but Alexander Le Blanc was standing in the hall holding two cups of Starbucks coffee, wearing his usual preppy outfit, and smiling at her, which made her suspicious. He seemed too darned happy, like a weasel in a henhouse.

"What are you doing here, Alexander?" She stepped into the hallway and closed the door to the attic so he couldn't see inside.

"I came to get my paper," he replied. "I brought you a Cinnamon Dolce Latte, your favorite." Alexander held out the cup.

"That's really considerate of you, but I'm not allowed to accept gifts from students." With everything going on, she still hadn't written comments on his paper. She resolved to do it first thing tomorrow morning.

"It's just a coffee for cripes sake," he said. "Call it a peace offering."

"Okay. Thanks." She took the cup. "I'm really sorry, but I haven't had time to retrieve your paper from Professor Schmutzig's office with the police barricade and all."

"Yes, a tragedy." He was staring at her with an impenetrable look on his greasy face. "Aren't you going to taste your coffee?"

She put the cup to her lips. "Hmmm...delicious. I promise

that I'll read…um, have your paper for you tomorrow. For sure this time. I swear. Just come back tomorrow afternoon." She had her back to the door and her right hand on the doorknob. She wanted to slam it in his skinny face and disappear inside. If only she'd been more responsible with her grading, she wouldn't be in this mess. Jessica didn't mean to be such a screw-up, but somehow she always managed to float into the rapids. Her stomach bunched into a ball and she thought she might hurl.

"Until tomorrow then, my lady," Alexander said, turning on his heels.

She was so relieved her sigh echoed through the stairwell. She retreated into her attic nest, sat the latte on the windowsill, and began rifling through the stack of papers piled in the corner of the room. She found Alexander's paper, "Beyond Common Morality, Raskolnikov as Übermensch." Raskolnikov as nuisance, more like. She tucked it into her book bag and went back to preparing for the Red X party at Tau Kappa Epsilon Fraternity. Lolita had told her to wear something sexy. That meant breaking out the little black dress. She texted Lolita and reminded her to bring some shoes.

According to the plan they'd made at Blind Faith, they were going to meet at the Brentano attic before going to the fraternity party to give those assholes a taste of their own medicine. She wasn't sure of the exact plan, but it involved catching the most notorious fraternity on campus in the act of slipping date rape drugs to unsuspecting girls. Personally, she planned to find that friggin' quarterback Kurt and make him drink some of that shit.

Wriggling into the dress, she noticed a hint of Cinnamon Dolce. She fumigated herself with vanilla spice body mist until coughing from the vapors, she opened the windows to let in some fresh air. The sounds of spring floated in on a magnificent evening breeze. For some reason, she was in good spirits. She knew she shouldn't be. Her dead advisor thought her thesis was crap and her new advisor wanted her to write about menstruation. The other faculty member qualified to serve on her committee had seen her passed out in his pajamas, and she was living in a musty attic without two dollars to her name. She was almost looking forward to going home to backwater Montana to face her depressed mother for the first time in almost a year. Alpine Vista trailer park with its dumpy doublewides. She sighed and rolled her mind's eye.

Jessica took out her braids to emulate her grandmother's wavy hair from faded photos where she was wearing those magical dresses with her hair done in neat finger-waves. Next, she went downstairs to the bathroom to shave her legs in the sink. Hiking up the dress, she lathered her legs with liquid hand-soap from the dispenser, then shaved and swished, shaved and swished. She lifted her dress to wash under her arms with paper towels and then splashed water on her face. She was overdue for another shower at the student rec center.

When Jessica got back to the attic, Lolita was waiting for her armed with a whole arsenal of shoes, dresses, make-up, and jewelry. She was wearing her signature black leather pants and a pink baby doll top under her motorcycle jacket.

"Why so many dresses?" Jessica asked.

"Amber," she answered. They both laughed.

Once inside, she handed Jessica some black patent leather platform shoes. "Here, try these on." She did as she was told, stood up, and tottered back and forth across the room.

"I see a face plant in my future."

"You'll get used to them. Let me do your make-up."

Jessica sat on the desk while Lolita applied eye shadow, eyeliner, mascara, foundation, and blush. "Not too much," she begged, but knew Lolita would do as she pleased. She closed her eyes and as her friend worked her magic on her face, Jessica's mind wandered to the diary. She had a moral dilemma, mention her suspicions to the police or handle Fingal herself. Of course, she couldn't tell the detective they'd stolen the journal. Then again, Donnette had stolen it from Schmutzig's office. Maybe stealing operated according to Hegelian logic. Maybe a double larceny was like a double negative. It turned theft into gift.

"Do you think I should confront Fingal?" Jessica asked, eyes still closed. "Or maybe I should tell someone he plagiarized Wolf's book?"

"Are you sure he did?" Lolita asked.

"Come on. Fingal O'Flannery hasn't published anything in decades. And conveniently upon Wolf's death, he sends off a book manuscript on the ear and the eye," she said, opening one eye.

"Could be just a coincidence. You don't want to accuse him unless you're certain." Lolita handed her a mirror. She had an artist's touch--must take after her father and his preference for abstract art. Jessica's face was an Expressionist painting, with its thick layers of contrasting colors. She wiped at her cheeks with a tissue.

"Stop it," Lolita ordered and batted her hand away from her face. "I'm not done."

"What are the chances The Wolf just finished writing a book called *Phenomenology of Painting and Music* and Fingal sends off a book called *Phenomenology of the Eye and the Ear*?" Jessica shook her head. "Absolutely none."

"Hold still or I'll mess up your face," Lolita said. Given recent revelations about Lolita's family history, Jessica smiled at the double entendre, and tried to talk without opening her mouth.

"What was it Dirty Harry said at the wake about Fingal taking Wolf's Endowed Chair?" Jessica asked. "Is he for real? He must be nuts. They'll never give him that Chair." Fingal had been a professional partier for the last twenty-five years. No way he'd written a book worthy of a Distinguished Chair. Anyway, those babies weren't just passed on to whoever was left alive.

"Why not? Assuming he didn't steal the manuscript," Lolita said. "Close your mouth and hold still. I need to apply lip-gloss. How do you know Fingal didn't kill the professor so he could submit the book in his own name? Or maybe Dirty Harry killed the professor and stole the manuscript for his lover."

"You think Fingal had Wolf killed to get a publication?" Jessica asked. "Interesting *hypotenuse.*"

"Well if Fingal or Harry *did* kill the professor, you may want to confront them in public with plenty of witnesses."

There was a knock at the door, and Jessica hopped off the desk to open it. Jack saluted and sauntered into the attic with Amber in tow. She was sporting a stained paisley moo-moo and her usual Uggs with her snaky hair in two Pebbles tails sticking up off the top of her head. Jessica looked at Lolita and they both laughed.

"What's so funny?" Amber asked.

"Good thing we have another hour," Lolita said. "Here, sweetie, try on these dresses."

"Why? What's wrong with my dress?"

"I said sexy, not hippy."

"What's the difference?" Jack asked, and squeezed Amber in a hug.

Forty-five minutes later, Amber's makeover was remarkable. Lolita had transformed her from a hippy earth mother into an elegant ethereal creature. Amber's long serpentine hair was no longer threatening, just wild enough, and once Lolita applied lipstick, her little oval mouth became a perfect orange kumquat.

Lolita held up an emerald green dress with lace sleeves and a flared skirt. "Try this one."

The extravagantly plunging dress showcased Amber's braless breasts and narrow waist. Too bad she and Lolita didn't wear the same size shoe. Her dirty Uggs were rough cobs at the end of silk stockings. Distracted by that impressive cleavage, Jessica doubted if anyone was going to notice Amber's feet.

Jack looked up from his book. He had been rereading Nietzsche's *Beyond Good and Evil* while the girls were primping. "Supposing truth is a woman?" he asked.

"Then philosophy's cruel gravity is not the proper way of winning a woman's heart," replied Jessica. Quoting Nietzsche made her think of the last time they were all together in Brentano Hall with the Wolf lying dead in his bathroom. She cringed.

Jack turned to his girlfriend. "Apricot, you take my breath away. You are my truth. I'm going to glue myself to your sexy hip lest some natty frat boy steal you away."

"What are you drinking?" Jessica asked in alarm. "That's not my coffee, is it?"

"What, I just had a sip," he said, and put the cup back on the windowsill. "Too sweet for me anyway."

"Alexander brought that to me earlier," she said. "Let's hope Lolita was wrong about the poisonous gift."

"Alexander Le Blanc may suffer from delusional disorder," said Jack. "But you're starting to sound like you suffer from paranoid disorder. Must be this PhD program making you pathological."

"What's delusional disorder?" Amber asked.

"Delusions of grandeur," Jack said, "defensive formations against low self-esteem and depression. I mean, think about it. Alexander is this scrawny, acne-faced, introvert seeking acceptance by the most popular guys on campus, the football players and frat boys."

"We'll see to those fuckers," Lolita said. "We're going to give those thick-necked footballers and their fraternity buddies a night they won't forget." She flipped her ebony hair into her helmet.

"Let's go." Lolita started out the door. "Jimmy's waiting in his cruiser around the corner from the party. Jack, you drive Jessica and Amber. I'll meet you there." The Russian commandant was in her element, barking out orders.

"Remember girls," Lolita looked stern. "Don't drink anything." She turned to Jack. "Did you bring the drugs?"

"Oh, right. Ketamine, crushed and ready to go." When he handed her a snack-sized baggie of white powder, she tucked it into the pocket of her motorcycle jacket, and then bounded down the stairs.

On the way to the car, Jessica thought she spotted Alexander hiding behind a tree. She focused her eyes in the dark. No one. She must be seeing things. Probably hallucinating him out of guilt for not reading his paper. Or maybe Jack was right and she was paranoid. She didn't care. Tonight, she planned to kick some ass on her first feminist revenge caper.

CHAPTER THIRTY

JUBILANT, JESSICA JAMES was looking forward to a celebration, even if they were on a retribution mission. After
the stress of Schmutzig's death, the revelations about Amber's
parentage, and the secret of Lolita's grandparents, she needed to
blow off steam.

"How are you holding up?" Jessica asked, reaching over from
the back seat to touch Amber's shoulder.

"I'm okay I guess," Amber said, turning around. "I'm not
speaking to my mother." She took a vial from her purse and placed
several drops of homeopathic elixir under her tongue. "I don't
know if I should tell my dad or not. I mean my mother's husband.
I guess he's not really my dad."

"He's your step-dad and he loves you. You don't think he
already knows?"

"No, I don't think so."

"How do you think he'd react?"

"Probably divorce Mom." Amber took out another tiny bottle
and dropped another extract under her tongue.

"No wonder she wanted to bury that journal," Jack said. "You
don't think Bald-Dick... sorry, Wolf, threatened your mom to tell
your dad, I mean Mr. Bush, do you?"

"We'll never know," said Jessica. "But the last entry said he planned to tell his mother she had a granddaughter."

"Wow, Zelda Schmutzig is my grandmother," Amber said. "Weird." She sprayed some kind of mist into her mouth.

"What are you doing?" Jessica asked.

"Rescue Remedy," Amber said.

Jack handed her a joint. "Here, try this Sweetie," he said. "The best herbal remedy in the world."

Lolita's bike was parked outside the fraternity house by the time Jack pulled up in front. There were banners hanging across another converted mansion: Graduation Weekend: Red X Party. At the front door, a clean-cut frat boy stamped a red X on the back of Jessica's hand, and said, "Welcome to the hottest party on campus." He stamped Amber's hand with a red X and motioned her inside. He made Jack pay a $10 cover charge and stamped his hand with a black X.

"Red for girls, black for boys," Amber said.

The frat boy laughed. "Not exactly. The bar is around the corner. You girls drink for free." He winked at them and rubbed his hands together. As if to prove his point, he stamped the gangly long necked girl behind them with a black X. Inside they noticed all of the boys had black X's while some of the girls had red ones and some had black ones. By the end of the night, most of the girls with the red ones would be in the hospital.

As they headed towards the bar, Jessica reminded Amber not to take a drink from anyone.

"Not even Jackie?"

"Jack, keep an eye on her."

"I'll keep more than my eye on her." When he took Amber's tiny hand in both of his and kissed it, her grin lit up the room.

The three friends met Lolita at the bar. "Spread out and stay on your toes." The bartender checked their hands and handed the girls punch in red cups. Jack tapped himself a beer from a keg. "Remember, no drinking," Lolita whispered. "We'll meet back here in half an hour."

Jessica circulated around the party looking for suspicious frat boys, but they all looked pretty harmless. Most of them were well dressed and clean cut. Some of them were downright cute. Since her break-up with Michael, she'd been seeing attractive men everywhere, boys she'd never have given a second look a week ago. She overheard a drunken frat boy say to his buddy, "Look for the sluts with the red Xs. They're tonight's rape-bait." She high-tailed it back to the bar to find her crew.

She found Amber standing at the edge of the bar, picking at a pile of tiny wrappers.

"Where's Jack?" Jessica asked.

"He was tired and queasy so he went to take a nap in the car," Amber said.

"Oh shit," said Jessica. "I hope it wasn't Alexander's latte."

"I gave him some Revive drops. He'll be fine."

Lolita soon joined them. "Where's Jack?" Amber insisted that they let Jack sleep it off in his car. "Don't worry. I realigned his cortices." Doing a strange cat's cradle maneuver with her fingers, she demonstrated.

Lolita gave her report. "If the doorman deems a girl "hot" she gets a red X, while "dogs" and boys get black ones. Then "hot" girls are offered the "special" punch at the bar. What did you two find out?" she asked.

"A frat creep said the red Xs were for their rape-bait," Jessica said, arms akimbo.

"I found these cute wrappers," Amber said. She presented her palm to reveal three little envelope wrappers stamped with Boris and Natasha.

"Let me see those," Lolita demanded. Amber dumped them into her outstretched hand. "Where did you get them?"

"I found a few on the floor over there." Amber pointed to a corner of the room.

"These are what they wrap drugs in," Lolita said, examining the papers.

"I have an idea," Amber said. "Give me some of that vitamin K."

"Why?" Lolita asked, discretely handing her the baggie.

"You'll see." Amber flattened the tiny wrappers on the bar and some of the white sprinkled powder into each one, and then carefully folding the corners, rewrapped them into tiny packages.

"Come on, " she said grabbing Jessica's hand. "Let's go dance."

Jessica stumbled along behind the hippy goddess onto the dance floor. Amber pulled off her Uggs and tiptoed barefoot into the mass of gyrating dancers. The bass from the loud house music reverberated through the wooden floor, and a mist of perspiration emanating from the throng of dancing bodies formed a cloud in the middle of the room. Amber smiled, and the flared skirt of her dress twirled as she circled around the boy who had stamped their hands earlier. She hiked up her dress with one hand and caressed his face with the other. Jessica danced nearby and watched as the boy grabbed Amber around the waist with one hand, holding his drink in the other. She whispered something into his ear and he pulled back with a gleaming grin and held out his cup. She sprinkled some powder from one of the little wrappers into his drink, stirred it with her finger, then put her finger to his lips and he took it into his mouth. With her encouragement, he downed the rest of his drink and after a few more minutes of flirting, she left him sulking and moved on to her next victim, telling him that the powder was Ecstasy and would make sex even more fun. Jessica couldn't bring herself to sidle up to one of those frat creeps even to give him a taste of his own medicine, so she squeezed out of the throng and headed back to the bar. She really wanted a drink and wished she'd brought her flask of whisky.

Before she'd reached the bar, Lolita flew by, grabbing her arm on the way. "It's Emily," Lolita said. "Come on."

"Who's Emily?" Jessica asked.

"My roommate, Emo, as you call her."

Jessica sprinted to keep up with Lolita as she strode across the crowded room towards the back where two fraternity brothers were hauling Emily out the door. One on each side, they were dragging her through the damp grass towards a gazebo in the back corner of the lawn. The girls slowed their pace and fell back into the shadows. The boys were laughing as Emily staggered between them, groaning.

"I hope she doesn't heave," said one of her captors.

"You get sloppy seconds since I found her."

"What if she has a disease?"

"That's what penicillin is for. We can just go back to the pharmacist." The tall clean-cut, square-jawed creep laughed as his dark-haired muscular friend pulled Emily into the dark gazebo. They were wearing matching khaki pants, button down oxford shirts, and contrasting ties.

Watching the frat boys haul Emo across the lawn, Jessica was wondering if this was such a good plan after all. Maybe they should go for backup. She hoped Lolita wasn't counting on her to take out one of these guys. Lolita pointed at the one with his pants down, and on cue, Jessica leaped onto his back, pulled his hair, and kneeing him in the kidneys. The rapist fell on top of poor Emily. A black leather lightning bolt, Lolita's foot crashed into "sloppy seconds" left ear. As his head whiplashed back, she landed a dead-on kick to the groin. Thwack and he was writhing on the floor. Jessica sat on the other one's chest, a cowboy boot pining each of his arms to the ground. After she'd finished with "sloppy seconds," Lolita pulled the other one's pants off the rest of the way and then removed his boxer shorts. Jessica scooted up to the rapist's shoulders to give her friend more room. The frat boy squirmed but could get loose.

"Hold his head!" Lolita shouted as she kicked him in the side. Jessica heard a cracking sound as the frat boy yelped.

"Pull his head back by his hair and make him open his mouth," Lolita commanded. She followed orders, tugging on the rapist's hair, and then her friend reached into the baggy and dumped a mighty pinch of white powder into his mouth.

"See how *you* like it asshole," she said.

Sloppy seconds was trying to crawl toward the door, and Lolita kicked him in the face so hard his nose gushed blood like a crimson geyser.

"You're not going anywhere until you get your dose, fucker," Lolita said.

"Hold his head," she commanded, and Jessica yanked this one's head back by the hair. He tightened his lips shut, so she had to pinch his nose until opened his mouth, gasping. Then Lolita gave him a generous dose of Ketamine. "See how you like being helpless. You're falling through the K-hole, asshole."

"How long does it take?" Jessica asked, and had her answer when she glanced over and no-pants was lying on his side, staring straight ahead drooling.

"Go get Jimmy. Hurry."

Instead of trying to get back through the crowded frat house, she galloped across the lawn, and leaped over the hedge, running along the sidewalk around the corner. She was breathless by the time she got to Jimmy's cruiser. He sat up at attention when he saw her coming full bore at his car. She motioned for him to roll down the window. "Hurry," she panted. "Lolita has a couple of rapists trapped in the gazebo behind the frat house."

The campus cop called for backup and then rocketed out of his cruiser and sprinted towards the party. Jessica ran after him, but couldn't keep up, so she fell back to catch her breath. When she reached the gazebo, Jimmy already had the two creeps handcuffed, and Lolita was holding Emily in her lap, rocking her back and forth. "Go find Amber," she told Jessica. "I'll take Emily home, but you guys make sure this doesn't happen to anyone else tonight."

Jessica went back to the bar, but Amber was nowhere in sight. She was sitting at the bar waiting, when the bartender insisted she take another cup of punch or move on. Glaring at him, she took it, and then went from room to room, looking for Amber. Her brain was vibrating from the blaring music, and the colored flashing lights were making her head hurt. *Shit.* She glimpsed Alexander Le Blanc in her peripheral vision, and before she could duck into another room, he started towards her. She tried to slip away, but he caught up to her.

"What are you doing here?" Alexander asked.

"I could ask you the same."

"Are you feeling okay?" he asked.

"Why do you ask?" Jessica was suddenly very self-conscious. She was dressed like a tart and at a party talking to one of her students, a student who had probably figured out by now that she hadn't read his paper.

"Your face is flushed," Alexander said. "My dear, you look like you're on fire. Maybe we should go outside and get some fresh air." She was hot and a cool evening breeze sounded good. But she wasn't going anywhere with this Existentialist weasel. Without thinking, she downed her punch. *Shit!* She couldn't bring herself to do a bulimic number in the bathroom. Could they have poisoned all of the punch? Everyone was drinking it. No way the entire punchbowl could be spiked with Roofies.

Quarterback Kurt Willis appeared out of nowhere, and slapped Alexander on the back, almost knocking him down. The lumbering quarterback was wearing his XXL varsity football jacket.

"Well if it isn't Little Miss Hottie." Kurt was licking her with his eyes again, making her want to take a scalding shower. When she tried heading for the door, Kurt held her by the arm.

"Hey, Zander, got anything for me?" she overheard Kurt yell into his ear over the noise of the party. Alexander opened his jacket and pointed to his inside pocket. "You mean Boris?"

"Boris, my BFF!" Jessica was queasy--probably the company--so she jerked her arm away from brute, and headed into the crowd. Maybe Amber was on the dance floor. Sucked into the throbbing throng of dancers, her head was pounding and the room started spinning. She had to get outside into the fresh air. Before she understood what was happening, someone had lifted her off her feet from behind. Her vision was blurred, but she recognized Kurt the quarterback's thick arms and strong Old Spice deodorant. Struggling to free herself, Jessica elbowed him in the chest and kicked her legs. But it was no use. She was fading in and out of consciousness and he was just too strong. As he carried her through the crowd, she tried to scream, but only gasped. The music was deafening, so even if she could scream at the top of her lungs, no one would hear her. The quarterback carried her through the front door, and her limbs were heavy and everything was off kilter as she gazed back at the party wishing someone would help her.

Cool night air prickled her face, and the noise from the party was fading. Streaks of light zipped past. Swooshing sounds. She could hear the pounding of her heart in her ears. Something had her in a tight grip. She was caught. She tried to kick her feet, but they wouldn't move. It was as if someone had cut the nerves that sent signals from her brain to her limbs. She smelled alcohol on Kurt's breath, almost barfed. Where was he taking her? Warm tears were running over her temples into her ears.

Jessica heard yelling and then a cracking sound. A loud explosion went off close to her ears, and her head smacked into the ground. Pain. Lots of pain. The wet grass was cold against her cheek, and she tried to burrow into the dirt, clawing at the earth, digging to escape. She was aware of dull thuds and then sensed vibrations on the ground beneath her. Someone was running, running away.

A hand touched her on the shoulder. Startled, she tried to pull herself up, but paralyzed she couldn't move her limbs. She heard her name. *Ms. James. Ms. James.* The buzzing baritone was familiar. *Detective Cormier?* The hand was now stroking her hair, and the bass voice was soothing. Jessica tried to hold onto it, but couldn't. "Amber," she whispered. "Find Amber." Everything went black.

PART THREE

CHAPTER THIRTY-ONE

"WHERE'S AMBER?" JESSICA James mumbled. Slowly, the room came into focus. Northwestern University Hospital. She made out voices, soft women's voices, and followed them with her eyes. Lolita and Amber, whispering back and forth, were wearing the same clothes they'd worn to the fraternity party. The party. *Oh no, Kurt Willis.* The last thing she remembered was feeling dizzy and being carried outside.

"What happened?" Jessica asked.

A familiar baritone voice replied, "You were drugged with GHB at the Tau Kappa Epsilon Fraternity. Fourteen other girls and eight boys have also been hospitalized."

"Detective Cormier?" she asked. She was unclothed except for her flimsy hospital gown, and even under the blanket, she was shivering. So many clothed people standing around staring at her, especially the handsome detective, was awkward.

"We apprehended Kurt Willis outside the TKE house. How do you feel?" the detective asked, moving closer to the bed and looked down at her with a warm smile.

"Like I've been bucked off a bull and then trampled," Jessica answered. "Did he…" her voice trailed off, tears pooling in her eyes as she looked down at the bed covers. Why did she drink that punch? She was so ashamed she wished she could disappear.

"Luckily, the detective tackled Kurt before he got very far," Lolita said. "That rapist quarterback has made his last pass."

"How did you know?" Jessica asked. "Why were…"

"Truth be told, I've been following you since our chat at the police station," Detective Cormier interrupted. "I saw the big guy carrying you and you were struggling. When I shouted at him, he dropped you and ran."

"Of course, Kurt's not locked up where he belongs," Lolita said. "Mommy and daddy bailed him out this morning."

"I assure you that with your help Ms. James, we'll take the case against him as far as we can," said the Detective. "Although he may not have sexually assaulted you--thank God--he did poison and abduct you."

"Could I have some water, please?" she asked.

Amber filled up the plastic water pitcher from the sink in the corner of the room, and then filled a little plastic cup, added a straw and handed it to her. She gulped it down and asked for another. No amount of water could quench her thirst or wash away her shame.

"You are dehydrated from the drugs," Amber said. "Here, let me give you some electrolyte drops." When she sat on the edge of the narrow bed, Jessica leaned closer to her friend for warmth. She opened her mouth, a baby bird waiting to be fed. Amber took out a vial from her mammoth purse, extracted a cobalt blue glass vial, unscrewed the black rubber dropper, and counted out 15 drops into her awaiting mouth. The "medicine" tasted bitter, but Amber's sweet touch was all she really needed. She couldn't help herself. She was crying. Amber put her arm around her. "There, there sweetie," she cooed. "It will be okay."

"Where were you?" Jessica asked through her tears. "I went

back to find you and you were gone." Turns out Amber had left the party with some nerdy guy on Northwestern's chess team to play a game of chess in his dorm room.

"When I ran out of vitamin K, I looked for you guys. On the dance floor I led a few of those A-hole frat boys through the K-hole," she said with a giggle. "But I couldn't find you. So I left a note for Jackie in the car." She pulled one of her serpentine locks into her mouth and started sucking on it. "He was still asleep. So I left with Gary." Her makeup from the night before was a swirling mask. Blue and black streaks had smeared down her cheeks and her once adorable kumquat mouth had become a shriveled apricot. Her breasts were spilling out of her plunging neckline, and strange uneven brown streaks stained her emerald skirt. *Bloodstains?*

"That geek didn't hurt you, did he?" Jessica asked. She took a tissue from her tray, spit on it, and began wiping at Amber's cheeks.

"Who? Gary?" Amber asked, closing her eyes. "Of course not."

"Well what's that on your dress? It looks like blood."

"Don't be silly. Gary invented a new dessert called Twisted Twix. You smash Cheetos Twists and Twix bars in a bowl, then mix them with honey. It's scrumptious."

"What about your campaign against processed sugar?" Jessica asked.

"Honey is an antiviral and antibacterial, and chocolate is an antioxidant. So it's practically a health food!" Amber smiled. "Don't worry, I took some detox drops this morning."

Jessica shook her head and her matted hair flopped from side to side. "So you ate this stuff and then what? Did he make any moves on you?"

"Of course he made moves, we were playing chess. I took his queen and won." Amber waved her small fists in the air in a victory celebration.

Jessica smiled. *Amber, idiot savant chess champion.* She ceased Amber's warm hand mid air and held it in both of hers.

"Girls, sorry to interrupt, but could I speak to Ms. James alone?" Detective Cormier asked. He turned to Jessica, "I need to ask you some questions, if you're up for it." She nodded, and then her friends both hugged her and left the room.

Alone with the cute detective, Jessica became self-conscious again about her nakedness. She pulled the blankets up under her armpits and sat up in bed. She was plugged into an IV machine, so every time she moved the needle stabbed her in the crook of her arm, and somehow she was both hungry and queasy at the same time. As if her thoughts had conjured breakfast, an orderly brought in a tray and sat it on the wheeled bed table. She tentatively lifted the heavy brown plastic lid to see what lurked underneath. It had to be more appetizing than the thick brown bowl of gluey oatmeal insulated with sweaty plastic wrap.

"Why were you following me?" Jessica asked.

"It's not every day I interrogate a girl with a gun hidden between her legs." Detective Cormier smiled. "Seriously, why were you carrying a weapon?"

She blushed. "How did…"

"Surveillance video. Standard procedure during questioning," Detective Cormier interrupted.

"It's not my gun. I just found it in my pocket."

"You found someone else's gun in your pocket?" The detective narrowed his eyebrows.

"Actually, it wasn't really my pocket either," she said with a sheepish smile.

"Not your gun, not your pocket," Detective Cormier said. "Whose are they then?"

"The jacket and the gun belong to Nicholas Schilling," she said. "I mean, Nicholas Charis."

"Which is it Ms. James?" Detective Cormier was no longer smiling. He took out his notepad and began writing. He had wheeled over the chair from the corner of the hospital room and was sitting next to the bed, so close Jessica could smell the lemony scent of his aftershave. The scent helped calm her stomach. She stared down at the breakfast tray. Amber must have ordered her meal because the milk was chocolate flavored. She hadn't had chocolate milk since she was a kid, a delicious surprise. *Thank you Amber.* She made a mental note to buy chocolate milk if she ever had a kitchen or refrigerator again.

"Schilling or Charis, Ms. James?" the detective demanded.

"Actually, he goes by both names. His father is also called Nicholas Schilling, so he uses his mother's maiden name Charis as well," she said. "He's an art history professor at Northwestern."

"Is he your boyfriend?"

"I broke up with my boyfriend last week," Jessica said staring at the bedcovers.

"What is your relationship with this Schilling or Charis? And why did you have his gun? Why did you bring it to the police station?"

"He lent me his jacket and I didn't know the gun was in the pocket," she said. "Those cops… uh, officers, rushed me out…"

"I see," said the detective. "You didn't feel the gun in the pocket?"

"No, it was so tiny and everything happened so fast," she said. "Nick gave me his jacket because I was only wearing, uh, I was cold."

Jessica hadn't thought of Nick Schilling, or Charis, yet this morning, even though she'd been wearing his jacket day and night. He'd been sending her enticing email messages inviting her to art openings and cocktail receptions. But she'd ignored them. It didn't seem right to go on a date with one of her professors. At least she hoped they would be dates. Of course, if they weren't dates, then why not? She sometimes met other professors for coffee or even drinks. Maybe it was all completely innocent. Maybe she should accept if he invited her again. An art opening would count as a field trip since he was an art history professor and a working dinner would be perfectly normal.

"Ms. James, did you hear me?" The detective's deep voice broke through her daydreaming. "I asked why this professor would have a gun."

"I have no idea," she said. One of the most attractive men she'd ever met was a billionaire art collector and university professor who carried a mini revolver to high stakes poker games. He led a double-life as his father's heir, a wealthy playboy, and a mama's boy passionate about art.

She was relieved when the detective changed the subject. He asked her what happened at the fraternity party and what she knew about drugs on campus.

"For the last year, I've been trying to bust a Russian mafia ring supplying rape drugs to colleges. I've been following the local campus dealers all the way back to the source, and I'm determined to stop the drugs feeding the campus rape epidemic. I think there's a connection between the GHB in the punch at the fraternity house and Professor Schmutzig's overdose," Detective Cormier said.

"What? How?" Chocolate milk was dribbling from her straw down her chin. She wiped it off with the back of her hand and decided she'd had enough breakfast.

"The coroner is about to release a report indicating Professor Schmutzig was poisoned with GHB. The coroner found traces on his lips and we found it in a Starbucks cup taken from his office."

"Did you say it was in his cup?" She thought of the latte Alexander had brought and of Jack out cold in his car. Then she remembered the diary. The last entry said Alexander was bringing gifts. Should she tell the detective about the diary? How they'd stolen it? Donnette would be devastated. She believed Wolf's secrets were buried forever along with his body.

"We're now convinced that Professor Schmutzig must have been murdered," Cormier said. "He didn't die from a heroin overdose. He died from a deadly dose of GHB. Toxicology reports the levels of GHB in his blood stream were lethal. We suspect the GHB we found in the professor's body and the GHB at the party come from the same source. In both cases, the GHB appears to have been cut with the tranquilizer Kolonpin."

"Murdered? But what does…did Wolf have to do with rape drugs on campus? You mean one of the frat boys murdered Professor Schmutzig?" Her brain was throbbing and she couldn't think straight. The lecherous Professor Wolfgang Schmutzig had been murdered with a rape-drug.

"We mean to find out," said the detective. Detective Cormier was passionate when he talked about the *rape epidemic*, and his impassioned speech reminded her of Lolita. The two of them should team up. They would make a wrong righting, injustice fighting, power duo to wipe out sexual assault on campus. Jessica cringed remembering the bloody scene in the gazebo and sloppy second's gushing nose and broken jaw after Lolita kicked him in the face.

"What happened to the guys Lolita caught with Emily?" Jessica asked.

"They were taken into custody. Miss Durchenko incapacitated three more potential sex offenders who were arrested last night as well. And seems your other friend poisoned several others with a drug called Ketamine, also associated with campus rape."

"Is Emily okay? And the other poisoned girls?" Fourteen girls, all stamped with the Red X. TKE must have set a record for most incapacitated "rape-bait" in one night.

"Yes thankfully they've all recovered. But those fraternity brothers who tangled with your friend weren't so lucky. They're going to be nursing more than bruised egos, perhaps for the rest of their lives."

"What do you mean?" she asked, wondering if Lolita could be charged with battery.

"One of them has teeth missing and broken ribs. Another has a broken jaw and nose. One has head injuries and a concussion. And they all have contusions on their faces and bruised groins. She gave them a beating they won't soon forget." The detective tried to repress a smile. "And, seems they accidently drank some of their own spiked punch."

"Is Lolita in trouble?" she asked.

"Those guys are too embarrassed about getting beaten up by a girl to press charges," he said. "And they were injured while attempting to commit felony crimes. The entire fraternity is charged with conspiracy to drug and rape. This will be quite an investigation."

CHAPTER THIRTY-TWO

WHEN JESSICA JAMES returned to Brentano Hall, she discovered someone had broken into her attic hovel and rifled through her stuff. Panicked, she ran straight for the desk, opened the bottom drawer, but there it was, right where she'd left it, her computer. Student papers were scattered all over the room, and her great-grandmother's dresses had been thrown out of their box into a pile. The case to her bass was open, but the instrument was still there. As she folded the dresses and then gathered the papers, she wondered how this week could get any stranger. The fact that the burglar didn't take anything made it even creepier. Maybe she should move over to Lolita's dorm room and sleep on the floor next to Emo's bed. Or maybe she could stay with Amber in her tiny studio apartment and put up with permanent fixture, Jack.

Was Jack okay? He'd drunk her latte and then passed out at the party, probably not a coincidence. She should take the rest of that coffee to be tested for drugs. Alexander must have spiked it. She winced remembering she'd barely escaped becoming Kurt Willis's next victim. Thank God Detective Cormier had been following her. She hunted for the Starbuck's cup, but it was gone. Maybe

Dmitry had thrown it out. She went to the janitor's closet to ask about it and found him in an intense discussion with Lolita.

"I was just coming to find you," Lolita said. "We need you to help us with Donnette."

"Dmitry, did you take a Starbucks cup from the attic?" Jessica asked.

"I never take anything that doesn't belong to me, Miss Jessica."

"No, it was trash, but it's important that I find it," she said.

"I haven't cleaned your room yet," he replied.

"Where's Jack?" Jessica asked.

"How should I know?" Lolita said. "Probably at Amber's."

Jessica tapped her cell phone awake and called Jack. He sounded awful. She invited him to treat her to a late lunch at The Blind Faith Café. All she'd eaten so far today was the chocolate milk at the hospital. He agreed to meet her there in an hour.

"Will you help us with Donnette?" Lolita asked. "We need to get the key to the professor's office, just for a few minutes. If anyone can do it you can."

"Why?"

"The key ring the professor gave Donnette has a small key to a safety deposit box. That must be where the professor put my dad's paintings."

"I need to get those paintings back," Dmitry said. "It's urgent that I find them."

"Okay," Jessica said. "I'll see what I can do."

Jessica crept downstairs into the main office. Friday afternoon of graduation weekend, the building was deserted. The lights were off and Donnette was sitting at her desk staring off into space. Everything in the office was tidy and neat. Not a pencil out of place. Donnette was in full make-up and matching skirt set, sitting perfectly still. When Jessica cleared her throat so she wouldn't startle her, Donnette glanced up but didn't smile.

"Is something wrong, Donnette?"

"It just isn't the same without Wolfie." Her nail polish matched her lipstick, pale pink. Pink and white were the theme for today's ensemble. Her white bouffant reflected her outfit, and her thick shellac of hairspray had taken on the sheen of pink mucus. She sighed, took a matching hanky from her pocket, and dabbed at her eyes.

"Speaking of Wolf," Jessica said, "could I borrow the key to his office? A student wants his paper back from the Existentialism class and I need to get it from his office."

Donnette reached into her pocket and pulled out the key. Sure enough, a tiny sibling accompanied the bigger office key. Jessica reached out to take the key ring, but Donnette just sat there holding the keys in her lap.

"Amber won't answer my calls," she said. "Do you think she's okay?"

"I'm sure she's fine," Jessica said. "I saw her this morning." She didn't say she saw her at the hospital after a night partying at the fraternity, or in Amber's case, playing chess all night and getting high on Twisted Twix in Gary-the-geek's dorm room.

"Is she mad at me?"

"Um, I don't think so," Jessica lied. She couldn't tell her Amber had found out Mr. Bush wasn't her biological father. "I'm sure everything will work out."

"I don't know why she doesn't like me. I've done everything for that girl."

"I'm sure she likes you," Jessica said. "She loves you." She could tell by the tears welling in her eyes that she was edging onto thin ice. "Just give her time, Donnette," she said. "It'll be okay. Amber's a sweet girl." In many ways, Donnette treated Jessica more like a daughter than she did Amber.

"I suppose you're right," Donnette said. She was folding and unfolding a paperclip, gouging her hand. "I've never been able to get close to that girl. She's too much like her father." The paperclip ripped the skin on her thumb and she was bleeding. "Dear Lord, now look what I've done," she said, wrapping her pink hanky around her red thumb.

"Are you okay?"

"Never mind me."

To change the subject, Jessica asked if she knew who might have rummaged through her stuff in the attic. Donnette said it was probably "that cursed Russian."

"Why do you dislike Dmitry so much?" she asked.

"I don't dislike him, honey. I just don't trust the commie bastard."

Jessica wondered if she was just jealous because Wolf wanted Dmitry to fetch his pizza and do his laundry instead of her. "Do you still think Dmitry killed Wolf?" she asked, skating out even further.

"Well, if not the cursed Russian, then who?"

Jessica made a mental list of possible killers: Fingal O'Flannery, the Skokie mafia, *Bratva*, or any one of Schmutzig's many disgruntled graduate students, one of the undergrads he'd flunked, or even Donnette to keep her secret about Amber. Or, maybe it was Michael. The Wolf had failed him at his dissertation exam, a first in Northwestern's history. She imagined Detective Cormier interrogating her cheating ex-boyfriend under a bright light, maybe a little waterboarding for good measure.

"Good question," Jessica said finally, pausing for what she hoped was an appropriate amount of time before asking again for the key. "Could I borrow the key now to fetch that paper?" When she held out her hand again, Donnette acted surprised, then stood up and straightened her skirt.

"I'll open the door for you," she said. She headed out of the office and Jessica followed. Donnette's heels tapped as she climbed the wooden staircase. Close behind, Jessica noticed black lint on the back of her skirt and restrained herself from picking it off. She could hear Donnette's skirt swishing against the slip underneath. Tap, swish, tap, swish, tap, swish, tap, swish. Donnette slowly ascended the stairs, pulling herself up using the banister, breathing heavily. Jessica worried she might have a heart attack, and thought about giving her a boost from behind.

"There's black lint on the back of your skirt," Jessica said, hoping Dmitry would hear her.

"Oh, can you take it off, dear?" she asked. Jessica plucked at the lint using just the tip of her fingernails so she wouldn't have to actually touch Donnette's butt. They had reached the landing and were standing in front of 24B.

"I like your outfit," Jessica said. "Very pretty."

"This old thing?" Donnette said, smoothing her skirt. She patted her hair, pleased with the compliment, and took the keys from her pocket. She put the key into the lock and opened the door. "Get what you need, honey," she said. "I'll wait here."

Lolita appeared in the hallway. "Donnette," she said, "could you help me figure out my schedule for next semester?"

"Goodness, you scared me," she said as she turned around. "Of course, dear, as soon as we're done here."

Jessica gave Lolita a questioning look and shrugged. She picked up a paper from the top of one of the many piles in Schmutzig's office, and then glancing around to make sure Donnette wasn't looking, grabbed the blue binder containing her thesis, shoved it under the paper, and held it tight to her chest.

"Did you get what you needed?" Donnette asked as she locked the door.

"Yes, thanks." Jessica inhaled until her lungs might burst.

Finally, she'd retrieved her thesis and that damning post-dated letter, but she hadn't managed to get the key away from Donnette.

She and Lolita followed Donnette back downstairs to the main office. The two friends were lip reading behind her back, miming a plan to get the key off her.

"Let me get on my computer," Donnette said, "and then I can help you with your schedule." She may have hated her father, but she liked Lolita. She always seemed to enjoy helping the girls, and took pride when they succeeded at the university. She poked at her keyboard until her dinosaur computer came to life. It was three years old, already obsolete.

"You know, I forgot to get another student's paper from Wolf's office," Jessica said. "Could I borrow the key to run up and get it?"

Absorbed in the screen, wordlessly, Donnette handed her the keychain and kept searching on her computer. Lolita leaned over the back of her chair to keep her occupied. Jessica ran up the stairs and slid into the janitor's closet. "Here," she said, out of breath. Dmitry quickly took the keys, slipped the small key off the ring and replaced it with another the same size. Without exchanging a word, he handed it back to Jessica, and she bounded back down the stairs. Donnette and Lolita were right where she'd left them, Donnette staring into the computer screen and Lolita looking over her shoulder.

"Thanks," Jessica said, handing the keys back to Donnette.

"Donnette, you're the best," Lolita purred. "What would we do without you?"

Donnette beamed. "You're such good girls."

CHAPTER THIRTY-THREE

J ESSICA JAMES AND her three friends gathered in their regular booth at The Blind Faith. Except for Amber, they all ordered Jolt Awake coffee, a special blend of coffee and ginseng. Amber was fussing about the evils of caffeine when Jessica reminded her of the Twisted Twix incident. Jack narrowed his eyes and tightened his lips.

"But caffeine is poison," Amber said, twisting her hair around her finger.

"Speaking of poison, TKE is lucky no one died," Lolita said.

"No one dies of fatal truths," said Jack, "there are too many antidotes."

"*Human all too Human*," Jessica said.

"Why don't you two get a room and have your love affair with Nietzsche in private? No one else gets off on it." Lolita finished her coffee, and then said under her breath, "Sometimes I think you two are proselytizers for the Anti-Christ." She waved the waitress over and asked for another cup.

"With comments like that, we'd better make it a *ménage-a-tois*." Jack laughed.

"What?" Amber asked, pulling the curly lock out of her mouth.

"Stupid Nietzsche joke," Lolita said.

"Oh, that dumb game they play," Amber said. "Guys, this fraternity stuff is serious. What's going to happen to them?"

"I heard that national TKE is going to suspend Northwestern's chapter," Jack said, looking more pale than usual. He hadn't changed his clothes from the night before, his shoulder-length wavy brown hair was stringy and flopping over his smudged wire-rimmed glasses, hiding one of his puffy eyes, and Jessica could smell him from across the table, pungent cheese.

"Good. They should be suspended, but from ropes attached to their balls," Lolita said. She was using her compact mirror and touching up her lipstick.

"That's not very nice," said Amber.

"Well, drugging and raping girls isn't very nice either," said Lolita, glancing up from applying her makeup, and then put the compact back in her jacket pocket.

"I think Alexander is supplying the rape drugs," Jessica said. "When Kurt asked him about Boris, he showed him something inside his jacket." She opened an imaginary jacket and pointed to the inside pocket.

"Boris is the name of the drug syndicate. They have Boris and Natasha stamped on the cocaine envelopes and GHB wrappers," Lolita said. She was on her third cup of Jolt. Night prowling and pouncing on would-be rapists seemed to agree with her, she was fresh as a lettuce.

"Those cute wrappers?" Amber asked, her head on Jack's shoulder. At least she'd washed her face and changed back into one of her nightgown moo-moos. Trying to see signs of Wolfgang Schmutzig in her features, Jessica recognized his round nose, wiry hair, and flashes of Wolf's brilliance behind Amber's wacky ways.

"We're going to bust those bastards." Lolita slammed her cup onto the table.

"Shouldn't we let Detective Cormier do the busting?" Jessica asked. She hated to think of what Lolita meant by "bust." She'd already broken some bones. The frenzied outburst in the gazebo scared her and she worried for the lives of those frat boys, as disgusting as they might be, and she didn't want her friend going to jail.

"How many more girls will be raped while the detective is waiting to get enough evidence to move in?" Lolita said. "I plan to administer more doses while he's dicking around filling out paperwork."

"Detective Cormier thinks there's a correlation between rape drugs on campus and the overdose that killed Wolf," said Jessica. "The police determined it was murder, an overdose of GHB."

"I wish I'd known him," Amber said. "Who'd want to kill him?"

"Anyone who knew him," Jack said. "And a few who didn't." He had scarfed down his burger and was inhaling his sweet potato fries.

"Donnette thinks Dmitry did it," Jessica said.

"My dad? Why would he kill the professor?" Lolita asked, sipping her coffee. She was too cool to eat in public.

"Maybe Schmutzig was blackmailing him," Jessica said, raising her eyebrows up and down.

"What do you mean, blackmailing?" Lolita asked.

"Well, Wolf had your dad running around like his personal valet, delivering his dry cleaning, picking up pizza."

"I wouldn't call picking up pizza blackmail. My dad was just humoring him because he thought the professor was inept."

"What about Fingal O'Flannery?" Jessica asked. "He certainly benefited from Wolf's murder. I still think he stole Wolf's book to salvage his career."

"Donnette did it," Jack interrupted. "If she couldn't have her boy toy then nobody would." He started tickling Amber. "Your mother's crime of passion was a humanitarian deed."

Jessica imagined Donnette in the throws of passion, accidently stabbing Wolf in the eyes with her fake fingernails or rolling over and suffocating him with her bird's nest hairdo. Donnette probably thought that giving someone a roofie was something nasty coeds did on a roof.

"The strongest drugs Donnette has in her medicine cabinet are stool softeners and judging by that stick up her ass," said Jack, "she rarely touches them." Laughing at his own joke, he snorted his coffee and started sneezing.

"That's not funny Jackie," Amber said. "You're mean. I can't believe my real dad is, was, a university professor. It's so weird to find out you're not who you thought you were."

Jack patted her springy curls. "I'm just teasing you, Apricot. I'm sure you're mom uses her stool softeners." Amber fake punched his shoulder.

"I wonder if the detective thinks I did it and that's why he's following me," Jessica said. "I shouldn't have written I wanted to kill the Wolf on my Facebook page."

"That's hilarious," said Jack. "You actually put that on Facebook? What an idiot." When she kicked him under the table, he caught her foot between his ankles and wouldn't let go.

"You're the one who broke into his office. You're the one celebrating his death."

"Okay kids, quit your fighting," Lolita said. "What about our local drug dealer Alexander and his poisonous gifts?"

"What about him? You think he killed Wolf? Why would Alexander want to kill Wolf?" Jessica asked. "Just because he didn't grade his paper?"

"He may not have a motive, but he does have the means," said Lolita.

"If Alexander is working for the mob, maybe they had Wolf killed," said Jessica. "Maybe Wolf was somehow involved with drugs on campus. Maybe he was Alexander's boss."

"That's preposterous. Bald Dick mixed up with the Russian mafia?" Jack said. "You've been reading too many crime thrillers."

"Maybe not," said Lolita. "I've got to go." She stood up and grabbed her leather jacket and helmet. She swung her long hair to one side, wound it up into a bun, and put her skidlid on. One after the other, she stretched her long arms into the tight Harley jacket, and then threw a hundred-dollar bill onto the table.

"My treat," she said. "Later." Lolita didn't even wait for the waitress to refill her coffee. She was out the door.

CHAPTER THIRTY-FOUR

AFTER HER FRIENDS left the café, still shaken by the break-in, Jessica James didn't want to return to the Brentano attic. Since Amber wasn't there, she ordered a Double Dirty Chai, chai tea with two shots of espresso. Alone in the booth, she scraped their scraps onto one plate and stacked the others, pushed them across the table, brushed the crumbs onto the floor with the back of her hand, and then took out her computer to do some research. Trying to please her new advisor, she started searching Nietzsche's writings for any mention of menstruation. "Write with blood." Was that close enough?

He mostly railed against the vices of Christianity: solitude, fasting and abstinence. Whatever her other vices, Jessica wasn't guilty of those three, at least not as long as her friends kept feeding her pancakes. Since her break-up with Michael, she was wondering about the third. Maybe abstinence was best. Sex was too confusing, especially when it came to distinguishing between sex and love. She wanted Michael, craved him with the pain of an amputated limb, and the aching nausea pervading her very being must be evidence she still loved him. Even so, she wasn't about to take him back. Her mom had taught her, once a cheater, always a cheater. Of course, her mom had been talking about poker.

Jessica was deep in thought when someone slid into the booth across from her.

"I was hoping I'd run into you." Nick Shilling aka Professor Charis gave her his designer smile. "You haven't answered my messages."

Speechless, she stared at him for a few seconds. "I've been busy." It was true. She had been busy. Busy drinking and passing out again. But that wasn't why she hadn't answered his messages.

"If you aren't busy this evening, would you like to accompany me to see a painting that I'm considering for my Russian art collection?" Nick asked. "Given your thesis project, it could count as research."

"Clever," Jessica said. "Luring me out with promises of homework."

"This would be more like a field trip. But if you like, we could do some homework afterwards," he said, a twinkle in his eyes.

"Do I need a permission slip for this field trip? Maybe a signed waiver from my mom in case of unforeseen dangers?" she asked. "Probably safer to do my homework myself." She considered her vow of abstinence, but then Michael's stabbing infidelity pierced her heart again, and more than anything she needed to even the score. She wished Michael would walk through the door and see her with Nick. Her stomach sunk and she closed her eyes, and yet again the words in Michael's diary were daggers stabbing her in the gut.

"What time?" she asked, closing her computer so forcefully heads turned from the snapping sound.

"I'll pick you up at 6:00. Where do you live?" When Nick reached across the booth, she flinched and jerked her hand away.

"You can pick me up here," she said, cheeks on fire. "I want to finish what I'm working on."

"What are you working on?" he asked.

Her cheeks were so hot, she imagined they were blood-red by now. She was embarrassed to tell him that her new advisor had her researching menstruation. "I can't go with you unless I finish this," she said. "So get out of here and I'll see you in a couple of hours."

Once Nick left, she took stock of what she was wearing. Jeans, high-tops, and a stinky T-shirt with a picture of Mr. Spock with the caption: *Are you out of your Vulcan mind?* She hadn't showered in three days. She glanced around to make sure he was really gone, then gathered up her stuff. When she stuffed her computer into her book-bag, it got hung up on something. *Shit.* It was Alexander's paper crammed into the bottom of her bag. She'd been carrying it around for the last week, but still hadn't read it. *Tomorrow. First thing.* She promised herself.

She jogged the mile and a half back to campus, then took the stairs of Brentano two at a time. Panting, she dug through her clothes and found one clean shirt, a royal-blue western snap-front with a black embroidered yoke. She pulled off her t-shirt and jeans, and then sniffed her right armpit. Phew. She recoiled at the pungent odor of her hairy armpits. She grabbed her toiletries bag and then peeked out into the hall. In her underwear, she glanced around as she crept downstairs to the bathroom. She scrubbed her armpits using hand-soap and paper-towels, and then did the same with her nether-regions.

Once back in the attic, she slipped on the clean shirt, snapped it shut, ripped off her dirty jeans and wriggled into slightly cleaner ones, and then tugged on her Ropers. To top off her cowgirl kit, she added her grandfather's bolo tie, a small silver horseshoe with an onyx stone set inside. Then, she unzipped the inside pocket of her satchel, removed Nick's goofy little gun, dropped it back into the jacket pocket where'd she found it, and threw the jacket over her shoulder. On the way out the door, she hesitated, dashed back inside, and dropped the jacket on the desk. She unsnapped her shirt, withdrew her new bra from the top drawer, fastened its clasps, twisted it around her torso, bent over, and pulled it up under her breasts. Securing the miracle bra in place, she straightened up again, re-snapped her shirt, grabbed Nick's jacket, and rushed out of the attic and down the stairs. She needed a miracle.

Two hours later, Jessica got back to The Blind Faith just in time to catch her breath and open her computer before Nick arrived. Looking up over her rebooting computer, she watched Nick walking towards her across the café. He was wearing black jeans and a black shirt under a black leather jacket. His purple shoes added the only color to his outfit. She dug the sexy undertaker vibe. One lock of wavy chestnut hair hung over his left eye, and when he bent over to kiss her cheek, she fought the urge to brush it behind his ear.

"Are we going to a funeral?" she said. "Where's the stiff?"

"I am," Nick said. "You've shot me through the heart, Jesse James." His icy blues set her heart galloping, and then his warm smile gave it the spurs. She hadn't been subjected to such a powerful rush of hormonal adrenaline since her first weeks with Michael. She could barely breath and her skin was on fire, every tiny hair on her entire body standing on end.

"Dolce, you look lovely, as always, a regular rodeo princess."

"I'm not a princess and this isn't my first rodeo." *Try, second.* "I'll have you know, I was junior barrel racing champion."

"Apologies. I'm sure you're an experienced cowgirl," he said with a wink as she sat down across from her.

"As my father always said, if you climb in the saddle, you'd better be ready to ride." She stared straight into his icy blues.

"I'll remember that," Nick replied, reaching across the table for her hand.

She pretended to shut down files and packed up the computer she'd just unpacked. When Nick stood up and offered his hand again, she scooted out of the booth, trembling. Instead of taking his hand, she hauled her backpack from the booth, flung it over her shoulder, and held tight to its straps with both hands. Nick lightly pressed his hand on the small of her back as they walked out of the café. Outside, she was greeted by another perfect spring evening, the night air smelling of sweet lilacs and lilies.

As Nick led her to his car, she tried to stay just a step ahead to avoid the electricity radiating from the palm of his hand touching her back. The tingling sensation was so distracting she couldn't think straight. When Nick pressed a button on his keychain remote, the car started automatically. In the streetlights, she couldn't tell if the sparkling Porsche Boxster was blue or black, and she wondered if this crazy rich dude had actually bought a new car for their date. *It's not a date. It's not a date. It's not a date.* He opened the door and the smell of luxury leather struck her hard, Nietzsche's proverbial whip. "When you go to woman, don't forget your whip." She laughed to herself.

"Maybe we should skip the field trip and move straight to the homework," Nick whispered in her ear as he opened the passenger door. The smell of his cologne went to her head and she was tempted to kiss him, but jerked back when she spotted Detective Cormier watching them from across the street. She pushed Nick away, fell into the passenger seat, and slammed the door behind her. Between Detective Cormier following them and Nick's appointment with the art dealer, she was not in any danger of losing her "womanly virtue" as her grandmother would say.

They were meeting the seller at a restaurant in Skokie. She'd already been to the Russian neighborhood several times with Lolita and loved the colorful vegetable and flower markets and the bakeries filled with powdery Russian pastries. As they drove past, she admired St. Simeon Orthodox Church, radiant with its dark red bricks and blue onion domes topped with golden crosses. Several times before, Lolita had taken her inside the ornate building to appreciate the icons and architecture, and her friend also introduced her to Russian and Ukrainian delicacies at Pavlov's Banquet. Some were tasty and some were just plain weird. Cold beet soup. Meat jelly. Salty fish eggs. At least she knew what *not* to order for dinner.

Pavlov's Banquet was just as she remembered it, a boxy brick warehouse spruced up with a bright red ribbon painted across its neon orange and pink facade, making it look like a gaudy Christmas present. A tiny patio jutted off the parking lot, separated from the asphalt by a spindly wrought iron fence and some scraggly plants. Tattered purple paper lanterns hung from a trellis above the anemic courtyard. Nick parked near the patio and dashed around the car to open her door before she managed to pry the heavy thing open on her own. This time she let him take her hand, and when he did, she felt like she'd been zapped with a cattle prod. The jolt surprised her and she let out a little gasp. Still holding her hand, he wrapped his arm around her waist and pulled her closer. With her free hand, she opened the front door of Pavlov's Banquet.

The hostess led them past a wooden dance floor with red, yellow, and blue lights illuminating it from the rafters. No matter how many times she visited, Jessica was always amused by the heavy burgundy curtains with golden braided cords adorning window scenes painted on every wall, 19th century tableaus of men and women in formal eveningwear and carriages, scenes of old Moscow. This time, she noticed the red curtains clashed with the dirty-carrot colored carpet.

"Nice place," Jessica said. "Is this where you bring girls to help them with their homework?"

"What? You don't find dusty plastic flowers and Christmas lights romantic?" Nick asked.

"There's a red velvet love seat in the backroom," she said,

pointing past the balloon-filled foyer. The cavernous restaurant had lots of secluded spots where lovers could spoon feed each other *salo* and link arms to do shots of vodka. Lolita loved that combination, raw pork fat and Russo-Baltique Vodka. Maybe in Russia it was considered an aphrodisiac, like oysters in the U.S., or rhino horns in China. She couldn't stomach the raw fat, so she hoped the vodka might work its magic on its own.

"Hmm. And have you had many liaisons in Pavlov's backroom?" Nick asked, raising just one eyebrow. She was impressed. She'd never been able to raise just one eyebrow even though she and Jack practiced by watching Mr. Spock on *Star Trek*. She remembered the episode where Mr. Spock's Pon Farr (the urge to mate) nearly drives him mad but there's not another Vulcan on the Enterprise. She knew how he felt.

Each section of the humongous dining hall had table settings and chairs with their own patterns and color schemes, making for a festive scene. The hostess led them to a red and blue themed table with chairs dressed in blue satin with red sashes tied in bows behind their backs.

"There's always a first time," Nick said.

"First time what?" she asked, "being in a restaurant where the chairs are better dressed than your date?" She held up the sash on one of the chairs.

A matching blue tablecloth adorned their table, and a large vase of plastic red roses sat in the middle encircled by gold-rimmed plates nestled like Russian nesting dolls. Each place setting had three crystal wine glasses lined up from tiny to large, the largest a carved red glass sprouting a blue satin napkin. The colors reminded her of a circus and she imagined the waiter bringing out an elephant wearing a colorful headdress.

A burly man in a somber suit approached the table.

"Mr. Schilling, Mr. Popov is sorry to keep you waiting." His serious demeanor and earpiece made her think Secret Service. "He had some business to attend to." The stone-faced agent waved for a waiter. "Bring our guests something to drink while they wait." Then the bodyguard disappeared as quickly as he'd appeared.

"Why don't you order for both of us since you've been here before," Nick said to Jessica. "Anything but schmaltz herring." She scanned the menu trying to remember what Lolita always ordered. The weight of the choices and responsibility for ordering made her stomach sink. Tightening her lips in concentration, she scanned the menu. She wasn't hungry, at least not for food. "I wonder who translated this menu. Listen to this." She read out loud from the appetizer menu, "Pavlov Blini, assimilates well with a shot of frozen vodka." They laughed.

"Perfect. Two shots of frozen Russo-Baltique Vodka and an order of blini," Nick told the waiter.

Jessica had just slammed her third shot of frozen courage when Mr. Popov finally showed up.

CHAPTER THIRTY-FIVE

WHEN A ROTUND man wearing a green smoking jacket over a maroon vest the size of a tablecloth paraded through the restaurant with his entourage and stopped right in front of their table, Jessica James drooled vodka down her chin. After three shots, she found Mr. Popov amusing, with his foppish comb-over, manicured nails, and rotund belly, and she couldn't stop giggling.

"I'm Vladimir Popov." The fat man extended his hand to Nick.

"You mean like *priest* in Russian?" Jessica asked.

"We're not in Russia," Popov said. "Who's this little girl and why is she here?"

"My apologies, Mr. Popov," Nick said. "Let me introduce you."

"You should have come alone, Mr. Schilling," Popov said.

"Should I go wait in the car?" Jessica asked. Vladimir Popov would have been one scary dude, if he didn't look like a colorful hot air balloon. Jessica stifled another giggling fit.

"Tell your girlfriend not to ask so many questions," the balloon said.

"I'm not his girlfriend." When she corrected him, the dirigible glared at her as he put his fat finger to his lips.

"Shhhh…"

"Perhaps this is not a good time, I could come back later on my own," Nick said.

"You could, could you?" the airship laughed. "No need, my friends. You're here now, so we might as well get to it." He heaved himself forward, leaned on the table, and after several attempts, hoisted himself to his feet.

"Come to my office and we can do business," Fatty said, motioning for them to follow. Nick took her hand and they trailed behind the fat man until he stopped at an elevator. He reminded Jessica of the character Gutman in *The Maltese Falcon*. He was even wearing perfume and sporting an embroidered hanky in his breast pocket. She imagined his sidekick Peter Lorre's Joel waiting for them in the elevator to deliver the black bird.

Jessica squeezed Nick's hand as the Zeppelin led them down a dark hallway and into his "office," a parlor with dizzying floral wallpaper and overbearing chandeliers. For an art dealer, he sure had garish taste. His place was more tired bordello than art gallery. On either side of the room, grand mirrors with gold gilded baroque frames reflected her scruffy image into infinity, and now instead of *The Maltese Falcon* she was in the last scene from *The Lady from Shanghai*, only with the older, fatter, greaser version of Orson Wells leading the way. Their images blurred together into a fun-house monster, and mesmerized by the mirrors, Jessica ran smack into the wall in front of her. Once through the threshold of another musty, dark, cavernous room, Fatty motioned for them to sit down in ornate wooden chairs painted gold. She was afraid to release Nick's hand, but took a chair anyway, then slid her sweaty palm along her jeans, and sat at attention in case she had to bolt.

"Would you like something to eat or drink?" the blimp asked. When he snapped his fingers, a diminutive waiter appeared out of nowhere. Maybe he'd been hiding behind the curtains. The fat man said something in Russian and the little man scurried away.

"No, thank you," she said.

"I wasn't asking you, dearie," he said. "Mr. Schilling, might I offer you something?"

"No, thank you," Nick said, his eyes catching fire.

"I don't trust a man who doesn't accept my hospitality, Mr. Schilling."

"I don't trust a man who insults my friends, Mr. Popov," Nick replied.

"Mutual distrust, the best way to conduct business." His balloon belly continued reverberating long after he finished laughing.

Soon, the waiter returned with a tray of liqueur glasses filled with viscous amber liquor, along with tiny square pastel pastries. He offered them to her first. She looked from Nick to Vladimir, and didn't know if she was supposed to take something or not. The waiter took a dessert plate rimmed with English roses from a cart and used tongs to place two petit fours on her plate, then he placed the plate and a glass of liqueur on the side table next to her.

Jessica wished she hadn't just downed three shots of vodka, especially if she was expected to keep drinking now. Flushed and hot, she unsnapped her shirt part way and fanned herself with her napkin. She wanted water but was too afraid to ask, so she took a sip of the syrupy liqueur. *Yuck!* She cringed and discretely wiped her tongue off with her napkin. When the waiter reappeared with cups of strong tea, she smiled and nodded. As soon as he'd placed her cup on the side-table, she snatched it up and gulped it down. It burned her throat but at least it chased away the treacley taste of the nasty liqueur, and she hoped it would help sober her up. She nodded again as the waiter offered to refill her cup from the silver samovar on the cart.

Another hulking suit appeared carrying a framed painting, and then leaned it against a chair across from Nick. Straining to see it, she leaned forward in her chair, but Nick was blocking her view.

"May I?" Nick asked pointing to the painting. When the Gut-man-look-alike smiled and nodded, Nick stood up, went to the painting, picked it up, and held it out at arms length. He studied it for several minutes. When he glanced over at her, he was wearing his poker face, and she couldn't read his eyes.

"Where did you get this painting, Mr. Popov?" Nick asked. "Can you verify its authenticity?"

"Where did I get it? Can I verify its authenticity?" the Aerostat repeated, putting down his pastry and glaring up from his plate at Nick. "Of course I can." He picked up the pastry and popped it into his mouth. "Where did I get it? Can I verify its authenticity?" he mumbled, his mouth full. He shook out his napkin and brushed the crumbs off of his lap, then finished his tea and waved for the waiter to pour him another from the samovar. "An associate in Russia has an extensive art collection and for a reasonable price, he's willing to part with this Kandinsky."

"If your associate wants to sell the painting, why doesn't he auction it at Sotheby's or Christie's? That's the way it's usually done. "

"Like many people in Russia these days, he prefers a more discrete and private transaction." He said, dabbing at his thick lips with an embroidered napkin.

"Jessica, come and take a look," Nick said, gesturing to her with his head. Trying not to make any noise, she carefully sat her plate on the glass side table, then tiptoed over to his chair, watching Fatty out of the corner of her eye. Nick patted the armrest of his chair, and she sat down. He'd sat back down and maneuvered the painting on his lap so she could see it.

"Darling, did you by chance bring the tiny magnifying tool from the other night?" He gave her a meaningful look. "I may need it later to examine the painting."

"Yes," she said, playing along. "Let me know if you need it."

She would have been calmer if she understood what game they were playing and why. He put his arm around her waist, and his hand was pressing into her (or his) jacket pocket.

"How much does your friend want for it?" Nick asked. Now he had his hand inside her pocket and was palming the tiny pistol, slipping it out, and sliding it along her back. She sat as rigid as a pole for fear she might knock it out of his hand.

Jessica didn't like the odds in whatever game they were playing. She never bluffed in poker and she didn't know if Nick was bluffing or not. In addition to the Hindenburg and the waiter, three bulls legs were standing nearby waiting for orders. All Nick's toy pistol could do is give one of the thugs a pierced navel before the others ground him into the paisley carpet.

"How much are you offering?" the fat man asked, a slight tremor in his voice.

"Get me a certificate of authenticity and then we'll talk."

"I'll give you 72 hours to make up your mind, Mr. Schilling." His round face became a hothouse tomato. "Then I'll offer it to another buyer."

Nick lifted the painting so she could see it. "Beautiful, isn't it?" Her mouth fell open, and she brought her hand to her face. *Oh My God.* She caught her breath to stop herself from gasping.

Nick narrowed his eyes. "We'd better be going. I'll get back to you soon, Mr. Popov. It's been a pleasure."

Once outside, Jessica hightailed it to Nick's car. She must be imagining things again. Out of the corner of her eye, she glimpsed that weasel Alexander pop into Pavlov's Banquet. But that didn't make sense. The car started itself from a block away, and she was barely in the passenger's seat when Nick kicked the accelerator and the Boxster roared onto Gross Point Road. Neither of them said a word until they were on the freeway. When he merged into the center lane, he exhaled loudly, "Whew."

"What did you think of that painting?" he asked.

"It's Dmitry's Kandinsky," she said. "I'm sure of it."

"Who's Dmitry?" he asked, weaving in and out of traffic, passing cars right and left.

"Dmitry's the janitor at Brentano Hall," she said. "He's obsessed with that particular Kandinsky composition. He paints it over and over."

"So you could tell it's a forgery?" he said. "Good eye, Miss James."

"It's not a forgery," she said. "It's one of Dmitry's paintings. I bet it's the one missing from Schmutzig's office."

"I'm not following," he said. "The janitor paints Kandinskys to decorate the offices at Brentano Hall?" He swerved into the right-hand lane and exited the freeway. "I want to meet this artist janitor. Where can we find him?"

"He's staying at The Residence Inn north of here in Wilmette," she said. "Why?"

He asked Siri for directions to The Residence Inn and headed towards Edens Expressway.

"We're going right now? Can't it wait until tomorrow?" she asked. "What if they're in bed? Why do we have to go now?"

Nick didn't respond; he was listening to Siri.

"What's going on? Maybe we should call Detective Cormier and tell him Vladimir has the missing painting," she said. "The one from Schumtzig's office. I'm telling you, that was the painting Dmitry gave to Wolf. It has the same frame and everything."

"Who's Detective Cormier?" he asked.

"The detective who saved me from Kurt-the-rapist. The officer who questioned me," she said, "Twice."

"You mean I have competition? I thought I saved you from Kurt the rapist," he said. "I'm worried about that jock's obsession with you."

She regretted mentioning Kurt-the-rapist. She didn't want to explain she'd drunk the poisonous punch, passed out, and landed in the hospital. It had only been just last night, but it seemed like a week ago. She pulled her phone out of her book bag.

"Are you calling the detective?" He sounded alarmed.

"No, I'm texting Lolita," she said. "Dmitry's her dad."

"Lolita the Poker Tsarina?" he asked. "Her father's the fake Kandinsky?"

CHAPTER THIRTY-SIX

BEFORE DMITRY DURCHENKO could stop her, his daughter had opened the door to whoever was knocking this late at night. He recognized her friend Jessica. She stepped inside the apartment and grabbed his daughter's arm. "We found your dad's painting," she said. She wasn't alone. There was a man with her. *Trouble always travels with a companion.*

Dmitry joined his daughter at the door. "Miss Jessica, what are you doing here?" he asked. He stared over her shoulder at the stranger standing behind her. "You found my paintings? Where did you find them?" he asked.

Dmitry was tired. He'd been waiting up for Vanya to get back from walking Bunin and then planned to go to bed, and was wearing his bathrobe and slippers. He was embarrassed to see Jessica outside of Brentano Hall, especially in his nightclothes. Judging from the color of her cheeks, she felt the same way. He didn't like late night visitors. He tightened the tie on his robe and stepped further into the doorway, pushing the visitors out into the hallway. And he didn't want them to disturb Sabina.

He was worried about his wife. She had yet to recover from the fire and still seemed shaken. The worst of it was the night terrors, when she'd wake up screaming. He knew how she felt. But his trauma wasn't the result of one horrific event, but a childhood filled with horrors beyond words at the Hospital. *Beautiful Sabina.* He wanted to shield her and Lolita from that kind of unspeakable pain. He didn't know what he would have done if Bunin hadn't dragged Sabina out of the burning house. Without her, he never could have left Russia or his mother. Without her, he never would have gotten on that train to escape the harsh life of his father and *Bratva.*

"The fat man at Pavlov's Pork Chop has the painting," Jessica said, talking fast and waving her hands.

"You mean Pavlov's Banquet," Lolita said.

"That's what I said!"

Dmitry shrunk. She'd only found his copy and not the original. He was still staring at the handsome man who had both arms around Miss Jessica. She must have noticed because she apologized and introduced them. As the man released Jessica and stepped around to shake his hand, Dmitry took stock of the stranger as if they were about to enter the ring. He wondered about this man dressed in all black with goofy purple shoes.

"Mr. Durchenko, your Kandinsky is uncanny," the stranger said. "How did you do it?" Jessica's boyfriend pushed past him and walked into the room as if he'd been invited. Dmitry hurried over to shut the bedroom door where his wife was sleeping. He had been doing all of the shopping and cooking to make sure she got as much rest as possible to recover from the smoke inhalation and a bad case of nerves. Things were stressful enough living out of a suitcase, their house and belongings gone, all their money turned to ash, the paintings missing, and now this bothersome stranger barging in in the middle of the night.

"I asked you how you copied that Kandinsky so exactly," the stranger said, "an unbelievable feat."

Dumfounded, Dmitry glanced from Jessica to Lolita. Who

was this *mudak*? He walked across the hotel room and herded his guests into the kitchenette.

Lolita intervened. "Would you like some vodka or tea?" she purred at Nick, then turned and winked at her friend, "Mr. Schilling, was it?" Dmitry wondered what was going on between his daughter and these people. Opposites must attract, because there was no other way to explain the friendship between Lolita and Jessica.

"Both would be lovely," Mr. Schilling replied.

"Spoken like a true Russian," Lolita said, laying on the charm.

"You must be Lolita, the Poker Tsarina," Schilling said.

Dmitry awoke from his daze. "What did you call my daughter?" he asked.

Both Jessica and Lolita glared at Mr. Schilling. Dmitry wondered and worried.

"I asked if…." Mr. Schilling stuttered, "if she's from Herzegovina." He cleared his throat.

Dmitry swore he'd heard something about poker and the Tsar. He didn't trust this Mr. Schilling.

"No," Lolita said. "I'm from here. My parents are from Russia." She ushered them to the table and gestured for them to sit down. If they weren't Lolita's friends, Dmitry would have thrown the intruders out on their ears.

"What were you doing at Pavlov's Banquet? And what's this about my dad's painting," Lolita asked, looking over her shoulder at Dmitry.

Lolita was up to something. Sometimes, he wondered how his daughter could afford tuition at Northwestern University, wear expensive designer clothes, and ride a fancy motorcycle. He knew the allowance he gave her didn't buy all of that, but he'd learned not to ask her too many questions.

When Lolita offered them seats at the tiny table, and the

intruders pulled up chairs like they planned to stay. Lolita poured them frozen Stoli shots and he made a pot of strong Russian tea. By the looks of it, it was going to be a long night.

"So you saw my painting at Pavlov's Banquet?" Dmitry asked. "Is Vladimir the Pope trying to sell it?" He asked as he slumped back in his chair. "What did he tell you? That it's an original Kandinsky?" He scoffed. "Only an idiot who knew nothing about art would fall for that." He was exhausted and wanted to go to bed.

"I don't know, Mr. Durchenko," Mr. Schilling said. "That's the most impressive copy of any Kandinsky I've ever seen. It almost had me fooled."

"Are you a collector, Mr. Schilling?" he asked. "How did the Pope find you?"

Mr. Schilling smiled. He did a shot of vodka and held up his glass for another. "How long have you been forging Kandinskys, Mr. Durchenko?"

"Nick!" Jessica cut him off. "Dmitry isn't a forger."

"Let's hear from Mr. Durchenko, shall we?" Mr. Schilling said. "You don't happen to have any scotch, do you?" This guy had some nerve, making accusations of forgery and then asking for whiskey. Dmitry wished Vanya would get back. He didn't like this Mr. Schilling. Miss Jessica could do better. He imagined the pleasure Vanya would take in carving his initials into Mr. Schilling's too beautiful face. He shivered.

"Nick, it's late. I think we should go," Jessica said. She was tugging at the sleeve of his leather jacket. He ignored her, but Dmitry agreed with Jessica. "Yes, you should go."

"Mr. Durchenko, I compliment you on your forgery," Mr. Schilling said. "It's truly the best I've ever seen."

"Nick, please," Jessica got up from the table. "I'm so sorry," she said to Dmitry. "Lolita, I had no idea. Really, I'm sorry." She blushed.

"Sit down," Lolita commanded. "Calm down everyone. My father is not a forger. He paints as a hobby. He copies the masterworks like any other art student. So what? Forgers are criminals who dupe people into buying fakes for profit. My father is not a forger!"

Dmitry sat staring at his hands in his lap. "Yes, Lolita is right," he said, after an awkward silence. "It's a hobby." *Maybe Schilling's a cop.* This was worse than the police interrogation.

"Where did you study the original, Mr. Durchenko?" Schilling asked. "To paint something like this, you had to have sat for hours in front of the real thing."

"As a boy, I saw it on a field trip to Tretyakov Gallery in Moscow," he said softly. He felt like he was back in grade school, being scolded by a teacher.

"Mr. Durchenko, I'm sure you know *Fragment number 2 for Composition VII* has never been in Tretyakov Gallery." Schilling took another vodka shot. "Perhaps you're thinking of the full canvas for *Composition VII?*"

"Nick! Please," Jessica raised her voice.

"Perhaps," Dmitry said. He wished that this nightmare would end. "Why do you care? You know perfectly well the painting is not a real Kandinsky. No one is forcing him to buy it. In fact, it's mine and it's not for sale."

"Where is the original *Fragment number 2?*" Schilling asked.

The walls were closing in and Dmitry was feeling claustrophobic. "How would I know?"

Mr. Schilling leaned towards him. "It was sold at Tajan auction house in Paris twenty-five years ago to a Russian collector." He downed another vodka and stared at Dmitry. "The only way you could have painted that picture is by sitting in front of it for weeks, months, even years. You know where it is, or was, don't you?"

"I'm sure I don't know," Dmitry said. *Where the hell was Vanya and his switchblade when he needed him?*

"And I'm sure you do know," Schilling said. He pulled a tiny pistol from his pocket and placed it on the table. "Do you know why I got this Colt 1911 New Agent?" he slurred. Obviously, Mr. Bigshot couldn't handle his vodka and wasn't man enough for a real gun.

Jessica shot up from the table. "What the hell are you doing, Nick?" she yelled. She tripped on her untied shoelace and fell backwards, taking her chair with her. Lolita grabbed her under the arms from behind and lifted her to her feet.

"Mr. Schilling, it's not polite to wave your gun around in our hotel room," Lolita said. "Even if it is just a toy."

"I assure you, Tsarina, it's no toy," Mr. Schilling said. "And I'm not waving it. I'm just making the point that collecting Russian art can be dangerous." Calmer now, he took a pack of cigarettes from his inside pocket. Mr. Schilling offered cigarettes around the table. Lolita took one, and Miss Jessica took one, too. Dmitry waved the pack away. Mr. Schilling lit them one by one, starting with Jessica's and finishing with his own. They were filterless *Gauloises*. Jessica almost inhaled but choked instead. Much to Dmitry's dismay, Lolita smoked like she'd been doing it all her life.

Mr. Schilling picked up the pistol. "I bought this gun because so much Russian art is handled by *Bratva* these days," he said. "I learned the hard way."

Dmitry scoffed. "You're going to need something bigger than that to deal with *Bratva*," he said. "Big voyages require big ships." What was this joker doing with that toy gun? He was going to get himself killed.

"It may be small, but it's deadly," Schilling said with a smirk. "And I'm a damned good shot."

"An axe is no match for a chainsaw," Dmitry said. "Pull that toy gun on any *Krysha* or Torpedo and they will show you what a real pistol looks like."

"Bratva? Krysha? What are you talking about?" Jessica asked.

"Bratva is the Russian Brotherhood," Lolita said, "Kryshi are their enforcers."

Mr. Schilling interrupted. "Do you know Mr. Durchenko, when Vassily Kandinsky first started painting, he signed his name in the bottom right corner of his work," he said. "But after he met his wife Nina, he changed his signature to a large letter V with a smaller letter K inside." He took an expensive pen from his inside pocket and drew it on a napkin to illustrate. "His initials, you see."

"Fascinating, Mr. Schilling," Lolita said. "But what does this have to do with my father's painting?" She stamped out her cigarette on the Residence Inn saucer.

"Do you know how I could tell your painting was not authentic?" Mr. Schilling took a long drag of his cigarette. "The one thing that made all the difference?"

"The tiger lily," said Dmitry without thinking. He thought of his mother and their afternoon picking tiger lilies in the French countryside. Appropriate that her favorite flower was a tiger lily. He wondered if his mother still picked tiger lilies, if she was even still alive. What had happened to her after he escaped with the valise she'd stolen from his father?

"Tiger lily?" Mr. Schilling asked, picking up his gun and then putting it back into his pocket. Dmitry waited. "No, Mr. Durchenko, the signature."

"Kandinsky didn't sign his studies or fragments," Dmitry said. He saw where Schilling was going and he didn't like it.

"Exactly. But you signed yours, didn't you. Why?"

"Why are you interrogating him, Nick?" Jessica asked, coming to Dmitry's defense. "He's not a criminal and you have no right to treat him like garbage."

"Why did you sign your painting with the initials V.K.?" He pointed at the mess he'd drawn on the napkin. "Odd that a forger would choose to copy an unsigned painting and then sign it."

"In that case," Jessica said, "If he'd wanted to forge it, he would have left off the signature, right?" This girl had a very logical mind.

"Strange that you would perfect Kandinsky's *Fragment*, sign it, but get the signature wrong," Schilling said. "You connected the V and K, instead of putting the K inside the V. Why's that?" He drew another more legible symbol on the napkin, a W with an extra leg kicking out to the right. He may be a *mudak*, but he knew his Kandinsky.

Lolita grabbed the napkin. "That's the logo for *VKontakte*, the largest social network in Russia," she said. "It's like Facebook. VK is the equivalent of FB." She stared at him. "What does it mean, Dad?"

"What's your game, Mr. Durchenko?" Schilling asked. "Why this symbol?" He pointed at the napkin again.

"A goat will find garbage anywhere," Dmitry said. He grabbed Schilling's lit cigarette from the saucer where it was balanced and dropped it into his teacup. He stood up and took the cup to the sink. He took the Stolichnaya bottle from the freezer and poured himself another shot. He threw his head back, downed it, then slammed the shot glass onto the dinette table. "If you must know, Mr. Schilling," he said, "it's a message for my mother. Not that she'd ever see it. I opened a VK account in the name of Kandinsky. A desperate attempt to make covert contact. Are you happy now Mr. Schilling? I risked my life to send a message to my mother. I just want to know if she's still alive."

CHAPTER THIRTY-SEVEN

"GO BACK TO bed, *lyubimaya*," Dmitry Durchenko said when the door to the bedroom opened and a feverish Sabina staggered out in her nightgown. He glowered at Schilling. "Now you've woken my wife. It's late Mr. Schilling. I think perhaps you should go."

"Please go, Nick," Jessica pleaded.

"I'm sorry to have bothered you, Mrs. Durchenko," Mr. Schilling said to Sabina. He turned to Jessica and said, "Let's go, Dolce." He got up from the table and put his hand out to Jessica.

"I'm staying," Jessica said, voice shaking. Her face was flushed and tears were welling in shining blue eyes. Schilling put his hands on her shoulders and tried to caress her neck, but she flinched and shook off his touch.

"Let me take you home, Jessica," he said.

"Lolita can take me home," she said, moving further away from him.

"Yes, Lolita can take Miss Jessica home," Dmitry said, nodding at Lolita.

"I'd like to take you home," Schilling said to Jessica, and then leaned closer to whisper something in her ear.

A banging on the door and a barking Bunin interrupted the

negotiations. He loosened the chain and peered through the crack. Bunin was panting and so was Vanya. "Open up, Dima," he said. As soon as Dmitry slid off the chain, his cousin barged into the room, holding a baggie, looked Schilling up and down, and then wrinkled his nose. Schilling was as full of shit as the baggie, and Vanya's disgusted scowl suggested he thought so too.

Schilling pushed past Vanya on his way to the door, then looked back at Jessica. "I'm leaving. Are you coming or not?"

"You go without me," she answered. "I'm staying."

Dmitry walked the arrogant ass to the door.

On his way out, Schilling turned to him and asked, "Do you know who purchased Kandinsky's fragment in Paris, Mr. Durchenko?" He didn't wait for an answer. "I do. It was Mr. Anton Yudkovich. Does that name ring a bell, Mr. Durchenko? Or should I say Mr. Yudkovich?"

Dmitry's eyes widened. He was stunned. How the hell could this *mudak* know about his father? He jerked back when Schilling reached for something from his jacket pocket, but Schilling only handed him a card, "If you ever have any real Kandinskys for sale, give me a call."

Dmitry responded by shutting the door in his face. When he turned around, he ran smack into Vanya who was hopping from foot to foot behind him. "Can we talk, Boss?" he asked Dmitry, "in private like." He glanced nervously around the room at the visitors. The only place they could go without disturbing Sabina was the small half bathroom on the other side of the kitchenette wall. Dmitry led Vanya into the lavatory and shut the door behind them. There was barely enough room for the two men to stand between the toilet and the sink, so Dmitry closed the lid of the toilet and sat on it.

"What's going on, Vanya?" he asked.

"Who was that *súka*?" Vanya asked in return, pointing towards the bathroom door.

"A friend of Lolita's friend. What's wrong? I'm exhausted and want to go to bed."

"Mind if I take a leak?" Vanya asked. "I was out so long and I gotta go."

"For Chrissakes Vanya," he stood up and moved along the wall towards the sink. "What the hell is the matter with you?"

"Your mother is here."

Dmitry whipped around and grabbed him in mid-pee. A stream of urine sprayed back and forth behind the toilet. "What do you mean my mother is here?"

"Chill out, Dima," he said, pulling himself loose. He zipped up his fly. "Like I said, your mom's here."

"What do you mean, she's here? Where?"

"Here, in the U.S.," Vanya said. "She called the Pope from the hospital and told him to have you call her back."

Dmitry held onto the sink and stared into the mirror but didn't recognize his own reflection with its sunken eyes, inflamed cheeks, and disheveled hair. "That's impossible," he said to himself. "Unless…"

Dmitry slid to the floor and put his head in his hands. Two decades of looking over his shoulder, worrying about his father finding him and planning his escape, hadn't prepared him for this moment. If that idiot kid Alexander hadn't stole the professor's damned painting and sold it to the Pope. If only the professor hadn't discovered him in his office when he was hiding the paintings under the floorboard, he wouldn't have had to give him his copy.

Just a week earlier, he could have returned everything, the money down to the last ruble, and the paintings if necessary. But now the money, just paper, had burned up with his house, and the paintings could be in some vault or safety deposit box anywhere in the city, or any city. All he had left to pay with was his life. And, probably not for very much longer, knowing his father. His hands were trembling as he remembered all too well what his father did to traitors, especially his flesh and blood. Anton, the Oxford Don, had already had his oldest son executed. Why not kill the youngest one too?

Again, he was back at the Hospital staring into Sergei's mangled face, smelling the blood, tasting the fear, hearing the cracking of the frozen concrete walls, feeling the weight of his Wool's cool steel grip. As if it were yesterday, he heard the echoes of the gun's crash to the floor and the two shots following him out into the frigid night. His father's words came back to him, "Dispose of him, you are a man not a mouse." Was his mother now leading him into a mousetrap? Did she even know? He ached to see her again, and would do anything for her, even if it meant giving up his own life.

"Here's her number, Cousin. Call and find out what she wants." Vanya pulled his cell phone out of his back pocket. "Here, use my phone." He bent down and handed it to Dmitry who was still sitting on the floor leaning against the door.

The past was like a fungus. Just when you thought it was gone for good, you caught yourself scratching again, and Dmitry was itching all over. He wanted to crawl out of his skin. Should he call her or run away? His whole world closing in on him in this cramped, windowless cubicle. It was no use running now. There was nowhere to go. He took the phone and tapped it on when someone knocked at the door.

"You two okay in there?" Lolita asked.

"Give me a minute, *kotyonok*," Dmitry said. "We'll be right out."

He asked Vanya to read him the number. He was

hyperventilating as the phone rang but managed to steady himself against the door. Each ring ratcheted the tension in his cardiac veins until they were wound around his heart so tightly around his heart it might burst.

After six rings, a small voice answered, *"Zdravstvujtye,* ah, Hello." He had obviously woken her up. He had forgotten how late it was.

"Mamochka." His voice cracked. "It's Dmitry. Is that you, Mama?"

"Dmitry, *lyubimyj,"* the soft voice said, "I've waited so long to hear your voice, *malysh,* my baby boy." Sobbing on the other end of the phone made him want to reach out and hold her, his beloved mother, weeping with pain or joy, he didn't know.

The last time he'd seen her had been on the train platform, a lifetime ago, his daughter's lifetime. His mother had been wearing her blue fox coat and hat, wiping the tears from his eyes with her perfumed handkerchief as they parted, pushing him away in order to save him.

"Mother," Dmitry said trying to steady his voice, "Where are you?"

"Come to us, *milyi,"* she said. "Come immediately. We are at the Mayo Clinic in Minnesota."

"Why?" he said. "What's wrong?"

"You will know everything when you get here," she said. "I can't talk now. You must come, my son."

"Mother, please tell me," he said.

"Dimka, know this. Everything changes. Nothing disappears."

For the past twenty years, Dmitry had heard her voice over and over again in his head, repeating those five words. Now, he wondered what they meant. Everything had changed and he was safe, or nothing disappears and he was dead... *Everything changes.* Could his father change? *Nothing disappears.* Did his mother still love him? Why was she giving him another code to decipher? Like the paintings? How could he tell her he'd lost them?

"Where are you?" Dmitry asked. He didn't know what he was asking. There was no roadmap to lead him to his mother's soul, no directions to her heart. For decades, he'd been searching in Kandinsky's *Fragment.* A fragment. He'd always only had a fragment of his mother. A fragment of his mother and a shard of his father. His relationship with his father was like glass, once broken, it could never be mended.

"Come to the Mayo Clinic in Rochester, Minnesota," she said. "Tonight. You must come tonight."

"Why?" he asked. Why had she forced him to leave Russia? Why had she come back? Why had she given him those two paintings?

"Dimka," his mother said, "you must come. Your father is dying…"

CHAPTER THIRTY-EIGHT

DMITRY DURCHENKO SAT on the bathroom floor listening to the dead phone line. He'd always thought of his father as immortal. Given *Bratva*'s reach, in a sense he was. *Everything changes, nothing disappears.* He had feared his father for so long and from so far away, he wasn't sure if the Anton he dreaded was real or imaginary. Even when they'd lived under the same roof, his father had been distant. And yet Dmitry was bound to him, tethered by the bandages of memory he'd wrapped around the wounds of his childhood.

"Are you okay, Dima?" Vanya asked. "Can we leave the toilet now?"

When they came out of the bathroom, the girls were having a heated discussion over tea.

"Girls, Cousin Vanya and I have to run an errand," Dmitry said. "We won't be back until late tomorrow night. Hopefully," he said under his breath, "If not by washing, then by rolling."

He wrapped Lolita in a bear hug. "Take care of your mother while I'm gone," he said. "*Ya lyublyu tyebya.*"

"I love you too, Daddy," Lolita replied. "Are you okay?"

"Where are you going?" Lolita asked, following him around

the small apartment. Dmitry's mind was turning in circles trying to figure out what he needed for the trip to the Mayo Clinic.

"A man must risk going too far," he said, "to see how far he can go." He was about to face the most dangerous encounter of his life, a reunion with his powerful father. Dying or not, Anton, the Oxford Don, Yudkovich controlled an army, and he had no doubt that he could reach beyond the grave to get what he wanted. His *Kryshi* were everywhere.

"I'm going with you," Lolita said. "Don't forget your phone." She unplugged his phone, picked it up from the window ledge, and handed it to him.

"No, *milaya*, please stay with your mother. She needs you," he said gently as he filled two Residence Inn Styrofoam cups with strong sweet tea, and then handed one to Vanya.

"Tell me where you are going," Lolita insisted.

He gathered his watch, keys and wallet before he realized he was still wearing his robe and slippers. Sabina had gone back to bed, and he debated whether or not he should risk waking her to get his clothes.

"Dammit, Dad, tell me what's going on," Lolita demanded. "Where are you going?"

"Be careful *kotyonok*," Dmitry said. "Both of you. And watch out for Mr. Schilling."

"Don't worry about Mr. Schilling," his daughter winked at her friend, "Jesse has him wrapped around her little finger. Don't you Jesse?" Jessica stuck out her tongue and made a face, and the girls burst out laughing.

Dmitry took in the scene, trying to memorize it. His daughter and her friend, happy, safe, and carefree. He seized the image with his mind's eye and took it with him to fortify himself against whatever the night to come might bring.

He cracked open the door to the bedroom to see if Sabina was awake. He was hoping she'd gone back to sleep. He didn't want to tell her where he was going, but he couldn't lie to her. His wife was a tiny leaf in the king sized bed. Kneeling down next to the bed, gazing at her sleeping face, he stroked her hair.

He leaned forward and inhaled her scent, sweet cream, and then kissed her on the forehead. She smiled but didn't open her eyes. "*Ya lyublyu tyebya,*" he whispered. "I love you too," she whispered back. This might be the last time he ever saw her. He knelt staring at her peaceful beauty with an artist's eye, trying to memorize it too. His heart ached with tenderness for his wife, but his love for her gave him the courage to leave her.

He stood up, tiptoed across the room, then slowly slid his jacket from the back of the easy chair and draped it over his arm. Next, he went to the closet and carefully gathered pants, shirt, and shoes with care, and then quietly left the room, shutting the door behind him. Back in the tiny bathroom, he quickly changed into his clothes. Until now, he'd never needed a gun, but he wondered if he should buy one on his way out of town.

When he emerged from the bathroom, Vanya was sitting on the couch with Lolita and her friend. He motioned for Vanya, and Bunin sprang up from the floor and came running. Together, the three of them left the apartment on what may be his last journey.

The GPS estimated it would take just over five hours to get to the Mayo Clinic. They should arrive before dawn. His mother said Anton was dying and he wondered if they would get there in time. He wasn't sure which would be better, if they did, or if they didn't. Did his father's death mean the end of his torment or just the beginning? His father was dying and instead of sorrow or grief, all he felt was dread. So his father would get to hell before him. Maybe his father was already there, waiting.

Dmitry cracked his window to get some air. Not even yet out of the city and already Vanya had turned the inside of the Escalade into a fire hazard. Vanya had insisted they stop at a convenience store so he could stock up on cigarettes and Snickers bars. Desperate to stay awake, Dmitry resorted to the foul liquid that tried to pass as coffee. With enough sugar and cream, it barely was drinkable. It was going to be a long night.

"Do you have a gun, Vanya?"

His cousin used his cigarette to indicate a duffle bag behind his seat. Dmitry needed both hands to pull the heavy bag close enough to open it. It didn't help that sitting between the bucket seats Bunin kept pawing at him, wagging and licking his face. He had to push Bunin away to drag the duffel bag closer. Puffing on his cigarette, Vanya nodded for him to unzip the bag.

No wonder it was so heavy. Inside, he found a Vityaz 9x9mm Parabellum submachine gun: closed bolt, blowback operated, Kalashnikov variant, standard issue for Russian military and police. And beside it was a Makarov pistol, semi-automatic, just like the one Yuri had used on his brother that horrific last night at the hospital.

He hadn't seen weapons like these since he'd left Russia. "Where did you get these?"

Vanya's smile gleamed. "Brought them from home." Dmitry didn't know if he meant his apartment in Skokie or his childhood home in Russia. He decided not to ask. Rummaging through the duffle bag, he found a PSS silent pistol just like the Wool he'd had in Russia. He took it out and turned it over in his hands. He saw D.Y. carved into the pistol grip.

"My Wool!" Dmitry exclaimed. "Where did you get it?"

He had often missed his Wool. He hated killing, but he'd always loved guns. Even as a kid, he loved to clean his father's pistols and rifles. A twinge of guilt pinched his heart. He didn't know if it was caused by his love for his father, or by his love of deadly weapons. In a way, his love for his father was a deadly weapon, luring him into danger.

Dmitry's father had given him the Wool on his thirteenth birthday, and he'd been proud that his father had given him such a powerful gift. Delighted, he had held the gun with both hands and instinctively pointed it at his father. Anton knocked the pistol to the floor and growled. "Don't point that at anyone unless you plan to kill him. Weapons aren't toys and you're no longer a child."

That same afternoon, his father had taken him to the shooting range to teach him how to use his first Wool. Once they arrived, they were both given ear protection and safety glasses. His father led him to the back where at least a dozen other grown up men were standing in their designated slots firing various guns. A paper target moved on a metal rack a hundred feet in front of them and as it zipped by, they shot at it. When they reached their designated slot, his father barked out instructions and he tried to follow, but his pistol wouldn't cooperate. It was heavy and hard to hold straight. He didn't hit a single target. Discouraged, he asked to go home. But his father had said, "Dima, quit sulking. We're not going home until you hit this target." After an hour, his arm hurt and he still hadn't pierced a target. When he started crying and begged to go home, his father yanked the gun from his hands and fired it five times, perforating the moving targets with every shot.

"Do I have to do everything for you?" his father asked. "Some day, I won't be around and you'll have to learn to take care of yourself."

Bunin barked and Dmitry put the Wool back and started digging through the duffle bag. Along with boxes of ammunition, he found a beautiful Damascus knife with a gold hilt and jade handle. He held it up so the jade caught the light.

"Gorgeous," he said.

"Was my father's," Vanya said proudly. "For skinning bears."

"It's a beauty," he said as he put it back. He zipped up the bag, pushed it back behind the seat, and Bunin resumed his place between them.

"One time we were hunting in Kamchatka," Vanya began in Russian. "We got off our snowmobiles and were on foot. We came around a switchback and seen a monster brown bear about twenty feet away." He laughed until he coughed. He put out his cigarette and took a drink from his water bottle. "Anyways," he continued, "that *Blyad* was ten-feet tall. I mean huge. I was only twelve and my father tells me to shoot it." He was laughing again. "My Mosin-Nagant rifle was bigger than me. And I pulled the trigger, fell on my ass, and pissed my pants. My father yelled his head off, but I shot the damn bear right in the heart. *Blyad* almost fell on my father." He started chuckling. "My pants were frozen where I pissed myself, like a popsicle, peesicle."

His laugh was contagious. His good humor, and the impressive arsenal in the duffel bag, reassured Dmitry. For the rest of the drive, they exchanged stories from their childhood.

As they reached the exit for Rochester, Dmitry asked, "Remember that time when we were playing together at my father's country house and you fell onto some rocks and broke your front teeth?"

Vanya gave him a metallic grin. "I didn't fall. You pushed me. But, I got even, huh, Cousin. That little scar behind your left ear."

"Remember how we hunted for your teeth?" Dmitry asked. "So we could glue them back on." They were both laughing.

They laughed about their childhoods only because they were so far away. As Dmitry got ever closer to his father's deathbed, his laughter was morphing into terror. When he spotted the exit for the Mayo Clinic, he grew sullen. He rode in silence the rest of the way to the hospital.

Another hour until sunrise, the brightly lit glass building illuminated the streets around the hospital, a beacon leading him not to safe harbor but his demise. Driving around the building, Vanya followed the signs for "Visitor Parking." The place was a maze and the corkscrew ramp to the parking garage made him queasy. As Vanya expertly swung the Escalade into a spot near an elevator, Dmitry's stomach soured and a film of stale coffee smothered his tongue. He took a swig from his water bottle. Before they'd left the Residence Inn, he'd filled it with vodka. His mother had scolded him when he was a teenager, "Vodka and good sense are mortal enemies," but with enough vodka, anything was possible. He took another drink from his water bottle and passed it to Vanya.

"No thanks, *chuvak*," he said. "I got some."

"Not like this you haven't," he said. "It's Stoli." Vanya grabbed the bottle and chugged. Fortified with liquid courage, he opened the passenger door and stepped out of the SUV.

"Should I come with, Cousin?" his cousin asked after him.

"No, I need to do this alone," he said, shutting the door.

CHAPTER THIRTY-NINE

JESSICA JAMES WAS snuggling with Lolita on the pullout sofa bed at the Residence Inn, watching an old Hitchcock playing movie on TV. Since she'd refused to let Nick take her home, she was stranded unless Lolita gave her a ride back to Brentano Hall. But even the thin lumpy sofa bed was better than a desk in the attic. She moved her bare feet back and forth across the smooth fabric of the hotel's cotton blend and realized how much she missed sheets. Sleeping in her dirty jeans and western shirt for the last week had been like sleeping in a straightjacket. Freed by a pair of Lolita's silky pajamas, finally her body could relax, even as her mind kicked into high gear.

"Nick was such a friggin' jerk. I'll never forgive him." She rolled onto her side facing Lolita. "And I didn't even get my revenge sex."

"Forget about sex, jerk or not, we need him," her friend said. "You've got to get him to bring the Pope to the Monday night game. The Pope will jump at the chance to swoop in on my territory."

"Do you think that's a good idea?" Jessica hadn't enjoyed her recent encounter with Vladimir the Pope and didn't relish another one.

Lolita lowered her voice, "Just get Nick to set up a meeting with the Pope to buy my dad's painting at the poker game and I'll do the rest. I'm determined to get my dad's Kandinsky back."

Jessica sighed and rolled over to watch the movie. Jimmy Stewart's character had just discovered his beloved Judy wearing the necklace depicted in Carlotta's portrait and realized she was an accessory to murder. Jessica always wondered how Hitchcock could make even mild mannered Jimmy Stewart into an abusive dickhead when it came to women.

"Can you do it?" Lolita asked.

"Do what?"

"Get Nick to bring the Pope to the poker game. Haven't you been listening to me?"

Jessica never wanted to see Nick Charis Schilling again, but when Lolita stroked her hair, she knew she'd do whatever her friend asked. Jessica reached across the side table for the remote and turned off the television so she wouldn't have to watch Jimmy Stewart throw Judy off the mission tower yet again.

Eventually, listening to her friend's rhythmic breathing put her to sleep. Fast asleep inside Lolita's embrace, Jessica woke up to pounding on the hotel door. Lolita flew up, sprinted into the bathroom, grabbed a towel, and wrapping it around her naked body, answered the door. Jessica yanked on her jeans over the top of the silky boy shorts PJs. *What the hell? It's 5 a.m.* Lolita peered out the peephole and shrugged, and then Jessica took a look. "What's he doing here?" Detective Cormier was holding her satchel. Astonished, Jessica opened the door.

"My book bag," she exclaimed. "Where did you find it?"

"May I come in?" Detective Cormier asked.

Lolita ushered him into the kitchenette, turned on a light, and put on water for tea.

"Please sit down, Ms. James," Detective Cormier said.

Jessica's heart did a nosedive when she remembered she'd left her satchel in Nick's Boxster.

"Your friend Nicholas Schilling has been in an accident," the detective said.

Jessica blinked in panic and immediately thought of when her mother got the news. A blizzard had cancelled school and little Jessica came home early to find her mom screeching and sobbing. Scared, she ran and hid in the barn, cowering in the corner of Mayhem's stall. Eventually, she got so hungry she snuck through the back door of the trailer into the kitchen. Her mom didn't say a word but just stared at her with puffy red eyes and Jessica knew something terrible had happened to her dad.

"Is Nick okay?" Lolita asked, putting her hands on Jessica's shaky shoulders.

"He'll be fine," Detective Cormier said. "But his Porsche is totaled."

"What happened?" Lolita asked.

"He ran a red light at the six way intersection at Milwaukee, North, and Kamen," the detective said. "His blood alcohol level was nearly .2 percent."

"The vodka," said Jessica, trembling. "I shouldn't have let him drink and drive."

"He won't be driving for quite a while with a DUI on his record," Detective Cormier said.

"It's not your fault he can't handle his vodka and is stupid enough to drive drunk." Lolita turned Jessica around by the shoulders. "It's a good thing you weren't with him."

"When your bag turned up among his possessions," the detective said. "I wanted to make sure you were okay."

"How did you find me?" Jessica asked.

Detective Cormier gave her a knowing look. "I have my ways."

After the detective left, Jessica locked herself in the bathroom, borrowed some toothpaste, used her finger to brush her teeth, then splashed water on her face, and gave herself a speedy sponge bath. She looked longingly at the shower. Maybe later.

As she emerged from the bathroom, Lolita was slipping into her leather pants and jacket. Tossing a confused Jessica a skidlid, her friend headed out the door. Following Lolita outside, Jessica inhaled the heavy perfume that hung in the sweet spring air, and her eyes started watering and her nose started running. She pulled a tissue out of her pocket. She loved the scent of lilacs, but it didn't like her. She wondered if it was a fact of life that people are allergic to what they love most. Jessica remembered Tigercat, her first love. Every night, the kitten had slept on her pillow, purring her to sleep, and every morning, she woke up congested, but still smitten.

Lolita started her motorbike and Jessica hopped on the Harley behind her friend. At least this time, she had on long pants. Still, the exhaust pipe was hot against her foot, and steam was rising from her damp high-tops. She clasped her hands around Lolita's waist and held on with all her might as her friend screeched out of the parking lot. The roads were deserted, and since Detective Cormier was following them, Lolita made a point of staying within the speed limit, for once. Their police escort waved and sped past as they turned into the parking lot of Northwestern University Hospital. As soon as the bike skidded to a stop, Jessica tumbled off and dashed into the hospital.

When she breezed through the sliding glass doors, the Starbucks inside the lobby was just opening and already the line was long. Nurses in zoo animal scrubs, orderlies in blue uniforms, and doctors with white lab coats, all waiting for their morning dose. Caffeine, the drug of choice for healthcare workers. Jessica ordered a Cinnamon Dolce Latte for herself and a double espresso for Lolita, who'd just joined her. With the help of strong coffee, the hospital was coming to life for morning rounds.

Jessica had already forgotten how much she'd hated Nick last night when he'd accused Dmitry of forgery. Now, she ached to see he was okay. She asked a woman at the front desk for Nicholas Schilling's room number, and then tried Charis. She and Lolita took the elevator to the fifth floor. As she walked along the antiseptic hallway, for some reason, Jessica remembered being sent to the principal's office in grade school for giving one of the Dalton brothers a black eye. She couldn't remember which one.

When they reached Nick's room, the door was shut and a nurse said they would have to wait. Jessica paced back and forth, and Lolita leaned up against the wall, one black boot firmly planted against the white wash. The hospital floor shone with polishing wax, but Jessica still didn't want to get too close to it. What doesn't kill you makes you stronger... *Unless it is flesh-eating bacteria.* When she put her satchel down and dropped on top of it, her friend gracefully slid down the wall and sat on the floor next to her.

"You have to convince Nick to help us get my dad's painting from the Pope," Lolita said. "We need to get it back before he tries to sell it."

"I'll try," she said. "But even if we can get Dmitry's Kandinsky away from the Pope, what about the real Kandinsky?"

Lolita pulled a tiny key from her pants pocket and held it up for inspection. "Any ideas of where this little guy's lock might be?" she asked. "We've got to find out how to get my dad's paintings."

When the door to Nick's hospital room swung open, Hello Kitty was blushing and giggling as she exited the room. *Slutty Kitty, more like it.* Jessica sprung up, brushed off her pants, and knocked on the door. Nick's single malt tenor bid beaconed her inside. She gasped and clapped her hand over her mouth when she saw Nick's face. He had two black eyes, stitches on his lower lip, and cuts on his nose and ears.

"You should see the other guy," Nick said. When she approached his bedside, he patted the bedcovers, and she sat down beside him. She took his hand, and then with her free hand, absently stroked his soft hair, remembering Tigercat.

"Nick," she said softly, "I'm so sorry about your accident."

"No, I'm sorry, I was such an ass," he said, sitting up in bed. "I should have known better than to drink vodka with Russians and I can afford a taxi." He put his head on Jessica's shoulder.

"Yes, you were an ass. You shouldn't have insulted Dmitry."

"It's just the last time I tried to buy a Kandinsky," he said, "I ended up in a Russian jail thanks to some Bratva double-dealing. I wanted to avoid a compromising situation, especially with you there." She put her arm around him. "Dolce," he said and closed his eyes, and she kissed his forehead. "Ouch," he said meekly.

Lolita cleared her throat. "Mind if I join you?"

Jessica nodded for her to cross the threshold.

"I was wondering if anyone had a clue about this safety deposit key?" Lolita asked, dangling the little key in the air again. "The real Kandinsky is in a vault somewhere in this city and I was just asking Jessica if she had a clue about the location of the professor's vault."

Nick bolted upright. "The real Kandinsky? You have Kandinsky's *Fragment 2* in a vault?" When his cheeks colored, his expression changed from wounded to wonder.

"It's in a vault," Lolita said, "but we have no idea where."

CHAPTER FORTY

DMITRY DURCHENKO STRODE through the garage to the hospital elevator and pushed the down button. As the elevator went down, his heart followed. His emotions were a jumble, his body one raw nerve. He stepped out into the hospital lobby and realized he didn't know his father's room number. He took a crumpled paper from his pocket and texted his mother. She texted back with the number, and he stopped at a reception desk to ask directions. His father's room was in the ICU in a wing separated from the rest of the hospital. The illuminated signs for the ICU had blocky blue letters, and he turned corner after corner following them to his final destination.

As he rounded the last corner into a dimly lit corridor, his mother emerged from the shadows, an apparition floating on air. Her long flowing dress wasn't what he had expected. He always pictured her in her Ermine fur hat and coat, standing on the frigid train platform. In his memory, she was encased in ice. Now, she was moving towards him, amethyst gown and white hair fluttering behind her as she walked. Unchanged by the years, he saw before him an older version of Lolita, elegant, lovely, and regal.

When she held out her hand to him, he fell into her arms, a boy again, reunited with his beloved mother. They clung to each

other until a nurse stopped to ask if they needed assistance. His
mother took him by the hand and led him down the hallway. Her
warm hand in his, tears welled in his eyes. On their way to his
father's room, in her soft familiar voice, she explained that Anton
had advanced pancreatic cancer.

"I brought him to the Mayo clinic as a last resort," she said.
"We have been back and forth to the best hospitals in Moscow and
New York for the last several months."

Dmitry took her hand. "I'm sorry Mother."

"At this point," she said with a quiet sigh, "nothing can be
done except make him comfortable."

They were walking in silence down an antiseptic corridor when
his mother stopped, turned to face him, and took his other hand.

"I've been trying to find you since you left Russia, my love,"
she said, holding onto both of his hands.

"How did you find me?" he asked.

"When Anton's art agent told him Kandinsky's *Fragment* was
for sale, I knew if I followed the painting, I'd find you," she said.
The corners of her delicate mouth turned up slightly. "I contacted
the seller, Vladimir Popov, who promised to get a message to you
on behalf of Anton. No one in *Bratva* dares to cross Anton, not
even on his deathbed."

"Not even on his deathbed," he heard himself saying.

"Your father is desperate to speak to you before he passes,"
his mother said. "He regrets asking you to…. to do such horrible
things." His mother looked away, brushing a tear with the back
of her hand. Clearly, she wasn't over Sergei's brutal death and his
father's cruel command that forced Dmitry to leave the country.

"I don't want to see him," he said. "I can't bear to see him."
He was ashamed he'd disappointed his father years ago, ashamed
he didn't want to see him on his deathbed now. Even though his
father had treated him cruelly, he was besieged by guilt. How was

it possible to have such contradictory feelings? Perhaps what truly made him afraid was he loved his father. His affection was more baffling than his abhorrence.

"Dimka, your father has changed," she said. "See him and you'll know. Like a snake, he has cast off his old skin."

"Even with a new skin, a snake is still a snake," he said.

"That may be," she said, "but his dying wish is to see you, my son."

"Why should I grant his last wish, when he wouldn't grant even my first?" he asked. "He told me to…to…" He couldn't say it. "How can I forgive him for the enormity of suffering he's caused? Especially to you." He gazed into his mother's bloodshot eyes.

"He is a dying man, my son," she said. "If you won't do it for him, do it for me, Dimka." He never could refuse his mother. Some things do not change and some things never disappear.

Dmitry knew they were nearing his father's room when he saw two *Byki* standing in the hallway flanking a door. The bodyguards were familiar, loyal bulls had been with his father all these years. As he drew closer, he recognized Yuri. Same craggy face, same St. Christopher's medal around his wrinkled neck. Yuri nodded at him, but neither of them spoke.

This was it. With his mother behind him, he was standing in front of the curtain across the door to his father's hospital room. Willing his legs to move, he staggered forward. His mother reached out and put her hand on his shoulder. "As the call," she whispered, "so the echo." His mother pulled open the curtain and gently pushed him towards the entrance to the room.

The sun was rising and orange rays spread from the window across the ashen floor, but the room was dark. Birdsong accompanied the beeping and clicking of the medical machines. His father's heavy breathing, each inhalation a rasp, each exhalation a rattle. He slid along the polished linoleum, soundlessly, trying not to pick up his feet. His chest tightened as he reached the end of the hospice bed. He saw a shape under the blankets, like a pile of bones under a napkin.

His mother was right. Physically, at least, his father had completely transformed. He had gone from the portly, even obese, man he had defied years ago to this skeleton lying before him. He might already be dead, if it weren't for the inescapable noises. Cold sweat streamed down his armpits and across his ribs, and he felt ill. When he turned back towards the curtain, he spotted his mother standing just inside motioning for him to continue towards the bed.

Everything moved in slow motion as Dmitry sat in the chair next to the bed. He stared at his father's face until it came into gradual focus in the hazy light of dawn, a death mask, chalky and dry. If he hadn't known this was his father, he would not have recognized him. He searched for signs of his father in that sunken face, that shrunken body, but he couldn't see any.

"Father," he whispered. He wished the unnerving rasping and rattling sounds would stop. "Father," he repeated. "It's me, your son, Dmitry." He waited for what seemed like hours. "Father," he said again, "Can you hear me?"

His father's eyes opened and the uncanny death mask lying on the pillow came to life. A beam of sunlight shot into the room, and when it doused Anton's face, Dmitry saw what remained of his father in the glassy orbs gleaming through the frail facade. His father was still in there somewhere, inhabiting this inanimate alien body.

A shriveled hand appeared from under the covers. Its fingers twitched, searching for something. The hand was grasping at the air, gasping like a fish out of water. Fighting the urge to recoil in horror, he forced himself to take the horrific hand. It felt like parchment, and his sweaty palm stuck to it like a cigarette paper to a lower lip.

"Father," he said. "I've come as you asked." After all these years, he was still compelled to obey his father.

The hand pulled him closer. It was stronger than he would have guessed. Struggling against his instinct to run, he leaned forward until his face was nearly touching the eerie mask. The smell of ammonia stung his nostrils. He could practically see vapors escaping from his father's mouth. The hand held him close, and the mouth started sputtering, misting his face with spittle. He involuntarily closed his eyes and tightened his lips. He tried to hold his breath to stop himself from inhaling those deathly emanations.

The mouth was moving faster now. The hand was pulling harder. The dark glassy spots in the mask pleaded with him. He didn't know what to do. He wanted to scream and run from the room. *Maybe he should call a nurse.* The rasping finally gave way to sounds, and the sputtering and popping finally gave way to voice, and his father murmured, "Dima, forgive me."

Then, the hand relented, the rattling receded, and the sheen disappeared from the two dark holes in the mask. Vapors floated up into the beam of sunlight piercing the room, and he realized this cloud of mist was all that was left of his father.

"Father," he cried. "Wait. Father. Please." Tears sprouted from his eyes and wrapped around his chest. They wound themselves tighter until he could barely breathe. They climbed over the form under the blankets, vines binding him to his father's corpse.

Dmitry peeled his hand away from his father's death grip. He gazed down at the tiny desiccated hand he'd just been holding. How could that be his father's hand? He didn't believe it. He tried to move, but couldn't. In life, his father had been a grizzly bear that chased him away. In death, his father was a scorpion that paralyzed him with its sting.

"Mother," he sobbed. "He's dead."

CHAPTER FORTY-ONE

WHEN NICK SPRANG out of the hospital bed and grabbed at the key, he took the sheets with him and Jessica James fell onto the floor.

"Hey, watch it," she said, picking herself up and brushing off her jeans.

"Let me see that key," Nick said, wearing just his hospital gown, and holding out his hand. Lolita leaned forward, looked him up and down, smiled, and then dropped the small key into his outstretched palm. "M. A. N. A. 307," he read out loud. "That's MANA art storage. It's on the Lower West side, near Chinatown," he said. "But you'll need the password."

"Password?" Lolita asked.

"Yes, they require a key and a password," Nick said. "Double security in case you lose your key and someone else finds it." He narrowed his eyes at Lolita. "How did you get this key?" he asked.

"Don't start with the interrogation again," Jessica said. "Or I'll kick your ass."

He smiled. "My ass is yours. Lolita, I'm sorry I was rude to you and your father. I hope you can forgive me."

"Forgiveness is irrelevant. Just help me get my father's paintings back."

"Paintings, plural?" his eyes widened.

Lolita told him about her grandfather, Anton Yudkovich, the buyer at Tajan auction in Paris, and her grandmother, Lolita Yudkovich, and how she'd given the Kandinsky and Goncharova paintings to Dmitry on the night he left Russia.

"You have a Natalia Goncharova too?" Nick was excited. "I would love to see one of her paintings. But we need your father's password."

"My father doesn't have the password and never did. He hid the paintings in Professor Schmutzig's office for safekeeping, but the professor discovered them under his floorboards and moved them to a vault somewhere. Then he was murdered."

"It wouldn't be the first time someone was murdered for art," Nick said.

"What do you mean?" Jessica asked.

"Obviously," Nick said, "the killer was looking for the paintings. Why else would anyone murder Professor Schmutzig?"

Jessica mentally scrolled through her list of suspects and their motives. More than one person had a reason to kill Wolf that didn't involve Russian art.

"We need that password," Lolita said. "How are we going to get it?" She was pacing the room. "Jessica, was there anything in the diary that might give us a clue?"

"Not that I remember. I gave the journal to Amber since it turned out the professor was her dad. I'll call her." She slid her phone out of her back pocket and tapped in Amber's number.

"Did I wake you up? Sorry. Hey, Amber, any idea what Wolf might use as a password?"

"Could be the same as his email password." Amber replied, "Fritz 10-15."

"How do you know that?" Jessica asked.

"Gary and I hacked his email," she said. "I just wanted to know more about my biological father."

"Twisted Twix? You two hacked Wolf's email? How'd you do that?"

"Gary showed me how," Amber said. "It was easy. Like chess."

"10-15, Nietzsche's birthday, Fritz, Nietzsche's nickname." Jessica mumbled into the phone.

"Fritz was the name of his first cat," said Amber. "His security question was name of your first pet."

CHAPTER FORTY-TWO

DMITRY DURCHENKO FLEW past his mother and the bodyguards to escape the suffocation. He couldn't get out of the hospital fast enough and plowed through the first exit he saw. He found himself outside in a bright courtyard and the penetrating sunrays stung his eyes. He braced himself against the void, holding his arms out in front of his torso, and stumbled onward, tears streaming down his face.

His father's death had broken the flukes of hatred and fear that had anchored his existence for so long, and far below the surface of the everyday the pain he'd suppressed was cut loose. For most of his life, he'd been riding the hook along the surface of a wide sea of emotions, not dredging the depths of his being. Now, the tension holding his life together had gone slack, and without his father, he was unmoored. Without his father, he was free.

Dmitry spent the rest of the day wandering the grounds of the Mayo clinic. He hadn't eaten or slept, or showered or shaved, since he'd left home. His eyes were so swollen from crying that he was looking through stinging slits, and his mouth was so dry his tongue felt like cracked rubber. Joggers stared at him as he staggered around the pond behind the clinic. On another day, he might have appreciated the manicured grounds with flowers and trees neatly placed around the walking path in perfect balance of colors and symmetry of shapes, but he knew nature was not so peaceful. These attempts to bring order to the chaos of life were vain, temporary supports that would soon give way to violence.

He walked in circles around the grounds until his knees ached and the sun was setting. Sometime after dark, a familiar voice caught up to him, "Boss, Boss. Come on now." And his cousin's strong grip led him by the arm back to the parking lot. It was near midnight by the time Vanya forced him to rest in the Escalade. At dawn, he noticed his cousin open the door and exit the SUV in a cloud of smoke, leaving Dmitry to sink back into an agitated sleep in the backseat. He woke up when the doors opened again and Vanya and his mother peered back at him from the passenger side of the SUV.

"Where did you go?" his mother asked. "I was worried when you rushed out. Thank god for cousin Vanya." Her skin was dusty and dry like she'd aged twenty years overnight.

"Where did you spend the night?" he asked his mother, afraid of the answer.

"I stayed with Anton until they took his body away. Yuri is making arrangements for his body to be sent back to Moscow for a funeral. I've got to get back, too."

"Please stay for a few days to meet your granddaughter. You can stay with us," he said, and then remembered they were living at a Residence Inn. "Or, I can get you a hotel room. You'll love Lolita. You two are so much alike." Dmitry was so exhausted he felt nauseous. Vanya must have noticed because he ran back into the hospital and returned with three coffees from the cafeteria. When Dmitry sat up in the backseat and took the coffee, Bunin wriggled between the seats from the back compartment and licked his face. He got the cup into a cup holder just in time. Nose in the air, the husky barked, and then wagging his tail so hard it whacked

Dmitry in the face, he nuzzled his muzzle into his mother's lap. After Dmitry pushed his hindquarters down and Bunin was laying between the seats, he took his cup into both hands and guzzled the tepid liquid, trying to wake up. Luckily, he didn't have to drive, and Vanya was so full of nicotine he never seemed to need sleep.

On the ride home, Vanya and his mother reminisced about the times "little Ivanovich," as she called him, stayed at their country house for the summer. She hadn't seen Vanya since his father had been killed and the rest of the family had been forced to leave Russia.

"I remember when you were just *a little Cossack* getting into trouble and leading Dimka astray." She laughed. "Remember that afternoon at the Count's when I told you the story of the prince and the tiger?" His mother turned and looked over the seat at him. "Anton and I were like the prince and the tiger, bound together through pain. I met him when I was only fifteen," she said. "He was thirty. My mother took me to see The Nutcracker Ballet at the Bolshoi Theatre and Anton was sitting alone in our loge box. I was drunk on the ballet and that's when he wounded me with his first arrow."

Dmitry stared into his half empty coffee cup as if it might hold the answers he sought.

"My parents disapproved of Anton," his mother said. Dmitry's maternal grandparents were respectable upper-class industrialists.

"They knew of Anton's reputation," she said. "Everyone did."

"So why did they let you marry him?" Dmitry asked.

"They didn't," she said. "They forced me to choose. And I chose Anton. We eloped to Paris." His mother smiled and stared out the window. They rode in silence for the next few miles.

"On our wedding night," his mother said softly, "Anton made me a woman. That was the second arrow. We were back in Moscow only fifteen months before Anton took a mistress. Sergei was just a baby. That was the mortal wound."

"Why did you stay with him?" Like everyone else, Dmitry knew his father had been unfaithful.

"When I learned of his mistress, I went to Paris with the baby," she said. "That's when I met Count Volkov. Do you remember the Count? So different from Anton. He was everything Anton wasn't. Anton commanded the center of attention. Konstantin preferred the periphery. Anton was gregarious and so aggressive with everything and everyone, while Konstantin was reserved and circumspect, a man of integrity." She gazed out the window and said softly, "Strength may open the door, but only virtue enters."

His mother leaned her head against the seat and closed her eyes. He watched her in the rearview mirror, her face relaxed and peaceful. He wondered if she was napping. She must be exhausted. She had been keeping vigil with his father in the hospital for a week, sleeping in a chair by his side. She jolted forward and he grabbed the back of her seat as Vanya swerved off the highway onto an exit.

"What are you doing, *chuvak*," Dmitry yelled at his cousin.

"I'm about to piss my pants, Boss." Vanya tamped out his cigarette in the overflowing ashtray. "And there's a Krispy Kream at this exit." He grinned into the rear view mirror at Dmitry.

Krispy Kreams and more weak coffee lifted Dmitry's spirits and the ride back home went faster.

"Why did you go back to him?" he leaned forward to ask his mother when they were back on the highway again.

"I didn't," she said. "He found me and took me back. Always, for Anton, the belly was full, but the eyes were still hungry."

"Why did you stay?" Dmitry had always wondered why his mother and father stayed together. They had nothing in common. Yet, for some reason, his mother was fiercely loyal.

"If you're given a choice between apocalypse and pastry," she said, "you don't ask what kind of pastry." She paused and he waited for her to explain. "A broken heart isn't fatal," she finally broke the silence. "I couldn't leave alive," she said, "but I made sure that you did."

"Why did father let you live after you betrayed him?" It sounded like an accusation and he regretted his words as soon as they'd left his mouth. His mother had betrayed her husband to save him. She'd risked her own life to spare his.

"Betrayal." His mother laughed. "I didn't betray Anton by bringing you the valise, my son," she said. "I had already betrayed Anton by loving you more than life." She stared out the window again. He followed her gaze to see what she saw out there. All he saw were fields of dirt waiting to be sown, but he suspected she saw something more, a future harvest to prove you don't always reap what you sow.

"Your birth was my revenge," his mother said, "and my salvation."

"Revenge?" he asked.

"You were born from love, Dimka," his mother said. "Because of you, I went back to Moscow with Anton."

"A broken heart isn't always fatal," he said softly.

"Anton's poisonous arrows may have wounded me, but they never pierced my heart," she said. "My heart never belonged to Anton. Only later was it stolen by another." When his mother reached her hand behind the seat toward him, he took it. She squeezed his hand, and said, "Dimka, my heart belongs to the love of my life. It belongs to your real father, Konstantin Volkov."

CHAPTER FORTY-THREE

JESSICA JAMES PEERED out the window of Nick's limo. It stopped in front of a mammoth maze of red brick building, a former factory on the southeast side of downtown. One part of MANA was square, another rectangular, and a third triangular, a geometer's dream. In the center of the whimsical shapes was a funky sculpture garden set amongst bright flowers and green shrubs in a neat courtyard. Nick's bruised and swollen face might draw suspicion, so he stayed in the limo. Jessica and Lolita got out of the car and met Amber in front of the building as she stepped out of a taxi Uggs first with her flowing paisley skirt close behind.

Just before they got to the glass entrance, Amber stopped and pulled one of her herbal potions from her vast purse. "Who's Raskolnikov?" she asked as she dropped liquid from a vial onto her tongue. Hair escaping in all directions, eyes wide, she looked frazzled and in desperate need of Rescue Remedy, but the tincture didn't seem to be working.

"The main character in Dostoevsky's *Crime and Punishment*. He murders an old pawn broker woman just to prove he can and then returns to the scene of the crime and gets caught," Jessica answered. "Why?"

"Alexander Le Blanc was writing emails to Professor…. uh my

dad, about him," she said. "He was comparing my dad to a teacher in some old Hitchcock film called *Rope*. Something about putting theory into practice."

"*Rope?*" Jessica asked. "The one where those crazy gay guys murder their friend, stuff him in a trunk, and then host a dinner party on it? Supposedly trying to prove their superiority. Love me some Hitchcock, but not my favorite film."

"I spent all night reading my dad's emails and rereading his diary," Amber said. "Learning about the professor is making me feel weird around my dad, I mean my mom's husband."

"Come on girls," Lolita said, holding the door open. "You can reminisce about the professor later. We have work to do."

The sleek inside of the building stood in stark contrast to its industrial outside. Crossing the threshold was like stepping through a time portal from the 19th Century into the 24th. Inside, everything was white: the walls, the floors, the ceilings, and the attendants' uniforms. They were even wearing white watches. A young woman with her slick hair pulled back in a tight ponytail, wearing a fitted white Chinese-style jacket and trousers, appeared at the door and asked if she could help them.

Jessica was gesturing for Amber to wipe the chocolate off of her mouth, but Amber just followed her finger with her eyes. Frustrated, Jessica pulled a tissue out of her pocket, licked it, and wiped it off for her. Lolita scowled. When the Chinese-jacketed woman asked again if she could help them, Lolita nudged Amber.

"We would like the paintings from storage, left here by my father," Amber said.

"Your father's name?" the attendant asked.

"Baldrick Schmutzig," Amber said. She sounded as if she'd practiced saying his name.

"Can I see some identification?" the attendant asked.

Amber pulled out her driver's license. "Amber Bush," the attendant read out loud.

"Yes. My mother remarried," Amber said with less conviction.

"Do you have the key?" the attendant asked.

Lolita held out the key to the attendant. She led them to a glass elevator looking out over floors of thick white walls with small black locks, rows and rows of them. On one wall there were small boxes, like post office boxes, white with black rims and black locks. Along another wall, there were a series of steel panels, reflecting back everything off their shiny surface, only slightly askew. They followed the attendant into the elevator and then out of the lift at the third floor. The expansive space was a futuristic maze, everything white with touches of black and steel.

Vault 307 was a thin steel door with two black locks and a computer touch pad like an iPhone only smaller. The girls exchanged glances.

"As I'm sure your father told you," the attendant said, "you need to insert your key, then enter your password, after which I will open the door with my key."

When Lolita inserted the key, the touch pad illuminated, and Amber wiped her hands on her moo-moo, then slowly tapped in Fritz 10-15. A red message flashed on the screen *Incorrect Password*. She tried again. Again, the threatening red message. The attendant asked, "Did your father give you the correct password?"

"Maybe it's case sensitive," Jessica said. "Try again, capitalize Fritz." It was freezing in the storage building but she'd broken into a cold sweat, and her hands and feet were clammy.

"Perhaps he used another password," the attendant suggested.

"Or, maybe he changed the password."

"Maybe it's his bank account password," Amber said. Jessica and Lolita gave her quizzical looks.

"Yes, that makes sense. Try his bank password," Jessica shook her head in agreement.

Amber tapped in another series of letters and numbers. "A.M.B.E.R. 2. 18," she said out loud as she entered the code. "My birthday," she said softly and dug in her purse for more herbal tranquilizers. A green light appeared on the screen. The attendant inserted her key and the vault opened. Inside were two paintings in large glassine envelopes sandwiched between cardboard. When Lolita reached in to pull them out, the attendant stopped her.

"We're going to take them now and close the account," Lolita said.

"Don't you want these?" the woman asked, holding out a pair of white gloves.

"Of course, thank you," said Lolita.

"Is your father dissatisfied with our service?" the woman asked. She emphasized the word father and glanced back and forth between the three girls.

"He's dead," Amber said.

"Dead," the attendant repeated. "In that case, I'm not sure we can release these until we hear from his lawyers."

"We have the key and the password," Lolita said. "Isn't that all you require? I thought that MANA had a reputation for confidentiality, that you prided yourselves on being discrete."

"That's true Miss, Miss," the attendant said. "What is your name? Are you also related to our client Mr. Schmutzig? Are you all his daughters?"

"Too many questions," Lolita said. "Come on girls, we're leaving." She turned on her heels and strode towards the elevator. Jessica and Amber scurried to catch up, and the attendant dashed after them.

"You still have to sign for them and settle the account," she said.

"No problem, how much?" Lolita paid the bill in cash, Amber signed, and then the trio rushed outside with their loot.

"Success," Lolita said as she opened the door to the limo. "I can't wait to show my dad."

Amber must have called Jack because he was waiting with Nick in the limo. When Nick asked if he could see the paintings, Lolita handed them to him. She was still wearing the white gloves. He motioned to her to give them to him, and he stretched his large hands into them, and then carefully opened the wrapping. "Natalia Goncharova's *Gathering Apples*." He sighed. "Gorgeous." He studied the painting for a few minutes while Jessica watched, entranced by the rapt look on his face. Then he opened the second. "Kandinsky's *Fragment 2 for Composition VII*. Stunning," he said. He turned to Lolita. "Your father is a very lucky man. Do you think he might consider selling either of these?"

Lolita shook her head. Jack popped the cork on a bottle of champagne he'd found chilling in the limo and poured them each a glass to toast their triumph.

"To Jessica, Amber, and Lolita," Nick said, "the Three Graces." He raised his glass. "Charm, Joy, and Beauty."

"Grace my ass," Jessica said. "The Three Fates, maybe."

"To the Three Fates then," Nick said, "Destiny, Peace, and Order."

"More like, Ready, Willing, and Able," Jack said, clinking glasses with each one of his friends.

CHAPTER FORTY-FOUR

WHEN THE LIMO reached the front of his apartment building, Nick kissed the back of Jessica James'
hand. "I was hoping you might tuck me in, Dolce,"
he whispered into her ear. She hesitated, but then on a whim
grabbed her book bag, scooted along the seat until she finally was
close enough to the door, and he helped her out. Nick turned back
toward the limo, "If your dad ever wants to sell these paintings,
you know where to find me," he called back to Lolita as he took
Jessica's hand and headed for his apartment building.

"See you at the game on Monday night," Lolita shouted after
them. "Remember to bring the Pope."

Still holding his hand, Jessica followed Nick into the black
glass building, past the doorman, and up the elevator. He had a
special key to use in the lift, and the doors opened directly into
his penthouse apartment. She was giddy from their caper at the
storage building, not to mention the three glasses of champagne
on the ride over. When Nick headed straight for the bedroom, she
dropped his hand, twitching her lips back and forth, and considered her options. She realized it was a bad idea, but couldn't resist
his bad boy smile and good hair.

"Won't you join me for a power nap?" Nick asked, gesturing

inside the bedroom. "I'm completely knackered," he said. "I really need to sleep."

"Just sleep?" She asked, following him into the bedroom. Gawking around at the artwork on the walls and the magnificent full-on view of the Chicago skyline, she tripped on the edge of a thick Persian rug and Nick caught her before she fell to the floor.

"At least sleep," he said gazing into her eyes.

Blushing, she turned away and looked out the window. She turned back just in time to see Nick strip down to his boxers and climb into bed.

"Just a nap," Jessica said as she pulled off her jeans, and then crawled under the plush duvet next to him, avoiding actually touching him. He rolled over and pulled her into a tight spooning embrace, and soon, exhausted from five sleepless nights on top of that hard desk in Brentano, she dozed off in spite her galloping heart.

She woke up to her cellphone ringing in the back pocket of her jeans. She freed her arm, climbed out of bed, dug the phone out, and glanced at the screen. Michael, what did he want so late on Sunday night? She turned her phone on vibrate, laid it on the night-table, and then climbed back into bed, snuggling close to Nick, suffering from the familiar stabbing pain in her chest from her ex-boyfriend's betrayal. Maybe she should have accepted his marriage proposal, if that's what it was. She still loved him, but she also hated him. She hated him more than she'd ever hated anybody. Well, maybe except for Wolf Schmutzig. What she needed was some good revenge sex. She rolled over to face Nick, admiring the smooth skin around his eyes. As she reached out to touch his sleeping face, her phone started buzzing and dancing across the nightstand. *Friggin' Michael.* She rolled back, grabbed it, and was about to switch it off when she saw a text message from Lolita. "Call me ASAP."

She sat up in bed and autodialed her friend.

"Jessica, meet me at Blind Faith in an hour. Bring Nick," Lolita barked into the phone, followed by silence. She'd hung up before Jessica could respond.

Jessica knew better than to cross the poker Tsarina, so she kissed Nick's cheek to wake him up. He smiled up at her with sleepy eyes, and then pouted when she tumbled out of bed and tugged on her jeans and then her cowboy boots. She lured Nick out of bed with promises of both "carrots and sticks" for good behavior if he drove her to The Blind Faith Café. He obliged and called his driver to meet them downstairs in half hour.

When they arrived at the café, Jessica was surprised to see Detective Cormier sitting across from Lolita at their regular booth. Nick pulled up a chair and Jessica slid into the booth next to Lolita.

"What's going on?" she asked, looking from Lolita to Detective Cormier.

"The detective wants our help," Lolita said. "Actually, he's made me an offer I can't refuse." Her eyes narrowed and she didn't look happy.

"I know you and Lolita run a poker game out of Brentano Hall on Monday nights," Detective Cormier said to Jessica.

"Is that illegal?" she asked. *Shit.* Breaking and entering, murder and perjury, a concealed weapon, and now illegal gambling. Goodbye graduate school, hello prison.

"A lawyer told me it's legal so long as we don't take a cut," Lolita said. "It's just a friendly recreational game."

"A judge may not see it that way," Detective Cormier said. "Especially since you make a pretty good living off this friendly game."

"The lawyer assured me it's not illegal," Lolita said. If you looked closely, you could see the very corner of her eye twitching. Her one and only tell.

"If you refuse to help me, then you'll have the opportunity to explain that to a judge. But, if you help, I'll take your word for it," the detective sipped his coffee.

"What do you want us to do?" Jessica asked. Nick was sitting so close to her, she sensed sparks flying between them, two electric eels. It was exhilarating and distracting as hell.

"Help me arrest Vladimir Popov," he said. "I've been trying for over a year. I'm sure he's the source of rape drugs on campus, but I can't prove it. A couple of years ago, I brought him in for an Internet scam with Russian brides, but it didn't stick. Now, I think he's somehow involved with Schumtzig's murder, but I can't prove it. I heard he was trying to sell a Kandinsky on the black market, and this is my chance…"

"Yes, he is," Nick interrupted. "But it's a fake. It's not an authentic Kandinsky. Lolita's father painted it." At least he didn't accuse Dmitry of forgery. He was being much more diplomatic since Jessica's promise of carrots to come.

"I know, it's the one from the Professor's office," said Detective Cormier. "But does Popov know that?"

"I'm not sure," said Nick. "Whether he knows it or not, he's trying to peddle the painting as an original."

"Perfect," said the detective. "Bring him to Ms. Durchenko's poker game tonight and I can charge him with racketeering and selling forgeries, stolen ones at that. I may not get him for supplying drugs, but I'll get him."

"As my dad says, when the claw gets stuck, the whole bird is lost," said Lolita.

"Mr. Schilling, since he approached you about the painting, would you be willing to purchase it for us? We need to catch him in the act. If so, can you accompany me to the station so we can wire you?" The detective bid them farewell and left the café with Nick in tow.

"The important thing is to get my father's painting back," Lolita said after they left. "This will be our last game, and without the game, this will be my last semester at Northwestern. I don't know how I'll tell my folks I'm not really on a scholarship. No game, no college."

"I'm sorry Lol," Jessica said. "What can I do?"

"You can play. Tonight, we're going out big."

"What? I haven't played since I was back in Whitefish."

"I'm going to stake you with everything I've got," Lolita said. "It's my only chance to pay tuition next year and graduate."

"No friggin' way. You can't bet everything on me!"

"I can and I will. You'll be the best poker player at that table." Lolita downed the rest of her coffee. The cup tapping the saucer was a call to attention. "And, if we're going to stop the Bratva syndicate's campus drug operations, we've got to get their drug dealer."

"Weasel more like," said Jessica.

"Yes, we've got to take out that Existentialist drug dealing scum, Alexander Le Blanc," Lolita said. "He's the missing link between Bratva and the fraternities."

"I'll bet he's the one who supplied the party favors at the Red X party."

"We're going to give the pharmacist a taste of his own medicine. But, we have to be careful." Lolita stared down something the others couldn't see.

"Why not just tell Detective Cormier that Alexander is dealing drugs?" Jessica asked.

"Because this will be more fun. Anyway, you heard him. Detective Cormier's been dicking around for the last year while the Pope and his pharmacist have been supplying the fraternities with enough Georgia Home Boy to incapacitate every girl on campus."

"*Pharmakós*," Jessica said under her breath. "Ancient Greek ritual of human sacrifice to purify the city, poison and cure."

"We're going to return the pharmacist's poisonous gift." Lolita stood up, grabbed her helmet, and was out the door.

CHAPTER FORTY-FIVE

I T SEEMED TOO easy and that made Jessica James nervous. Vladimir the Pope had agreed to meet them at Brentano Hall for the poker game. Lolita was right. He was eager to move in on her game and wanted to unload the painting as soon as possible. Jessica had heard the Pope was a dangerous man who could make people disappear without a trace. To compound the threat, she'd be playing for Lolita's tuition with her friend's entire savings.

When Jessica arrived at Brentano with Nick in tow, Lolita was setting up. Since her usual dealer was still sick, she'd had to hire Jack again. He was leaning against the wall smoking a joint and offered it to Jessica as she passed by, but she just waved him off. She needed a clear head if she was playing for Lolita's future. Anyway, the last time she smoke weed in Brentano, she'd found a dead body. Now she wished she'd been sleeping instead of spooning and fantasizing about revenge sex with Nick the night before. As tired as she was, she should actually have had sex instead of just dreaming about it. She smiled remembering how tempted she'd been to take a selfie of Nick nearly naked sleeping next to her, his luxury penthouse in the background, to send to cheating Michael.

She heard a bustling outside the door and looked up to see Vance Hamm saunter in, his Shuffle Master under his arm, the first to arrive, as usual. A few minutes later, the Pope made a grand entrance with his entourage, Alexander Le Blanc, flanked by two bulls. He leaned a small wooden crate against the wall behind one of the folding chairs and then plopped into it with a thud. Waving his fat mitt, he introduced Alexander as *Zander the Great*, and insisted the little creep sit next to him at the table.

"Only players at the table," Lolita explained. "Those are the rules."

"As they say, rules are made to be broken," the Pope said, snapping his fingers at the towering bodyguards. "And so are bones, if you know what I mean." The bulls moved to either side of Lolita and glowered down at her.

"Suit yourself, Mr. Popov," she said, gesturing for Alexander to sit down.

Just watching the thugs from a distance made Jessica's palms sweat; and she wasn't thrilled to see the weasal again either. She still hadn't graded his paper, and the way he looked at her with his narrow beady eyes made her uneasy. Something was up with the scrawny geek, and she was beginning to suspect he was more dangerous than he appeared.

When the rest of the regular players showed up, including the head of the Stock Exchange and a point guard for Chicago's professional basketball team, Lolita got them settled around the card table. Jessica glanced around at the rich men, broke into a cold sweat, and clamped her arms to her sides when she noticed the dark stains forming on the armpits of her good luck shirt.

"Tonight, my friends," Lolita said, "how about we raise the stakes? $10,000 buy in, $1000 big blinds, $500 little blinds?"

Jessica held her breath, dreading the possiblity of losing all her friend's money.

"Love it," Vance said, rubbing his hands together.

After Lolita collected the buy-ins and doled out the chips, the players arranged their color-coded piles on the table. The room was electric with anticipaction, and the fine hairs on Jessica's arms stood on end under her lucky shirt, a beat-up faded plaid western number. She'd inherited some of her mother's superstition about gambling. Her mom wore the same underwear for weeks on end if she was on a roll and Jessica had worn the same dirty outfit to sleep in for the last week. Maybe her worn out shirt was bringing luck alright, bad luck.

Vance started up the Shuffle Master. "May the best man win," he said and then glared over at Jessica and added, "or woman." Clearly, he preferred Jessica serving drinks instead of playing poker. But, she was used to playing with the boys. High stakes poker, like philosophy, was a man's game; and in both she was determined to give as good as she got, even if it killed her. Being the only woman at the poker table wasn't so different from being the only woman at a seminar table. The boys puffed themselves up, bluffing and upping the ante, trying to out do each other, especially if it meant humiliating someone else, particularly if that someone was a girl. She'd learned from both poker and philosophy, the boys could dish it out, but they couldn't always take it, not from a girl anyway. Whenever she'd stood up to them and given them a taste of their own medicine, things tended to get dicey and dirty. She'd had fellow students and professors make lewd comments and then laugh at her when she blushed. Even the Wolf, her advisor, had tried to sabotage her. She'd learned the hard way that in both academia and poker, with the deck stacked against her, sometimes cheating was the only way to beat the system. She thought of her mom saying, "if you can't be good, be careful." Tonight, she was determined to be good and careful in order to beat these tough guys at their own cut throat game.

"Did you bring my painting?" Nick asked, taking his

checkbook out of the pocket of his navy wool designer jacket and pointing his designer pen across the table at the Pope.

"Business can wait. It's time to play poker," the Pope replied. The painting was packed in a wooden box sitting behind his chair.

"Good man," said Vance. "Deal, Jacko."

"*The good man wants just two things,*" said Jack, "*danger and play.*"

"*And woman's the most dangerous plaything.*" Jessica finished the quote. "I'm about to show you just how dangerous."

Lolita waltzed between the players, delivering drinks and snacks, while smooth jazz played in the background and dozens of candelabras lit the cavernous room. The light flickering on the players' faces gave the scene an eerie feel and Jessica could almost hear the sounds of the professor's telltale heart beating under the floorboards. She hoped the Wolf was haunting Brentano Hall, waiting to reveal his killer and solve the mystery of the post-dated letter.

Expecting the Pope to be an aggressive player, Jessica sat to his left so she could be the last to call his bets. Everyone had a drink: Nick his Lagavulin, Vance his carrot juice with lime, the Pope his frozen vodka, and Jessica her whiskey and Coke. They were armed and ready to play Texas Hold 'Em. Lolita brought Alexander a poisonous gift, a new drink she'd invented V and K, frozen vodka and ketamine powder. Jessica reached for her Jack and Coke, but thought better of it and put it back down. She had to stay sober to win. And the last time she drank at the Monday night game, she'd ended up blacked out on the floor.

Jack dealt the cards and the game was afoot. Nick won the first hand with an ace high hearts flush with the ace and a queen in the pocket. The Pope called every bet but didn't win a single pot. After the first few hands, Nick was still the chip leader and the Pope was losing big.

"Zander," the Pope said, "go get me something to nibble on from the car. I'm famished."

"We have dinner catered at midnight," Lolita said. "The food should arrive soon."

"You do, do you? Well, I want something now. Something savory. Off with you, Zander." The Pope brushed his hand in the air, and Alexander rushed out, and then returned a few minutes later with a picnic basket. He made a show of serving little paper plates of Russian appetizers, tiny potatoes, raw pork fat, and little pickles. He moved Jessica's drink and sat a plate in front of her. The Pope maneuvered his plump bejeweled fingers, and plucking out one revolting tidbit after another, popped them into his mouth.

"Are we playing poker or having a fucking picnic?" Vance asked.

The Pope finished his food and drink, but Alexander hadn't touched his vodka. The weasel was too busy with his nose up the fat man's ass to drink.

"Take your shot before it gets warm, Zander," Lolita said, pirouetting around him to move his shot glass closer. But her encouragement was in vain as Alexander sat glaring across the edge of the table at Jessica. She wanted to drag him out into the hall and shake the little twerp silly.

On the next hand, Jessica was dealt big slick, an ace and a king, and came out shooting. But on the river, she still had only an ace and a king, and the Pope raised by $1000. Jessica was pot-committed, and so far the flop looked innocent enough, but she was already down half her stack of chips, and she had a bad feeling about his hand. She folded. Good thing too. The Pope won with three-of-a-kind, nines. He'd had the pair in his hole cards.

Jessica's hands were sweating as she picked up her hole cards, a measly three of diamonds and a seven of spades. She folded when the first two community cards were a pair of queens. She watched the actor and the Pope going head-to-head when Vance started his coffeehousing. "I know better than to cross you Vladimir, so I'm going to warn you that I've got the nuts on this one."

The Pope laughed. "You do, do you?"

"I swear on my mother's grave," he said looking the Pope dead in the eyes.

"Your mother's grave…" The Pope quit laughing, glanced around at the other players, and threw his cards down onto the table face up. The flop had given him a pair of meat hooks, nines. He'd folded with two good pairs.

Vance started giggling and turned his cards over. Nothing but a five and dime. "Gotcha, big guy," he said raking in the pot. "I'm good. I'm really good. Works every time, suckers."

Red capillaries had sprouted at the top of the Pope's head and were spreading all the way down his neck. He grabbed Zander's vodka shot and downed it.

"How about I refill everyone's drinks," Lolita said, picking up empties and placing them on a tray.

Vance was still giggling and dancing in his chair like a kid who'd just gotten a pony for his birthday.

"Do you know who I am, pretty boy? You'll pay for this. If your mother wasn't already in her grave, I'd put her there myself." When the Pope pounded his giant fists on the table, the chips bounced and a few skittled onto the floor. Jessica's drink tottered and the Pope caught it in his big paw, polished it off, and slammed the empty glass on the table so hard it shook again.

Before Vance could respond, Alexander sprang up from his seat, then immediately sat back down staring at Jessica's empty glass as he grabbed his hair like he was trying to pull it off of his head. "I've got to get something from the limo," he said, and left in a huff.

Jessica hoped the something wasn't an UZI to blow Vance's head off. The actor was now howling and his whiny laughter echoed through the basement. He was trying to speak but could barely get the words out he was laughing so hard. "My….my….. my mother's not dead, you idiot." He was on the verge of hyperventilating. *Actors! What an ass.* Jessica didn't like the Pope, but the way Vance reeled him in, made her sick. The Pope had gone all-in and lost his entire stack of chips on that idiot actor's stupid bluff.

"One way or another, I'm going to take you out of this game, pretty boy. I want another buy-in," the fat man said to Lolita. "You do take checks, don't you?"

"Of course you can have another buy-in, Mr. Popov." Lolita purred. "But this is strictly a cash only game."

"I could give you $100,000 in cash as a down payment on the painting," Nick said, pulling a briefcase from under the table.

The Pope nodded towards the painting and reached out for the case but Nick pulled it back.

"Is that a yes, Vladimir?" Nick asked, opening the brief case to reveal stacks of thousand dollar bills. "You're selling me the painting for five million and I'm giving you $100K down. Just confirming our terms."

"Yes, yes. Let's keep playing." The Pope waved his hand in the air over the briefcase. The weasel-sized dose of vitamin K in Alexander's vodka didn't seem to be affecting the Zeppelin.

When Lolita motioned for Jack to deal the next hand, Jessica wiped tiny beads of sweat from her brow with the back of her sleeve. Detective Cormier would be there any minute and she needed a good hand if she was going to recoup her friend's grubstake. After three more hands, she was dealt pocket cowboys, so she came out shooting again. Everyone called and the pot was a monster. When another king fell on the river, she knew she had the nuts. Vance started his bluffing table talk about having the better hand, but she ignored his bullshit and went all-in. Vance pushed his massive pile of chips into the center of the table and went all-in too. *Shit.* Maybe she'd miscalculated. Maybe she didn't have the best possible hand. The Pope did a rough count and called. Vance was the first to turn over his hole cards, a pair of aces. The Pope turned over a pair of sixes, for three-of-a-kind with the community cards. Her three kings beat them both. *Jesse James rides again.* She blew imaginary smoke from the tips of her index fingers on each hand and then racked in the pot. By the looks of the monstrous pile of chips, she'd just won over fifty thousand dollars, Lolita's tuition. Damn, it felt good to be back in the saddle!

Cursing under his breath, Vance went to the bar for another carrot juice, and she overheard him mumble something about "fucking bitch." She was still raking in the pot when a large hand stopped her. The Pope had grabbed her wrist and held it so tight his grip was cutting off her circulation.

"What do we have here?" The Pope asked as he pulled a card from her sleeve. She was stunned. "Annie Oakley here is a card cheat. Do you know what we do to cheaters in Skokie? Do you, little miss?" The big man reached across the table and took hold of both of her arms and was shaking her. He shook so hard she fell off her chair, bit her tongue, and then tasted the bitter blood coating her teeth. Trembling in terror, she kicked at him, trying to scoot away across the floor, but he still had ahold of her wrists. Twisted between the table leg and the fat man's feet, she didn't know which way was up.

"Vladimir, please," Nick said, getting up from his chair. "I'm sure Jessica isn't cheating."

"Oh you are? Are you?" From under the table, she saw the fat man glance at one of his bodyguards and jerk his head towards Nick. When the Pope dropped her arms, she scooted out from under the table in time to see the bull round the table and put Nick into a chokehold.

"Gentlemen, please," Lolita said. "This is a friendly game. Let's calm down, everyone." She walked up behind the Pope, bent down, and whispered something in his ear as she poured him another vodka. A sly smile split his giant face as he grabbed one of Lolita's bare arms and pulled her down onto his lap.

"You think you can run a game in this town just because you're the Oxford Don's granddaughter. You think you're so smart, college girl. Well, I'll teach you a thing or two." The Pope wrapped both arms around Lolita. "I own this town. Got that, sweetheart? Do you?" Lolita narrowed her steely eyes, reared up from his lap, elbows flying, and escaped the grizzly bear embrace. Then she twirled around and landed a black boot on the side of the Pope's head.

When she saw her friend attack the fat man, Jessica lunged towards the thug choking Nick. But by the time she reached him, it was too late. Nick's eyes had rolled back in his head and he'd collapsed into the bull's arms. When the thug released him, Nick's limp body fell to the floor at her feet.

CHAPTER FORTY-SIX

"FREEZE!" A FAMILIAR voice shouted. Jessica James turned and saw Detective Cormier in the doorway flanked by several uniformed officers. When she sensed a breeze behind her, she turned to see Jack slipping out of the back-door to the room.

"Everyone! Hands in the air. Now!" Detective Cormier moved into the room, gun first, heading straight for the Pope. Two uniformed officers followed him into the room, holding their pistols in both hands, surveying the room.

"Why if it isn't our city's finest?" the Pope remarked. "What's wrong detective? This is just a friendly game of poker. A family game really." He stared at Lolita.

"It's an illegal game," Detective Cormier said. "Everyone move away from the table with your hands in the air. Stand up slowly, and put your hands up. Now!"

"You've got nothing on me. You know this won't stick." The Pope smiled and folded his hands on the table in front of him.

"We'll see about that," Detective Cormier said, pointing to the painting with his gun. "Back away from the table and put your hands above your heads, all of you."

The Pope stood up and raised his hands, then gestured with

his head for his men to comply. Suddenly, he grabbed his chest and his eyes opened wide. In response, one of his bodyguards leapt at Detective Cormier. The detective was struggling with one thug when the other pulled a pistol from his pocket. A mass of bodies fell to the floor, twisting and punching. With their guns already drawn, the cops had the advantage and started shooting.

At the sound of the explosive shots, her instincts kicked in, and she covered her ears with her hands and dove head first under the table. The Pope's mountainous body quaked and he slumped back into his chair, his torso bent over the mound of flesh it rested upon. From her crouched position, Jessica was peering up into his bulbous dead eyes. She saw Lolita's red-nailed fingertips reach down and lift the Pope's phone from his jacket pocket. Jessica gasped, tears welled in her eyes, and she bit her lip. It wasn't any easier seeing a dead man the second time around. Shaking, she huddled under the table until the room quieted.

Once the shouting and shooting had stopped, Jessica slowly crawled out from under the table and scooped her chips into her satchel. She glanced down and saw the two bulls writhing on the floor. Both appeared to have flesh wounds, and the officers cuffed them and then hauled them to their feet. Detective Cormier called for backup and soon more officers appeared in the doorway.

"He's dead," he said, standing over the fat man's body. "He's not shot. Must have been a heart attack. Looks like Mr. Popov's going away for good, but not to prison. No one can escape the final justice. Take him away." It took three men to move the big man's body. Detective Cormier was holding onto his right arm above the elbow and Jessica noticed blood was running down his sleeve, dripping onto his black leather shoes.

When the officers laid the Pope on the floor, he seemed even bulkier stretched out flat with his massive mound of belly protruding from the floor, a mountain coming straight out of the sea.

His bug eyes were staring at the ceiling and his lips were turning blue. Sitting on the floor nearby, Jessica felt like she was going to vomit. She was relieved when one of the officers reached down and closed the dead eyes. On hands and knees, she crawled over to Nick. Semi-conscious, he was still lying on the floor by the bar where the thug had dropped him.

"Nick?" she asked, sitting next to him on her heels. He pulled himself up onto his elbows and gave her a weak smile. The shriek of sirens was growing closer as she glanced around the room. Lolita was sitting at the table along with the other poker players, the police officers were busy with the Pope and his men, and the detective sat down on the edge of the table, still holding his arm.

"Consider this a warning, Ms. Durchenko," Detective Cormier said to Lolita. "Your first and your last. No more poker Tsarina."

Lolita nodded.

"We'd make a good team, Ms. Durchenko," he said, extending his good arm.

"You take down the Russian Brotherhood," Lolita said, taking his hand, "and I'll take care of the fraternity brotherhood."

"That goes for the rest of you too, no more illegal gambling," the detective said to the players. "Leave your names and numbers with Officer Marino over there by the door. We'll need to get your statements. Marino will give you instructions on the way out." Except for Nick and Jessica, the other players left with Officer Marino.

Once they were gone, Nick picked up the crate leaning against the wall behind the Pope's chair. "I would like to personally deliver this to your father, if I may," he said to Lolita. "I need to apologize for the other night."

"I'm afraid we have to take that downtown," Detective Cormier said. "You too Mr. Schilling. We have to remove the wire and get your statement."

"My father is not a forger, detective," Lolita said.

"We'll get to the bottom of it, Ms. Durchenko. Don't' worry," the detective said. "But it's evidence in a murder investigation. I assume this is the painting stolen from the professor's office, but we'll know soon enough. Odd that nothing else was taken, not even his computer."

"How would you know nothing else was taken?" Jessica said a bit too forcefully. "His office is such a mess. He's got student papers piled up in there from three years ago… That reminds me, where's Alexander?"

"Who?" Detective Cormier asked.

"A student. Alexander Le Blanc, he was here with the Pope," Jessica said, her voice trailing off when she saw Lolita was narrowing her eyes and scowling. "He left just before you got here."

"Don't worry, we'll find him and pick him up for questioning," the detective said. "I'll coordinate with campus security." Detective Cormier called to security guard Jimmy, who was watching from the hallway. Two ambulances and a fire truck arrived, and loaded up the wounded bodyguards and the Pope's corpse. After the EMTs bandaged his arm, Detective Cormier escorted his men out of the building, and insisted Nick accompany them.

"I'll meet you at the station in a few minutes," Lolita said. " I've got to clean up here. Jessica can stay and help me." At the sound of her name, Jessica went to her friend, put her arms around her, and buried her face in Lolita's soft shoulder. She couldn't help it, she started sobbing.

"We'll need to get your statement too, Ms. James, once you're able. You too, Ms. Durchenko. Please come by the station when you've finished cleaning up. Jimmy, make sure they get to the station within the next hour." Jimmy nodded.

When the detective had gone, Lolita asked "Did you set up a meeting with Alexander at the café before he left?"

"I thought Jack was supposed to arrange to buy drugs from him."

"Jack is fetching something from the professor's office," Lolita said. "We'll get Alexander ourselves."

"No, you won't. Alexander may be dangerous," Jimmy said.

"Not as dangerous as we are," Lolita said. "Jimmy you stay here in case Alexander comes back." Jimmy stood with his mouth open, his sad eyes worshipping Lolita.

"Let's go," Lolita said turning to Jessica.

"Go where?"

"To the café, of course, after we fetch Jack from the professor's office."

"What? Jack went back to Wolf's office?" Jessica sat down on one of the chairs.

"We have some unfinished business. Come on." Lolita pulled her up from the chair, and then led her out of the door.

CHAPTER FORTY-SEVEN

WHEN JESSICA JAMES knocked on the door to room 24B, it creaked open, and she peeked in.

"Hey there, cowgirl," Jack said. "Look what I found." Grinning from ear to ear, he held up a manila envelope.

Jessica tiptoed into the office and glanced around. The police must have confiscated the trash because there were no more pizza boxes, candy wrappers, or half-full Pepsi bottles. Only books and stacks of papers still gathering dust in Wolf's creepy office. Jessica waited for Lolita to scoot inside and then shut the door behind them.

"What is it?" Jessica asked.

"Come see," he said, waving the envelope in the air.

"Let me see that," Lolita said, grabbing the envelope. "Is this the book Fingal O'Flannery stole from the professor?" She opened the envelope and pulled out a manuscript.

"Our Montana cowgirl came up with a thesis so brilliant, those boys were fighting over it." Jack laughed.

"What are you talking about?" Jessica asked.

"Take a look at this!" He snatched the envelope out of Lolita's hands and pointed to the address on the front, Oxford University

Press. Then he seized the manuscript and thrust it at her. As she fumbled through the pages, her mouth fell open.

"Holy shit. It's my thesis. What does this mean?"

"Amber found an email message confirming Bald Dick sent this manuscript to Fingal for feedback and then he planned to send it to Oxford. That's why I came back to snoop around his office. Obviously, when Wolf croaked, Fingal saw his golden opportunity. Jesse, your work is in high demand. Just change the return address on this envelope and you might have your first publication, Oxford University Press, no less."

"This is all very interesting, but we've got to catch that weasel Alexander before he gets away. He's supplying the fucking rape drugs on campus and we're going to bust his balls," Lolita said, then turned on her heels to leave the office.

"What about my thesis?" Jessica asked, running after her, pages flying as she went.

"Jack will stay here and gather it up and we'll sort it out later," her friend said as she strode down the hallway. "Right now you're going to the Blind Faith to find that drug dealing scum."

"Wait!" Jessica was scooping up papers off the floor and trying to put them in order.

"We've solved the mystery of the thesis and the post-dated letter. Come on, we've got to catch Alexander before Detective Cormier comes back looking for us!" Lolita started down the stairs. "Jessica, you're going weasel hunting. Jack will take care of your thesis and continue searching the professor's office. Now, let's get going."

"How do you know Alexander will be there?" Jessica asked.

"Because you're about to send him a message telling him to meet you there to discuss that damned paper you've been carrying around in your bag for the last week," Lolita said. "He'll be there."

"But, I haven't read… "

"Read it while you're waiting for him," Lolita said. "Jack, meet us at the café when you're done here. I'll pick up Amber. Her place is close to the café and I need her to do something for me. Remember, text me the minute he gets there. Now get going."

After Lolita dropped her off at the Blind Faith, abandoned by her friends, Jessica made her way through late night diners padding their stomachs before bed and summer-school coeds drinking their homework. She headed to the bar and sat down on a swiveling stool. She needed a drink after the deadly poker game and revelations about her stolen thesis. After downing a double shot of Jack Daniels, she decided to have dessert and splurge on a ten-dollar Cosmopolitan. She deserved it if she had to face Alexander's twenty pages of existential angst. She opened her book bag and pulled out Alexander's crumpled paper. It was frayed and stained from spending a week inside her only bag. If Lolita had succeeded in poisoning the little shit, she wouldn't have to read the damned thing. While she waited for her Cosmo, she started speed-reading the paper in hopes of finishing before Alexander arrived.

"Beyond Common Morality, Raskolnikov as Übermensch," by Alexander Le Blanc. Argg. She already wanted to puke.

Just as Nietzsche's Zarathustra divides the world into Supermen and sheep, Dostoevsky's Raskolnikov divides the world into extraordinary and ordinary men. Supermen or extraordinary men have the right to do anything. They are above the law. Most people live their lives like lice, thinking only of filling their bellies or finding pleasure...

Jessica grinned when her cocktail arrived and sat it on top of the deadly boring paper, admiring its sunset colors and the triangular shape of the glass. An orange peel tail spiraled off the rim of the pastel pink martini. She took a sip and pursed her lips when the collision of sweet and sour zapped her taste buds. Then she gulped and it disappeared. She needed to take the sharp edge off the rough night, so she ordered another fruity cocktail and went back to reading.

The idiot fraternity brothers who care only for drugs and sex and the prickteasing sorority girls who beg to be raped in their slutty clothes are ordinary sheep who deserve to go to slaughter. They are beneath my genius and I would never contaminate myself by touching them. Extraordinary men go beyond mere bodily ecstasy and face the abyss, the tragedy of existence, with courage and violence. They suffer from their superiority.

"What the fuck?" Jessica blurted out, spitting some of her drink onto the bar. She started the next paragraph, paying more attention to whatever it was she was reading.

Professor Schmutzig, you have inspired me.

He's addressing the professor in his final paper? What's this kid up to?

It is truly Nietzsche's "twilight of the idols." Perhaps it's apt, you are the only one who can appreciate what I am about to do. In your last class, you gave the example of a student, like Raskolnikov, himself a poor student, who kills one of his professors to prove that he is extraordinary. You, dear professor, reinterpreted Dostoevsky. You argued that Raskolnikov could never prove himself superior by murdering the pawnbroker and her retarded sister because they were clearly inferior to him and therefore in order to prove himself he needed to murder someone of equal stature.

Jessica blinked hard and stared at the paper. Without looking up, she picked up her drink and sipped.

That would be like me killing those idiot, drug-addicted rapists in Tau Kappa Epsilon, or one of their stupid slut sorority babes: "Woman is not yet capable of friendship. Women are still cats and birds. Or at best cows..." (Thus Spoke Zarathustra). *As Nietzsche says,* "God is dead. God remains dead. And we have killed him.... Must we ourselves not become gods simply to appear worthy of

it?" (The Gay Science, 125). *We must kill our idols. The* Übermensch *is not just an extraordinary man. He is beyond man and most
certainly beyond woman.*

Jessica sighed, flattened the paper on the bar, leaned her head
into her hands, and continued reading.

*Isn't it true that we repay our teachers best by going beyond them?
I will prove myself a superior man by going beyond even you, beyond
my philosophical idol. I will prove to you, Professor Schmutzig that I
am extraordinary. You will taste my bittersweet ascent.*

She couldn't believe what she was reading. Alexander was bat-
shit crazy! Maybe he was like Hitler and misinterpreted Nietzsche's
theories to justify killing. Could it be? Had he murdered Wolf to
prove he was a superior man? It would be ironic if Schmutzig's
twisted reading of Dostoevsky had inspired Alexander to murder him. She'd always wondered at Wolf's suggestion that Raskolnikov's mistake wasn't murder, or even going back to the scene
of the crime with a guilty conscience, but rather killing an old
pawnbroker woman and her half-wit sister, low-lives below even
the poor student's dignity. It made her queasy just thinking about
it. She downed the rest of her second Cosmopolitan and ordered
another shot of whiskey. She needed to think.

She'd last seen Alexander in Schmutzig's office the day before
he was killed. As usual, he was milking Wolf's office hours, sucking up and gushing about his passion for existential philosophy.
They were eating croissants and drinking coffees together as usual,
compliments of the little suck-up weasel. *Holy shit!* The diary. Schmutzig said Alexander was bringing him gifts. Lolita was right.
They *were* poisonous gifts. Alexander must have laced Wolf's coffee with enough GHB to kill him. Did the little weasel plant the
heroin and needle on the professor to make it look like a suicidal
overdose? *Whoa.* The scrawny kid was way more dangerous and
deranged than she'd ever imagined.

She rummaged in her satchel looking for her phone and fished around some more trying to find the detective's card. He'd written his cell number on the back of it. Her hands were shaking as she pulled it out of her bag. When she tapped in his number, the line went directly to voice mail. *Damn!* She quickly texted Lolita, "OMG. A killed W. HB2BFC!". She'd just poked send when someone snatched the phone out of her hands. Alexander Le Blanc was somehow sitting next to her at the bar. She shot up from her barstool. "What the hell are you doing?"

"Well, what did you think of my paper?" Alexander grinned and grasped her wrist.

She struggled to free her hand. "You won't get away with it."

"You're the only one who knows about this paper and my plan," he said. "My housemate Gerard makes a mean Cosmo, *n'est-ce pas?*"

Jessica stared at the empty glass, and her stomach sunk. "That's why you've been trying to poison me. It wasn't for Kurt."

"Kurt's an idiot," Alexander said. "Do you still think Raskolnikov is a superior man, justified in what he did? Have you heard of Nathan Leopold and Richard Loeb? They thought they were smart enough to commit the perfect crime, but they got caught. Getting caught is for fools and I'm no fool." He put his arm around her waist. She tried to push him away, but she was so dizzy she had to hold onto the bar.

"Alexander…" Nauseous, she could barely stand.

"I'll take my paper now, bitch," Alexander said. He pulled his paper out from under her elbows on the bar. She grabbed at it, tore off the first page, and held it tightly in her fist. When he pried her hand open and snatched it, she wobbled backwards, willing herself not to fall. She swatted at his hands trying to get her phone back.

"I think you've had too much to drink, Jesse dear. Don't worry, I'll help you get home safely," he said loudly, glancing around the crowded café. He was holding her around the waist, pulling her across the restaurant. As a few anxious faces turned their way, he said, "She's had a bit too much to drink, that's all." They looked away.

She tried to resist, but her limbs were heavier than lead. She opened her mouth to scream, but no sound at all came out. A waitress intercepted them near the door, but just then quarterback Kurt Willis showed up. "No worries, folks," he said. "My girlfriend is a little tipsy." Kurt scooped Jessica up and carried her outside, cradling her in his brutish arms. She kicked with all her might, but her legs weren't moving. She looked around for help, but the street was empty.

They were standing at the curb when Alexander's phone started singing, "You can be the President, I'd rather be the Pope. You can be the side effect, I'd rather be the dope."

"What the hell is that ghetto noise?" Kurt asked.

"Damn, it's the Pope," Alexander said. "Wait a minute, I have to take this... Hello, hello, are you there? Vladimir?"

"What's going on Zander?" Kurt asked.

"He hung up. He drank Jessica's spiked whiskey at the poker game, so I hightailed it out of there. At least Vladimir is okay. He owes me money." Alexander put his hand over Jessica's mouth. "Let's get her in the car and I'll give her another dose. The little bitch refuses to die."

"Can I bang her first?"

"Be my guest, if you must." Alexander's phone started another chorus of "You can be the President, I'd rather be the Pope. You can be the side effect, I'd rather be the dope."

"It's Vladimir calling back."

"What's with that ringtone?"

"Prince's *Pope*. Cool, eh? It's my ringtone for Vladimir."

"Hello, Vladimir? Hello?"

"Let's get Jesse into my car before someone sees us," Kurt said. Alexander's phone was rapping again. "Shit, the connection must be bad. I'll call him back from the car." The car was around the corner from the café, parked on a quiet street. Alexander was yanking at her hair from the other side of the car while Kurt shoved her body inside. Her legs scraped against the car door as they stuffed her into the backseat and metal ripped at her skin. Kurt pushed her inside, pulled down his pants, and threw himself on top of her. She tried to shove him off, but he was too heavy and her limbs weren't responding to her brain. His hot breath on her face and the stale smell of onions and beer, made her gag. She could hear Alexander answering his phone again in the driver's seat, "Hello? Vlad…"

"Freeze! Hands up!" Detective Cormier's baritone vibrated through Jessica's limp body.

Kurt elbowed her in the face as he scrambled to sit up. The detective opened the back door and pulled him out by his ankles and his face slammed the pavement with a satisfying thwack. Detective Cormier handcuffed him, read him his rights, and then turned him over to a uniformed officer. Jack crawled into the backseat, sat down beside her, cradled her head in his lap, and caressed her face. "Sweet, Jesse. Poor little cowgirl." He was whispering into her ear when she made out another noise from the front seat, a car door squeaking open, followed by the sounds of footfalls on the pavement. Alexander was making a break for it.

"Stop or I'll shoot," the detective yelled after a receding Alexander.

Jack helped her out of the backseat and out onto the sidewalk. She leaned against his body, and he held her around the waist.

Detective Cormier sprinted after Alexander and tackled him from behind before he got around the corner. The detective fell on top of the fugitive and flattened him on the sidewalk. Squirming,

Alexander tried to escape, but the muscular cop had him pinned. Detective Cormier flipped him over, cuffed him, then pulled him up off the ground, and dragged the puny kid back to the squad car.

Alexander laughed. "You won't have me for long. Vladimir will post bail."

"I doubt that," Detective Cormier said. "He's dead."

"Dead?" Alexander asked. "I don't think so. He called me just a few minutes ago."

"There's no need to lie. The autopsy showed Vladimir was poisoned with GHB and ketamine. You killed the Pope the same way you killed the professor. That's two counts of first-degree murder." Sirens screamed and lights flashed as an ambulance pulled up.

"Thank God we prevented a third," Detective Cormier said.

"Can I ride with Jessica to the hospital?" Jack asked as two paramedics lifted her onto a gurney. Everything spun as they wheeled her toward the ambulance.

"But who was calling me then?" Alexander asked, shaking his head. "It was Vladimir's ringtone."

Another smaller hand caressed her head. "There, there, it will be okay. Open your mouth, sweetie," Amber said. "Let me give you some detox drops." Jessica opened her mouth and bitter liquid dropped onto her tongue.

"Look what I can do," Amber said, tapping on her cell phone. Alexander's phone started singing again, "You can be the side effect, I'd rather be the dope."

"I hacked the Pope's phone. Cool, huh? I was distracting Alex the Pharmacist to slow him down so we could get here in time."

"I'd like to give that little fucker a side effect or two," Lolita said. "Sweet Jessica, we got here as fast as we could when I got your text. Detective Cormier, I found this cell phone under the table when we were cleaning up after the poker game." She handed it to him.

"No, this isn't possible!" Alexander shouted. "It was the perfect crime. I'm no fool and you can't prove anything. You idiots can't do this to me. It wasn't murder. I wanted to prove to Professor Schmutzig right by killing someone equally intelligent…" His rant faded into the distance.

Jessica threw up blood. Then everything went black.

CHAPTER FORTY-EIGHT

DMITRY DURCHENKO HUNG up the phone. His daughter had called to say she had a surprise for him, and he had one for her, too. He was feeling better after a good night's sleep, and his mother was still asleep on the sofa, a tiny silver leaf curled up under a cigarette burned hotel blanket. They'd stayed up too late catching up on the last twenty years. Dmitry hadn't had the heart to tell her the paintings were missing. As he made tea in the kitchenette, he remembered how much he'd loved tea and toast with marmalade when he was a boy. Sometimes he and his mother would have tea together in the afternoon when no one else was in the house, just the two of them.

His mother sat up, rubbing her eyes, and he brought her a cup of tea, then sat in the easy chair across from her.

"Can I ask you something, Mother? Why did you give me those two paintings? I've always wondered why those two in particular."

"That trip to Caën was one of the best times of my life," his mother said. "I was hoping the paintings might take you back there, in memory if not in body. We were like a real family then at Konstantin's estate, having picnics and picking Tiger Lilies instead of hiding behind bodyguards and living by violence."

"That was my favorite trip too," he said softly. He still hadn't come to terms with the revelation that the Count was really his father. Thirty-seven years being tethered to Anton Yudkovich could not be severed overnight, or perhaps ever. He'd tried to cut the cord his whole life, but he was still carrying the Oxford Don in the crypt of his unconscious.

"And, wasn't Kandinsky's *Fragment 2* your favorite painting?" his mother asked. "I wanted you to have it. As you know, Natalia's *Gathering Apples* was mine. I wanted you to have something to remember me by."

"I've thought of you everyday mother," he said. "I've missed you with all my heart." His eyes were watering, and he pulled a handkerchief from his back pocket to wipe them.

"My handkerchief!" his mother exclaimed. "You still have it after all these years."

Dmitry cradled the worn cloth in his palms. It had become such a part of his daily life, he'd forgotten his mother gave it to him all those years ago on the train platform. He stared down at the tattered fabric with its faded embroidery.

"Why do you love Goncharova so much?" he asked. He had never understood his mother's preference for those primitive blocky forms and folksy peasant scenes.

"Natalia Goncharova was an extraordinary woman," his mother said. "She was everything that I am not."

"You're extraordinary, Mother." Dmitry got up from the overstuffed chair and sat next to his mother on the couch. She smiled and took his hand.

"But Natalia was truly an independent spirit," she said. "People thought she was crazy. She painted flowers and elephants on her cheeks. She wore colorful nightgowns in public. When she was the belle of the *Ballet russe* in Paris as a costume and set designer, she became a Moscow fashion icon." His mother laughed. "Soon, the upper crust of Russian society were painting their faces and wearing nightgowns in public."

Dmitry smiled. He still didn't see why such antics appealed to his mother.

"Natalia valued what others denigrated," his mother continued. "Gathering wood, cutting ice, picking fruit," she said. "Picking flowers." She paused and looked as if she'd been transported to another world. Perhaps she was back on the bank of the river picking Tiger Lilies. "Natalia saw beauty in our peasants and our homeland. Even after she went to Paris, her heart belonged to Russia." His mother patted his hand. "She made her own way in a man's world, never caring what others thought of her or what risks she took."

"What will you do now, Mother?" he asked. "Sabina and I would love for you to stay here with us."

"Stay in this temporary apartment on a sofa bed?" she laughed.

"Of course not here," he said, his face warm. When he realized he had gotten used to the Residence Inn with its cramped quarters and lack of comforts, the thought worried him. He surveyed the room with fresh eyes. Of course they couldn't stay here.

"We'll buy a new house," he said, "one with a separate apartment for you."

"You are kind, *milyi*," she said. "But Konstantin is waiting for me. He has been waiting for decades, and now it's our turn for happiness. After I return to Moscow and make arrangements for your father… for Anton's funeral, I'll move to France to grow old with my beloved."

The door to the apartment burst open. Lolita bounded in. "You'll never guess what I've got," she said. She stopped in the foyer and gazed at her grandmother. She dropped her packages and dashed to the couch.

"Grandmother?" she asked, "Is it really you?" She fell to her knees in front of the sofa, gazed up, and then put her arms around her grandmother's waist. "Grandmother." She buried her head in her grandmother's flowing lavender pant suit, one she'd been wearing since the day before.

"Lolita, *moya lyubov*," she said, kissing the top of her head. "I've waited your entire life to meet you, *milaya*. Now I am whole. My heart is finally home."

Dmitry had been right. It was love at first sight. His mother knelt down and returned her namesake's long embrace. The two Lolitas on their knees holding each other for dear life. He hated to interrupt.

"The packages," he said when he couldn't wait any longer. "Is that the surprise? Did you find them?" Dmitry dashed over to the boxes and unwrapped the cardboard. He couldn't stand it and tore at the box. After ripping and clawing, the paintings appeared, two cylinders coiled neatly inside bubble wrap. Carefully, he opened the plastic and unrolled the paintings one by one, letting the Goncharova curl up again while he gazed at the Kandinsky.

"How did you find them?" he asked, caressing the edge of the familiar painting. Then he lost himself in the Kandinsky, his old friend. His mother came to his side, reached down, and unrolled her favorite Natalia Goncharova.

"How beautiful!"

Dmitry insisted that she take it home with her, but she refused. He couldn't bear to tell her that he would have to sell one of them, but it was the only way he and Sabina could afford to buy a new house.

Lolita and her grandmother were inseparable until her return to Moscow two days later. They cooked their favorite foods, drank vodka together, went shopping for summer clothes in the department stores downtown, and made plans for Lolita's to visit her grandmother at the Count's estate in Caën. When Vanya drove them to the airport, the two Lolita's sat side by side in the back-seat, holding hands and chatting. In the departure lounge, his mother handed his daughter a petite vintage overnight case, red alligator with gold locks. A leather patch under the handle had been embossed with the initials L.Y.

"This is for you, my dear," she said to Lolita. "Wait until I've gone to open it. Wait until I'm back in Moscow." They held each other in a tight embrace.

"Dimka, my son," his mother said, her eyes welling with tears, "please come and visit us. Konstantin, your father, is eager to see you again. You could bring your family." He kissed her cheek. He couldn't imagine calling the Count "father," but he had always cherished the memory of them fly fishing together again on the banks of the river.

"Take care of our darling girl," his mother said to him. "And take care of my Natalia, too."

Dmitry winced and stared at his shoes. He'd already arranged to meet Nicholas Schilling about the paintings. If he sold the Goncharova, he'd be betraying his mother, but he didn't have a choice. Kandinsky's *Fragment* was a piece of his soul, his best friend, and he'd relied on that painting to get him through many a dark night. He could never sell it, no matter what the price.

CHAPTER FORTY-NINE

DMITRY DURCHENKO FELT like he was back at the
Moscow Institute of Art, but he was in the rich art collector's fancy penthouse apartment, about to betray his
mother. Surrounded by Russian paintings, he longed to take brush
to canvas to cover his sins with thick oil paint. Perhaps now he
could paint something other than Kandinsky's *Fragment Number
2*. He knew Kandinsky by heart: every trickle of red, slash of black
ink, and hemorrhage of gold. Each dissonant note in its allegro,
the harmony in its adagio, and its deep blue intermezzo, formed a
symphony he had memorized in his body. He couldn't say if *Fragment 2* symbolized the Deluge, the Last Judgment, or the Resur-
rection. But it had become his religion, offering both redemption
and pain, themes he'd studied in some of the very works on Schilling's walls when he was a young man at the Institute of Art.

Schilling led him out of the foyer and into a sitting room with
a wall of glass facing downtown. When the art collector offered
him a seat on a white leather couch, Dmitry shook his head and
continued to gaze around the room. The contrast between the
shiny metropolis hollow and meaningless below and the thick
abstractions throbbing with life inside startled him. He stared at
the paintings, hanging in neat rows on the other three expansive

walls of the room, in what must have been the art collector's Chagall gallery, containing some works Dmitry had never seen before. His gaze flew from wall to wall, so much to take in. When Schilling went to the kitchen to ask his maid to bring them wine, Dmitry moved closer to examine a curious horned figure ascending, mouth open, to grasp stone tablets from hands emerging out of the clouds, all against a bright yellow background. This must be the famous sketch of Moses receiving the tablets. He'd read about it in school. Rarely on display, only a few people had ever seen it. He resented Schilling for keeping it to himself, but then he though of his own beloved Kandinsky.

Startled, Dmitry reeled back from the painting when Miss Jessica emerged from another room wearing an oversized men's bathrobe, pale as chalk with dark circles under her swollen eyes. Cohabiting with the devil, at least she'd be warm.

"It's good to see you up and about Miss Jessica," Dmitry said. She looked awful, poor girl. "I heard that you helped the police catch the professor's killer."

"Unbelievable, isn't it?" she said, curling up on the white leather sofa in the middle of the room. "Alexander Le Blanc poisoned him with GHB and used Dostoevsky to rationalize it. Raskolnikov's theory of extraordinary men from *Crime and Punishment* as an excuse to kill. Mix that with an unhealthy dose of misinterpreted Nietzsche, and you've got a lethal cocktail of wacked out homicidal existentialism. " She shook her head. "Absurd."

"He was emulating a character from nineteenth-century Russian literature?" Dmitry asked. "He should have read Tolstoy," he said under his breath. "Instead of wallowing in the turmoil and angst of his own soul, he could have worried about practical matters like national party politics or the effects of digital technology on farming."

"Or, maybe he would have just thrown himself in front of a

train like Anna Karenina," Jessica said with a smile, tucking the edges of the robe under her legs, wrapping herself in a cocoon of white terry cloth. Nick came back into the sitting room with his black clad maid in tow, sat down next to Jessica, and put his arm around her.

"How did you figure out Alexander was the killer?" Dmitry asked.

"I thought Alexander was harassing me because he wanted his paper back. And I thought Kurt was trying to…" she said, blushing. "It was almost a deadly misunderstanding."

"Deadly is right," Schilling said, gesturing for Dmitry to take a glass of sparkling wine. "He *did* want his paper back once he realized it was a confession and it wasn't in Wolf Schmutzig's office."

Dmitry sipped the bubbly wine wishing he had something stronger, a nice shot of frozen Russo-Baltique.

"I'm such an idiot," Miss Jessica said, sipping from a champagne flute.

"You're anything but an idiot, Dolce," Schilling said. "Alexander's the idiot."

"When I read his final paper after the poker game, I realized he was crazy, absolutely mad. He wrote about superior men killing people to prove their intelligence and specifically mentioned proving himself to Professor Schmutzig by killing someone worthy. That's when I put two and two together, and remembered Alexander was supplying drugs on campus, including rape drugs. His paper was basically a confession to this perverse murder. Once he found out I was grading his paper instead of Wolf, he tried to poison me."

Dmitry sighed and stared into his lap. "I should have stopped him. I knew he was dealing drugs for Bratva. And I saw him in the professor's office weekly."

"But there's more to the mystery. Tell Dmitry what Jack and

Amber found in the email and the office, Dolce," Nick said, taking Miss Jessica's hand and kissing it.

"Well, Amber hacked the professor's email and found a scanned manuscript he'd sent a couple weeks ago to Fingal O'Flannery to read. Turns out to be the very book Fingal is now publishing as his own, conveniently after Wolf's death. So the night of the poker game, Jack went back into the professor's office and found the same book manuscript tucked into a manila envelope addressed to Oxford University Press." Miss Jessica's face was bright red and her eyes were glistening like she might cry.

"But who really wrote that manuscript?" Schilling asked, nudging her with his elbow and then kissing her forehead. Dmitry blinked and squirmed in his chair.

"I guess I did. Turns out, it was my thesis," Jessica said, blushing. "That's why Schmutzig wanted me to drop out of graduate school. He stole my research and was planning to send it off to Oxford as his own. But after he died, Fingal took it and sent it out as his. I still can't wrap my mind around this level of sabotage and intellectual theft. It really wrecks my faith in philosophers and crusty old men."

Dmitry didn't know what to say. It made sense to steal money or paintings. But, a philosophy thesis, what worth could it possibly have?

"How did you know Alexander was dealing drugs on campus?" Jessica asked. "Was it mostly date rape drugs?"

Dmitry winced, wondering how many girls had been attacked because he had said nothing. "For a smart boy," he said, "Alex was very stupid."

"Those frat boys taking selfies while raping unconscious girls are about to learn their idea of entertainment is a felony crime." Schilling said, stroking Jessica's hair.

"They're dickheads," said Miss Jessica, moving away from

Schilling's caress. "I think sororities should hand out female condoms lined with razors." She stood up and starting pacing back and forth in front of the couch. "*Vagina Dentata*, that would fix the bastards."

Nicholas Schilling's maid served them coffee in silence. No one responded to Miss Jessica's gruesome solution. Vaginas with teeth, maybe American girls were even scarier than Bratva. Miss Jessica added extra cream and sugar to her coffee, and smiled as she picked up the cinnamon shaker from the tray.

Schilling finally broke the silence. "On to happier subjects. My mother will be thrilled with the Goncharova. I'm sending it to her for her birthday next week. I can't thank you enough, Mr. Durchenko." Schilling got up and went to a writing desk, sat down, and made out a check. When Dmitry saw the amount, his breath caught. It was enough to buy a whole city block, downtown. He detested having to sell his mother's favorite painting, but he and Sabina needed to buy a new house. They couldn't stay in the Residence Inn forever.

As he walked out of the building, Dmitry knew he might as well have just sold one of his own children, but there was no turning back. Schilling offered to have his driver give him a ride, but he decided to take the elevated train to the hotel. He needed time to think, time to mourn. When he got off the train, instead of returning to the Residence Inn, he walked to the lake. The temperature was perfect, neither hot nor cold, warm nor cool. A day when air and skin became one. The lake was a sheet of steel, steady dull silver. He hoped its steady sheen would calm his nerves, as he thought about how much his life had changed in just two weeks.

CHAPTER FIFTY

J ESSICA JAMES WAS pouring bright orange cheese powder into a dented pot, compliments of the Residence Inn. When she added boiling water the florescent dust turned into a sticky wad, so she pounded it with a wooden spoon, then added the macaroni. Holding up a spoon dripping cheesy goo, she pointed it at her friend and laughed. "Hey, hand me the Stoli. How about making this mac-ala-vodka?" She'd already had a couple of frozen vodka shots for an appetizer. Lolita passed the bottle, then used a paper towel to remove beef *piroshky* from the microwave. As she tossed them on the tiny table, she announced, "Dinner is served."

Curled up on the couch with Bunin, Sabina looked up and smiled when her daughter presented a doughy *piroshky* accompanied by a daub of mac-and-cheese, along with a vodka shot. "Bon appetit," she said setting the plate on the coffee table. Bunin slid off the sofa, nose touching the hot plate, and then glanced back at Sabina with questioning eyes.

Tail wagging, Bunin snatched the meat filled bun off the plate, then ran to the door to meet Dmitry. Shoulders slumped, Dmitry entered the hotel room, a black cloud ruining an otherwise sunny day.

"Did you hear about *Gathering Apples?*" Jessica asked, trying to cheer him up. "Nick was examining the painting and he noticed another painting bleeding through. He thinks it must be Goncharova's study for her *Self-portrait with Tiger Lilies.*"

"What?" he asked, freezing in the entryway, neck twitching, as if a cold breeze had grazed his neck with a ghostly caress.

"Did you say Tiger Lilies?" Dmitry asked, wild-eyed.

"Lots of times artists paint over other canvases and eventually the original image shows through," Jessica said, wondering what was wrong.

"Yes, I know. It's called pentimento," Dmitry said, running his hand through his thick hair. "I have to get that painting back."

"But Nick's sending it to his mother for her birthday."

"We have to stop him," he said, heading back out the door. "I can't lose her again. Call Schilling and tell him I'll trade for the Kandinsky."

"What?" Lolita asked. "Are you crazy? The Kandinsky is worth at least ten times as much as the Goncharova."

"The Tiger Lily," he said, "My mother's favorite flower bleeding through her favorite painting. It's a sign. I have to get it back. Call Schilling now!"

Jessica called Nick, but his driver had already left to take the painting to Federal Express.

"Stop him!" Dmitry yelled.

"Calm down, Dad. You stay here. Have some tea or something." Lolita said, then turned to Jessica and tossed her a helmet. "We'll get it back. Which FedEx? Come on."

"Downtown, in the John Hancock Center on Michigan Avenue," Jessica answered.

As usual, her speed demon friend swerved in and out of traffic on her murderbike. "Hold on," she yelled as she accelerated around a corner. She must be going over eighty miles an hour.

Jessica closed her eyes, clamped her legs down hard on the bike, latched her hands around Lolita's waist, and inhaled the thrill. The tail of Lolita's long hair was blowing into her face from under her helmet, so Jessica pinched her eyes shut even tighter and pressed her lips together. When Lolita skidded into the Federal Express parking lot and sprinted into the store, Jessica jogged after her. Her friend asked for a manager and explained the situation, but the package had already been posted, and the manager refused to do anything until he had personal authorization from Mr. Schilling in the flesh.

Jessica called Nick and then went outside to wait for him. Pacing back and forth in the parking lot, she took in the brilliant skyline and choppy lake the in the background. Every time she came downtown, she was awed by the skyscrapers with their sheets of glass reflecting fat puffy cotton clouds in an otherwise robin's egg blue sky. She noticed an ominous thunderhead on the horizon and wished Nick would hurry up.

Fifteen minutes later, he arrived in his limo, all business as he took Jessica's hand on the way past, then strode inside the Federal Express office. Lolita had been sitting on her Harley smoking a cigarette; she hopped off, ran ahead, and held the door open for them. When the manager explained the truck was already loaded and it was too late to retrieve the package, Nick glared at him and got out his wallet, then started placing hundred dollar bills on the counter, one at a time. He paused, looking the manager straight in the eyes between each bill. With every bill the manager's face brightened. Nick stopped at eight hundred, waited a few seconds, and then reached out to take the money back. Before he could, the manager snatched up the money, and dashed into the back of the store. Several minutes later, he returned with the package. Puffing out his chest, he refused to turn the package over to one of the girls and instead placed it directly into Nick's waiting hands.

"We need to get this back to my dad," Lolita said. "He's probably blown a gasket by now. I'll call him. You take Jessica and the paintings back to the hotel and I'll meet you there."

"If he's willing to sell the Kandinsky instead, I'm ready to make a deal." Nick said, grinning as he led Jessica to the limo.

"We'll see about that," Lolita called after him as she hopped on her bike.

When they got to the Inn, Dmitry was waiting at the door. He wiped his sweaty palms on his pants, then seized the package out of Nick's hands and placed it on the table. Sitting in the kitchenette, he used his carbide tipped scraper to pry open the crate. Carefully unrolling the painting, then flattening its edges with his fingertips, he sat motionless starting at Goncharova's *Gathering Apples*. Jessica looked over his shoulder at the vase full of Tiger Lilies bleeding through the peasant women picking apples.

"Mr. Durchenko," Nick said, taking a seat at the table. "I've heard you've had second thoughts and would rather sell the Kandinsky."

"My redemption, my pain," Dmitry mumbled.

"I'm sorry," Nick said. "What was that? Which painting are you selling?

"Neither." Dmitry stood up, took his wallet from his back pocket, removed Nick's check, ripped it into tiny pieces, and threw them into the air. Jessica stepped out of the way just in time to avoid getting run over by Bunin as he charged, biting at the falling confetti.

"Maybe it is time to stop running," Dmitry said rubbing his hands together. "No offense to your macaroni, girls," he said, smiling, "but who wants to go to Pavlov's Banquet for dinner?"

Much later that night, back in her attic hovel, Jessica James was packing for her trip home the next morning, back to her melancholy mother and depressive Alpine Vista trailer park. She chewed her fingernail as she stared at the photograph of Michael, the last memento of her first ever lover. She rummaged around in her pile of clothes, found his dirty blue cardigan, stomped on it, then stuffed it in the overflowing trash can. She skipped back to the desk, picked up the photo and stared at it again, remembering the early days of sparks flying and insatiable desire. She removed the photo from its frame, slipping it out from under the glass, then tore it into tiny pieces and scooped them into a neat pile on top of the desk. She struck a match and set the mound on fire, then watched as her "first" went up in smoke.

She wiped her eyes with the backs of her hands, then slid her phone out of her back pocket and tapped in Nick's number. One nail takes out the other. Her heart was galloping as the phone rang. When he answered, she jabbed the red circle and hung up. The thought of lying in bed next to him, his soft wavy hair and penetrating blue eyes, made it hard to resist calling him back to invite herself over for a proper goodbye.

A knock on the door interrupted her sexy daydreams and she realized her Shamanic burning ritual was still ablaze on the desk. She batted at the fire with a stinky undershirt she had been about to stuff into her duffle bag.

"What are you smoking in there?" She heard a familiar voice outside the attic door. "Let us in and we'll join you."

When she opened the door, Amber bounced through carrying a big metal mixing bowl. Lolita followed with a fifth of Jack Daniels in one hand and loaf of black bread in the other.

"What the hell?" Lolita rushed to the desk and tamped at the cinders with the whiskey bottle then beat at it with the loaf of bread. "Are you trying to turn Brentano into a tinderbox?" Lolita surveyed the room, scowling at the pizza boxes, stacks of papers, piles of dirty clothes, and overflowing trash can. "This place is a mess. Everywhere you go, chaos follows."

"Like life." Jessica sighed. "You need chaos in your soul to give birth to a dancing star."

"Are Nietzsche and his dancing stars going to clean up this mess or are you planning to leave it behind for my dad?" Lolita asked.

"Let's torch the place! That'll take care of the mess and every nasty vice and evil spirit left in Brentano Hall." Jessica smiled.

"I brought Twisted Twix." Amber's radiant smile lit up the tiny attic. "I got Gary's recipe. Here, try some." She peeled plastic wrap off the top of the bowl, then fished in her whale of a purse and pulled out three plastic spoons.

"Thanks but I think I'll start with my old buddy Jack," Jessica said raising her eyebrows and pointing toward the bottle in Lolita's right hand.

"A going away present," Lolita said, handing her the fifth and then breaking off a piece of dark bread. "I figured I'd slum it with whiskey tonight since you're leaving in the morning."

"Did you bring glasses?" Jessica asked.

"Who needs 'em," Lolita said, reaching over, unscrewing the cap, and tossing it onto the pile of trash.

"Okay. Game on." Jessica took the bottle, chugged a big slug of whiskey, wiped her chin with the back of her hand, and passed it to Amber.

"Guess what?" Amber took a sip from the bottle. "That's foul," she said, voice hoarse.

"What?" Lolita asked. "Hey, what about me? Give me that."

"What?" Amber asked.

"You said guess what, so tell us," Jessica said.

"Oh yeah. Professor Schmutzig...my dad, left me money for

college in his will, and I'm applying to Northwestern to study computer science. Gary is helping me with my application."

"Getting his recipes, filling out applications together, things are getting serious between you and Gary-the-geek," Lolita said with a wink.

"What about Jack?" Jessica asked.

"Your Jack or mine?" Amber asked, giggling.

"Either one."

"I haven't decided yet. Hand me that one." Amber took another sip, then scooped out a heaping spoonful of mashed chocolate Cheetos and stuffed it into her mouth. "It's getting better," she mumbled with her mouth full.

"So you're going to get a degree in computer science, become a professional hacker, and turn your twisted Twix episode into a virtue." Jessica laughed, took another swig from the bottle, and sat down on the floor next to Amber.

"Well you've somehow managed to make a virtue out of your obstinacy and gullibility, my Montana friend," Lolita said, leaning against the door since the kneeboard walls were too short to lean against.

"What do you mean? Anyway, you're a fine one to talk, my Russian friend, or should I say Poker Tsarina?" Jessica held out her hand for the bread, and Lolita bent down and passed it to her.

"Unfortunately, the detective has put a stop to my game and my income, at least for the time being." Lolita smiled her sly smile and lit a cigarette.

Jessica's phone started singing Lana del Rey's "Honeymoon," *We both know it's not fashionable for you to love me.*"

"It's Nick." She blushed, then turned her phone off. "I told him we have to cool it, especially if he's going to be on my dissertation committee."

"It was just rebound sex anyway," Lolita said.

"That's the best kind," Amber said, coiling a snaky lock of hair around her index finger.

"What sex? I'm taking a vow of celibacy until after I get my degree, or at least until the end of the summer."

"Which ever comes first?" Lolita asked, raising an eyebrow.

"Very funny."

"Like the whiptail lizard, Cnemidophorus neomexican? It reproduces without sex." Amber took another spoonful of goop, and did a little seated dance as she munched. Sitting cross-legged next to the bowl of sticky salty sickening crunchy goo, Amber and Jessica were taking turns scooping spoonfuls into their mouths.

"Breeding without sex? Why that's just the torture without any of the fun," Jessica said, spitting on a Kleenex and wiping some chocolate off of Amber's forehead. "The only thing I plan to birth is a doctoral dissertation. I'm going to get this damned degree if it splits me open." Jessica took another slug, then slammed the whiskey bottle on the floor in front of her.

"If determination has a name, it's Jessica James!" Lolita said, blowing smoke rings, still standing, one black boot up against the door. Springing forward, she bent over, seized the bottle, and raised it into the air. "We make a damned fine team. A toast, to us, the Three Fates: Destiny, Peace, and Order." She pointed the bottle at Jessica, then Amber, then took a swig.

"Pass Jack over here." Amber held out her hand. "More like, Ready, Willing, and Able," she said, giggling and waving Jack above her head.

"It's my turn with Jack." Jessica did a downward dog to stand up and tried to snatch the bottle away from Amber, but she passed it to Lolita.

"Hand him over," Jessica said, lunging at her friend. "It's my turn to make a toast." Lolita took a drink, taunted her with the bottle, then relented and handed it over.

Jessica swung the bottle over her head. "A toast," she slurred. "To the Cowgirl Philosopher, the Hippy Hacker, and the Poker Tsarina." She tipped up the bottle, and after the rest of the amber liquid poured into her mouth and dribbled down her chin, she threw the bottle against the wall, and laughed as it shattered with a loud crash, one jagged piece sticking into the wainscoting.

"Whoa there cowgirl," Lolita said. "We'd better tuck you in if you're going to get any sleep before your flight tomorrow."

"Don't remind me. I can hear my mom's voice already, 'Be good. And if you can't be good, be careful'. Guess I'm getting ahead of myself. I'm saying goodbye when I should be saying hello," Jessica said in a sing-song voice. "You say goodbye, I say hello, hello, hello," she howled, tugging on her Ropers, and tousling her dirty blonde hair. "Okay, just prop me in the corner until we're ready to saddle up. Alpine Vista trailer dump, here I come!"

"Come on, Amber. We'd better leave the Cowgirl Philosopher to sober up before dawn." Jessica stumbled into her friend's long arms and held her in a tight embrace. "Get some sleep, sweetie," Lolita whispered in her ear. "Morning will be here before you know it. I'll collect you at eight to drive you to the airport."

On the way out the door, Amber stopped and pulled a small glass vial from her purse, then handed it to Jessica. "Here, take this. It's milk thistle tincture. It prevents hangovers."

"Thanks. Love you guys," Jessica said, staggering backwards as she shut the door just a little too forcefully. Sighing, she looked around at her chaotic nest, then climbed up onto the hard desk, and curled into a little ball.

As she lay on the lonesome desk in the creaky old attic, she remembered an episode of Star Trek. Captain Picard lived an entire lifetime in the course of a few hours; instead of a ship's captain, he'd had a family and grown old playing the flute. The last two weeks had compressed her lifetime, as if she'd lived in this attic forever--her boozy mother, Alpine Vista's familiar haunts, and the wilds of Montana, existing in an alternate universe. As the dark walls closed in on her, and her eyelids grew heavy, she rolled to one side, pulled out her phone, and set the alarm. She didn't want to miss her flight home.

ACKNOWLEDGMENTS

Thanks to my tireless editor, Lisa Mae Walsh. Without her encouragement, comments, and inspired editorial advice, I couldn't have written this novel. Thanks to Alexandra for correcting my Russian, to Maddee for her creative cover designs, and to Jessica for copy-editing. Thanks to everyone who read earlier drafts and gave me helpful feedback, especially Teri, Chuck, Tracy, Elissa, Alison, Rebecca, Taunia, Claire, Colin, and Susan. I really appreciate it! And, thanks to Beni, who not only cheered me on, but also gave me great ideas and insightful criticism all along the way. Finally, thanks to my furry friends and family who kept me company for hours on end, happily purring next to me or on me. It would be a lonely endeavor without them.

ABOUT KELLY OLIVER

 WHEN SHE'S NOT writing Jessica James mystery novels, Kelly Oliver is a Distinguished Professor of Philosophy at Vanderbilt University. She earned her B.A. from Gonzaga University and her Ph.D. from Northwestern University. She is the author of fourteen nonfiction books, most recently, *Hunting Girls: Sexual Violence from The Hunger Games to Campus Rape* (Columbia University Press 2016), and over 100 articles on issues including campus rape, reproductive technologies, women and the media, film noir, animal ethics, environmental philosophy, and Alfred Hitchcock. Her work has been translated into seven languages, and she has published an op-ed on loving our pets in <u>The New York Times</u>. She has been interviewed on ABC television news, the Canadian Broadcasting Network, and various radio programs

Kelly lives in Nashville with her husband and her furry family, Hurricane, Yukiyu, and Mayhem.

For more information on Kelly, check out her website: kellyoliverbooks.com

COYOTE

(Jessica James Mysteries Book Two)

AFTER HER FIRST disastrous year in graduate school, Jessica James returns home from the big city to the backwaters of Montana for a summer job at an historic railroad lodge in spectacular Glacier Park. After her cousin dies in a gruesome accident at the lumber mill, Jessica is pulled into a fight against the corruption and greed ignited by the oil frenzy on the Montana plains. Her roommate, Kimi RedFox is determined to stop powerful Knight Industries, headed by Cheneyesque billionaire Richard Knight, from drilling oil on the Blackfoot Indian Reservation. "Kimi" means "secret" in Blackfoot, and the reticent Kimi keeps hers until it's almost too late. Kimi's not about to accept help from Jessica or anyone else, but she's resolved to find her missing sisters, even if it kills her. Corrupt Richard Knight has assigned his younger brother David to oversee fracking operations in on the Blackfeet reservation. Trying to overcome his reputation as a spoiled slacker, David wants to impress his brother and earn Jessica's respect. But is the handsome young businessman his brother's henchman or his dupe? And, will Jessica and Kimi quit sparring long enough to team up and expose sex trafficking, prostitution rings, and murder schemes involving some of the biggest frackers in the country? Or, will they become the murder's next victims?

PRAISE FOR COYOTE

"**A splendid mystery** *involving one of the most resonant issues of our dangerous times. Fans of Sophie Littlefield, Deborah Coonts, and Nevada Barr have something to celebrate.* **Jessica James is a new American original.**"

Author Jason Miller, *Down Don't Bother Me*

BOOK CLUB QUESTIONS

1. How does Jessica deal with sexism at the university? How should she have dealt with it?
2. Discuss the issue of party rape on campus. Is Lolita and Jessica's revenge against the fraternity boys justified?
3. Did you guess the killer? If so, how did you know? If not, who did you think killed Wolf?
4. Do you think Nick and Jessica belong together? They're both consenting adults. But is there a problem that she is a student and he is a professor?
5. Who was your favorite character and why?
6. What did you think of the alternating points of view between Jessica and Dmitry? Which was your favorite and why?
7. Do you think Dmitry should have left Chicago instead of confronting The Pope once Bratva found him?
8. Do you think Dmitry should have pursued a career in art or related to his interest in art instead of becoming a janitor?
9. What did you think of the strong women characters in the novel? What did you think of the relationships between

them? Between Lolita and Jessica? Between Jessica and Amber? Between Donnette and Jessica?

10. Was Alexander a good villain?
11. Did you learn anything about philosophy or art?
12. Which was your favorite subplot? The Russian art subplot or the feminist revenge subplot?
13. Is it important to the plot that Jessica is from Montana and used to be a cowgirl?